GIVE ME BACK MY HEART

Denise Robins

CHIVERS

British Library Cataloguing in Publication Data available

This Large Print edition published by BBC Audiobooks Ltd, Bath, 2007.
Published by arrangement with the Author's Estate

U.K. Hardcover ISBN 978 1 405 64096 1
U.K. Softcover ISBN 978 1 405 64097 8

Printed and bound in Great Britain by
Antony Rowe Ltd., Chippenham, Wiltshire

For
Louise and George Barden

CHAPTER ONE

The dance given by Lady Inverlaw for her two nieces who had just arrived from Casablanca was in full swing. Everybody who was 'anybody' in Edinburgh had been asked to the beautiful Georgian house in Moray Place, and it was a glittering affair, talked of for many a day after that night of frost and stars in the Spring that preceded the war.

Jean Inverlaw, herself childless, had not seen much of her brother, Harry Rutherfield, who for the last twenty years had lived in French Morocco where he was head of an important private shipping line. Neither did she approve of the fact that he had allowed his two daughters to be brought up in France rather than England.

But Harry was a wealthy man, and Jean a widow not as well off as she used to be, and he had offered her a handsome sum to entertain his two daughters for a spell. His extravagance (his Casablanca home, the Villa des Fleurs, was famous for its magnificence) was apparent to all Edinburgh tonight. Never had so many wonderful flowers been seen. A special dance band had come from London. The supper was lavish, and the two Miss Rutherfields themselves were obviously scoring a big triumph. Lady Inverlaw sat watching through

1

lorgnettes an eightsome reel. An elderly man, wearing a kilt, bent down and whispered:

'Which is the young lady who is engaged to be married?'

Lady Inverlaw indicated one of her nieces, a girl who was dancing with a mad grace which had never before been seen in this sedate drawing-room; she had tawny-coloured hair worn in a sleek pageboy bob which touched her creamy shoulders; wide eyes more green than blue, and a wilful red mouth. She was wearing a cream velvet dress which suited her slenderness. There were sapphires about her neck and in both tiny ears. On one shoulder a spray of orchids was pinned with a sapphire and diamond brooch.

A little too *French*, perhaps, for an Edinburgh drawing-room. But that was Jean Inverlaw's complaint. Harry had been so crazy about his wife, a Parisian who had died five years ago, that he had allowed her to have the up-bringing of the girls. Louise was like her mother's family. Fiona had her father's colouring and his Highland mother's name.

'She is the one engaged to a Frenchman,' Lady Inverlaw said, indicating Fiona. 'That younger one, fair, in blue, is her sister, Louise.'

The elderly Scot watched the reel for a moment, listening to the stirring music, the beat of the drums and the gay sharp cries of the young Scots who were executing their native dance. He made no comment upon

2

either Miss Fiona or Miss Louise Rutherfield. He was a man of few words, but he thought he had never seen anything so brilliant and lovely as the elder girl. The young one was pretty in a fragile way, with big blue eyes and fair curls. And there were other pretty girls in the room. But Fiona outclassed them all. She threw herself into the dance with a fascinating abandon. Many stories had been circulated around Edinburgh about the elder Miss Rutherfield. It was said that she would inherit half a million from her father one day, and she had been affianced from her childhood to the son of her father's French partner. It had apparently been one of these old French traditional *mariage de convenance.* There weren't many of them these days and the elderly Scot was intrigued and a little bewildered. He wasn't sure that he approved of it. A girl ought to be allowed to marry a man of her own choosing.

That was also Lady Inverlaw's private opinion. She always thought that engagement of Fiona's a monstrous arrangement. But knowing Harry and his cold hard business head, she was quite sure he had arranged it in order to ensure the financial bond between himself and his partner in the firm, Gaston d'Auvergne.

The reel ended. Laughing and clapping their hands, the young couples wandered off the floor, and toward the supper-room.

Fiona linked arms with her sister.

'Not too tired, darling?'

'No, I am enjoying myself, so don't start saying I ought to go to bed,' said Louise peevishly.

Fiona laughed.

'There, baby, you shan't be sent to bed!' she said. 'But don't overdo things.'

'I'm having a wonderful time,' said Louise, her fair cheeks flushed, her blue eyes watching a tall handsome young Scot who wore a MacLean kilt. 'This is so different from Casablanca, Fiona. We are so shut *in* there. We are like women in purdah . . . we go out with our father or Tante Marie, or friends chosen for us. Here we are free and I like these English and Scots boys. They are such fun. They are so much *nicer* than all the French or Spanish we meet. With the exception of Philippe, of course.'

Fiona did not answer for a moment. Her brilliant eyes clouded a little. She moved into the refreshment-room thinking over her young sister's words. It was true that they were tasting a freedom and a new fresh thrill here in Edinburgh which they had never experienced in Casablanca or Paris, where they lived most of the year round. Equally true that her father's countrymen seemed, on the whole, much nicer, cleaner, more attractive in every way than men of the Latin races. In Casablanca she rarely thought about it. But she knew that she resembled in many ways her British father, and ever since they were babies she and Louise had had a Scots governess. Their upbringing had not been entirely Continental. But there was always Philippe in the background . . . for her, Fiona.

Fiona was a little startled to find how far the thought of Philippe had receded since her arrival in Scotland. Yet he was her *fiancé* . . . the man she was going to marry the next time he came over from America.

She had seen a fair amount of him, on and off, ever since their formal betrothal on her sixteenth birthday. That had been an exciting event and it seemed to have pleased her father enormously. It had pleased her, too, at the time. As a romantic schoolgirl, she had found young Philippe d'Auvergne very much a Prince Charming. She had a miniature of him which went everywhere with her, and she knew every feature of that pale aristocratic face. He had sloe-dark narrow eyes, a smooth black head and exquisite manners. Whenever he was with her, he said the most beautiful things; away from her, he wrote poetic letters, and sent her magnificent presents. For the last three years he had been running a branch line of his father's shipping business in New York.

Vaguely Fiona remembered Philippe's more recent visits to Casablanca. Their parties there or in Paris—she herself always heavily chaperoned by their mother's sister, Madame

5

Duronde, whom they called Tante Marie. Only occasionally had Fiona been left alone with Philippe. Then he would make love to her in a desultory fashion, a kiss on the hand or a chaste salute on her forehead, a passionless embrace. Nothing that either roused or startled her. Philippe was waiting for her to grow up, he said.

She would be twenty-one in June. Now she felt grown up indeed. How could a girl stay altogether in ignorance in an exotic country like French Morocco? But she was still unawakened. She still felt for Philippe d'Auvergne what she would have felt for a dear brother. The marriage had been arranged. Papers had been signed. She knew that it was almost as binding as marriage. And later another marriage would perhaps be arranged for little Louise who was just eighteen. But Louise was delicate and had to be much petted and looked after, and for the moment nothing was being done about her future.

Looking with bright restless eyes around her Scottish aunt's reception-rooms, Fiona was conscious, not for the first time, of a trapped feeling . . . the feeling of a bird in a gilded cage. Lately she had begun to read books that the Scots governess, Miss Macdonald, and *Maman* and Tante Marie had so far kept out of her reach. Novels, books of philosophy, of psychology. Books from the English Library in

Casablanca, or which she found when spending the day in Gibraltar or Tangier.

She had begun to realise how unusual it was for a girl like herself to be bound down from the age of sixteen and to have no freedom or choice in love and marriage.

She *was* fond of Philippe. She imagined it would be exciting to become Madame d'Auvergne, to live with Philippe in New York or Paris. But tonight she wasn't so sure. It wasn't that any of these nice young men had awakened her interest. But just an odd touch of the hand . . . a warm word . . . an instant's thrill of proximity, and something told Fiona deep down in her heart that there was far more to this business of an engagement than *she* knew about. There was love, real deep breathless love, when one wanted to live and die for a man, not merely to be showered with jewels and enjoy a life of luxury and pleasure.

Suddenly Fiona pressed Louise's hand and whispered: 'Oh, *how lucky* you are!'

Louise stared at her sister. Lucky! *She!* How absurd. Louise had always been envious of her brilliant elder sister, and particularly of Fiona's betrothal to Philippe. From her childhood, Louise had had a penchant for the charming Philippe. What did Fiona mean?

Fiona told her what she meant.

'You are lucky to be still *free*, Louise darling,' she said. Louise, who was a little prim and had none of Fiona's restlessness of mind

7

and body, looked shocked.

She was still more shocked that next morning when she awoke to find a note beside her pillow from Fiona.

I've taken the M.G. and gone out for a run. I feel I can't go shopping with Aunt Jean this morning. I'll see you at lunch.

'Fiona must have gone mad,' thought Louise.

Fiona herself wondered if such was the case as she drove the small sports car which had been bought for the use of herself and her sister while they were in Scotland. Drove away from the city and out toward the Pentland Hills.

She had slept badly last night. Somehow the party, all those reels and dances, laughing and joking with boys like Gordon MacLean and Alex Munro, had disturbed her.

'Don't you know that you are the most fascinating creature I have ever known in my life,' Alex had said to her.

'Why are you engaged? Why must I meet my fate only to find she is not free?' Gordon had bemoaned.

And other men had said the same sort of things. All very distracting, especially when she remembered her bond with Philippe. She had laughed so much last night! She never laughed with Philippe. He had no sense of humour.

Fiona was quite sure now that she had very little of poor *Maman* in her. She was her father's daughter, and these Scots saw the funny side of things.

Disconsolately Fiona looked at the soft blurred line of the hills, at the budding trees, at the shaggy Scots sheep grazing in the fields. There was an east wind which whipped the rich blood into her cheeks. It was perishing cold after the heat of Casablanca, but she liked it. Somehow she thought without pleasure of the colour, the sensuousness, of her romantic home, the beautiful Villa des Fleurs, with its jade green shutters and enamelled doorways, and the fluted Moorish columns. It was beautiful in the sun and a poem in the strong white moonlight. What a contrast to the Scottish countryside, the blue shadows of those pepper trees, the feathery eucalyptus, the brilliant hues of magenta bougainvillaea against white walls, the sweet-smelling jasmine and the rose geraniums. Fiona could in imagination hear the harsh distant cries and discordant music from the bazaars; see the Arab women, heavily veiled, padding through the narrow alleys that were roofed with the wooden lattices to keep them cool.

It would all be marvellous if one had the right person beside one to enjoy the beauty; to experience the sensations of delight that could surely be extracted from all that colour and glamour.

9

But when Philippe came to the Villa des Fleurs things seemed no more beautiful to Fiona. She was only mildly interested. For that reason alone she had always guessed that things must be wrong. Today she knew it for a certainty.

'*You must be mad!*' her sister Louise had said.

Well, really, perhaps she was! For she had a very strong antipathy this morning for the tie that bound her to dear Philippe.

She was glad that her father's chauffeur had taught her to drive. At home, of course, she was never allowed to go out in the car without Tante Marie or two servants. It was wonderful, this driving alone through the wind in the pale Scottish Spring.

Fiona accelerated. A moment later she aimed off the main road into a lane. She wanted to get away from other vehicles . . . right into the very depths of the country. She turned perhaps a little too sharply and quickly and she did not see a young man on a cycle coming towards her. There was a horrifying moment when she did see him, too late. Her left wing caught his rear wheel. The next moment he was off the bicycle and Fiona had pulled up the M.G. with a jerk and sprung out, wondering whether or not she had killed a man.

CHAPTER TWO

An hour before that incident, Bill Lindsey, first officer of a merchant ship known as *The Falcon*, left the docks at Leith, hired a bicycle for the day and set off to explore the countryside.

It was not Bill's first visit to Scotland by any means. A seafaring man, he knew most of the big ports and several times a year *The Falcon* steamed down the Firth of Forth. But today was a special day in Bill's life. The captain had hinted this morning that he was due for retirement and that possibly, when *The Falcon* left Leith again for the Mediterranean, Bill Lindsey might find himself in command of the ship.

It was the dearest wish of his heart . . . to be Captain Lindsey and to know that *The Falcon* was *his* . . . His at the age of thirty. A very young captain, perhaps, but for the last two years he had had his master's ticket. As an employee of the shipping line of the Anglia Shipping Co. Ltd., he held a high reputation. All his life he had been at sea and loved it.

The only thing he didn't get enough of at sea was exercise and the green country which he missed. He had decided to go on this bicycling tour for the first week of his leave, and later, perhaps, visit London. He had no

11

parents, only an old uncle and aunt in London. He would like to see them but city life soon irked him. Fresh air and open spaces were essential to Bill Lindsey.

He was thinking about the possible command of *The Falcon* and whistling cheerfully as he cycled along the narrow lane that fringed the Pentland Hills. And then, a sports car coming at dangerous speed . . . and that collision. Bill was flung off his bicycle. His head came in contact with the road and after that there was a few moments of oblivion for Bill.

When he opened his eyes again, he found himself lying on the side of the road with his head on the lap of a girl. He heard a voice, a charming feminine voice, saying:

'Oh, speak to me, *please*! *Do* please say you are all right!'

A small hand was pressing a handkerchief against his forehead. He put his own hand up to it gingerly. He could still 'see stars' and the green world was revolving around him.

'Great grief!' he exclaimed. 'What the devil happened?'

The girl exclaimed:

'Oh, you *are* all right! Thank heaven!'

Then Bill sat up. Things were becoming clearer. Blinking, he looked at the girl in whose lap his head had been cradled. A little dazedly he looked into a pair of eyes so startlingly lovely that they took his breath away. Lord! they were green eyes, with fantastically long lashes. And the girl had an unusual face with high cheekbones and pure line of chin and long white throat. Her hair hung in a tawny satin mane almost to her shoulders. Where had he seen anything like this before? Only on the films. Who did she remind him of? Rita Hayworth, perhaps . . . that was the type. She used the most intriguing scent. As for those long slim legs in the gossamer stockings, he had never seen anything so perfect. He knew little about girls but he was sure the tweeds she wore were expensive, to say nothing of the rich fur jacket.

'Oh, please forgive me,' she was speaking again. 'I'm afraid I was driving much too fast.'

Then Bill recovered his equilibrium. He swung from admiration of this glamorous young woman to a righteous fury.

'Little fool!' he said through his teeth. 'What the devil do you want to drive like that for in a lane this narrow? You ought to have your licence suspended. You are not fit to drive a car.'

Fiona gasped. Never before in her life had she been so rudely spoken to. She blushed bright crimson. The *boor* to speak so harshly, even though she *had* knocked him off his bicycle. Didn't he know his manners? Her eyes flashed with indignation at him. His flashed back into hers and she had to admit that he had the bluest eyes she had ever seen. The

13

deep clear blue of the sea. And how brown he was . . . a deep bronze. In contrast, his light brown hair, thick and curly, was touched with gold. She noted, too, in that moment that his eyelashes were curly, tipped with gold, and that his chin was square and had a dent in it.

Who was he? He was tall and sparsely built, and he wore shabby grey flannels, a dark blue jersey and an old tweed coat.

'You ought to be locked up,' were his next words.

Then Fiona broke out:

'How dare you speak to me like that . . .'

Bill rose to his feet. He swayed a moment, a hand up to his head. Damn it all, he felt sick and dizzy. He had always said that women were a nuisance . . . if there was ever any trouble with the crew it was over a woman, and pretty ones were always a menace. This 'glamour-girl', now also on her feet, her tawny head reaching his shoulder . . . ought to be whipped . . . or kissed . . . he hardly knew which, but she oughtn't to be allowed to drive a car dangerously and ruin a man's holiday.

He opened his mouth to say something but no words came. He swayed a little more drunkenly. His head felt on fire. And the next moment he would have fallen if Fiona had not hastened to support him.

'I'm afraid it's your head,' she was saying, in a mollified tone. 'I think you'd really better let me drive you somewhere . . .'

14

'Drive me anywhere you like,' said Bill Lindsey. 'You're lovely, but you're a menace to mankind.'

'Oh,' exclaimed Fiona, crimsoning again.

But those were the last words she was to hear from Bill for some time. He nearly toppled over and she hastened to get him into the car. From that moment onward he seemed to pass into unconsciousness again. She felt horribly guilty. That wound on his head was bleeding afresh. She could not bear to see the red stain against the bright curls. He was very handsome, and very rude, and she had never met anybody in her life quite like him. 'A menace to mankind' he had called her! That was not at all the sort of thing Philippe said to her. She did not know whether to be furious or amused. But she knew that she must do something for her victim.

The bicycle, now a wreck, lay in the ditch. Fiona unstrapped the suitcase which was on the back of it and put it in her car. Then without further ado, she turned the M.G. round and drove back into Edinburgh.

She drove straight to her aunt's house in Moray Place. It was half past eleven. The butler said that her ladyship and Miss Louise were in Princes Street, shopping. Fiona, accustomed to giving peremptory orders to native servants in Casablanca, thereupon told the astonished butler to get another man and help the gentleman out of the car and into the

15

house.

'Put him in one of the spare rooms, Thomas. I'm responsible for the accident so I must look after him. I'll telephone for the doctor.'

With an injured air, Thomas did as he was told and wondered what her ladyship would say.

Her ladyship returned with Louise to find that a stranger had been put to bed in one of the many rooms at the top of the house and that the family physician had already come and gone. He had dressed the injury to the injured man's head and announced that he must not be moved for at least three days. He had slight concussion.

Lady Inverlaw stared at Fiona.

'You must be mad!' she exclaimed.

Fiona smiled.

'That's the second time I've had that said to me today. But really, Aunt Jean, I *am* responsible, and if I'd taken him to a hospital, perhaps he would have charged me with dangerous driving and there would have been an awful scandal in Edinburgh about your niece.'

Lady Inverlaw climbed down. There was something in what Fiona said. Better to let the injured man stay here a day or two and then let him go about his business. Who was he, anyway? She hoped he was a gentleman.

Louise Rutherfield looked at her sister with

large inquisitive eyes.

'Fiona, you are *impossible*. Whoever is he?'

'He's very handsome,' said Fiona calmly.

'But he called me a menace to mankind. Can you imagine such a thing?'

Louise giggled, and then with a sly look at Fiona, said:

'What would Philippe say?'

'I really don't know,' said Fiona with a yawn and a graceful shrug.

'But who *is* this man?' repeated Lady Inverlaw anxiously.

Fiona then delivered the information. Thomas, who undressed him, had found some identity papers. His name was William Lindsey and he was first officer of a merchant ship and Thomas imagined the ship was now in dock in the Forth and that the young officer was on leave.

Lady Inverlaw sniffed. An officer on a merchant ship didn't sound too good to her. She would have preferred it to be a Lieutenant-Commander in the Royal Navy. But Lady Inverlaw was a snob. Louise was asking a great many more questions and Fiona's answers slightly disturbed her ladyship. The young officer was very handsome and had a charming voice: a little rough, perhaps, in manner. But that, Fiona said, with a mischievous smile, might be accounted for by the fact that Mr. Lindsey had been flung off his bike and was naturally not over-pleased about it.

'Well, you leave him to Wilkie,' said Lady Inverlaw, at once forming the opinion that it was best to put the oldest and ugliest maid in the house in charge of the handsome stranger.

She then suggested that Fiona should write to the captain of *The Falcon* (Thomas seemed to have discovered the name of the ship) and inform him of the accident.

Left alone with her sister, Louise fixed her large blue eyes a trifle accusingly upon Fiona.

'You are so wild sometimes . . . you do such strange things. Why did you bring him back *here*? What *would* Philippe say?'

'Don't ask me that again,' flashed Fiona, 'and you are for ever reminding me about Philippe. Do stop it, Louise darling.'

'But you are going to marry him!' protested Louise.

Again that trapped feeling that she had experienced last night came over the older girl.

'Yes, I suppose I am,' she said slowly.

CHAPTER THREE

Bill Lindsey opened his eyes for the second time that day to find an exceptionally beautiful anxious young face bending over him. Drowsily he looked at it and then around him. Gee! What a room. Handsome, palatial, with

18

rich powder blue satin curtains and Chippendale furniture, and himself lying in a deep soft bed such as Bill had seldom slept upon before in his life. What a contrast, he thought, to his small cramped cabin on *The Falcon* and his hard bunk.

'Oh, I hope you're feeling better.' said a melodious young voice of great sweetness which had a soothing effect upon First Officer Lindsey. He lay in a kind of trance. It was altogether soothing in here. Drawn blinds dimmed the April sunshine. An electric fire warmed the room. And now he saw that the 'glamour girl' was no longer in tweeds, but in a silk afternoon dress that showed to even better advantage the lissom grace of her figure. Two rows of creamy pearls encircled her long throat. There were pearls in her ears. Bill said in a whisper:

'*You* did this to me . . . you menace to mankind.'

'I really am sorry,' Fiona said, 'but you need not be so horrid about it.'

'I feel horrid.'

'Aren't you any better?'

He put a hand up to his head and found it bandaged.

'I expect I am. Who tied me up?'

'Dr. Rich, and he says you're not to get up until he gives you permission.'

'Whose house am I in?'

'My aunt's—Lady Inverlaw.'

19

Gee! thought Bill Lindsey once more. He was indeed in a new world. A sumptuous house . . . belonging to a titled lady . . . and this amazing young woman with her glorious hair and distractingly lovely face.

'What's your name?' he asked dreamily.

'Fiona.'

'How do, Fiona,' said Bill in his friendliest manner. 'You remain a menace, but I forgive you, providing you never drive that darn' car of yours again.'

'Indeed I shall.'

'Then heaven help all cyclists,' he said drily.

'You aren't very polite.'

'Sorry, lady. I'm not much good with your sex. I live among men on the sea. I was taking my leave and enjoying it just before you put an end to it for me.'

Fiona bit her lip. She hardly knew what to say. Never before had she dealt with such an extraordinary young man. He was a bear . . . the antithesis of Philippe, who kissed her hand so gallantly and showed the utmost respect and homage. The expression in the clear blue eyes in that tanned, strong face left her no room for doubt that he had no use for her. She said:

'I'd better go, I'm not supposed to be in here, anyway. Aunt Jean's maid, Wilkie, is nursing you.'

His gaze wandered over her proud beauty.

'Oh. So *you* aren't making up for your crime

in person. You surprise me. I should have thought you would like to show your remorse by actions and not mere words.'

Fiona hesitated. She did not honestly know whether Mr. Lindsey was being sarcastic or genuine. But she did know that his whole attitude challenged the spirit in her. She said:

'I don't know that I'd be any good as a nurse, and anyhow, you're ungracious and ungrateful. I might have driven you to a horrid hospital.'

'And I might have died and then you'd have been charged with manslaughter,' said Bill severely.

It was strange how this man had power to make her blush. Fiona was scarlet now again as she sprang up from the bedside.

'Oh, how hateful of you! I'm sorry I ever came to see how you were getting on.'

Then Bill Lindsey softened and on an impulse caught one of her hands and pulled her back to the bedside.

'Listen, Beautiful. I'm a rough brute. I know it and I apologise. You were sweet to bring me back here. But I don't want to stay. Send for an ambulance. Have me taken away, do. And don't look as though you're going to burst into tears.'

Fiona gasped. The hot colour still flamed in her cheeks and the grip of Bill Lindsey's strong brown fingers filled her with an emotion that she neither understood nor welcomed in that moment. The way he *spoke* to her . . . why, it made her feel like a naughty child. She, the spoiled, sought-after Miss Rutherfield of Casablanca. She, Philippe's adored *fiancée*.

Bill spoke again.

'Gosh! My head feels like a top . . . spinning . . . Oh, gosh, what a holiday! Why did I ever leave my ship?'

Fiona snatched her slender fingers away from his grasp. She stared down at him. His eyes had closed. He looked very young . . . a brown handsome boy, lying there on the white pillows in the striped pyjamas Thomas had found in his case. Fascinated she looked at the tanned powerful column of his throat . . . the well-shaped hands . . . hands that looked as though they were always in the sun . . . and doing hards jobs. Very different from Philippe's, which were white, slender and manicured.

The wildest, queerest sensation rushed across Fiona, a desire to feel those strong brown hands gripping her wrist again . . . hurting her . . .

She said, breathlessly:

'Please be quiet . . . the doctor said you mustn't talk. Go to sleep at once. I'll send Wilkie to you.'

Then turning, she ran out of the room.

In a turmoil she joined her sister downstairs. It was already late afternoon. Bill Lindsey had been dozing until now and she had been full of remorse because she had spoilt his holiday through her carelessness. But how *dared* he treat her in such a familiar, off-hand manner? She wouldn't go near him again.

But she did. Much later that night, when Fiona was sitting in the drawing-room with some friends of her aunt's, and Louise and young MacLean were playing dance records on the big radiogramophone, Wilkie came in and asked to say a word in private to Miss Fiona. She whispered, would Miss Fiona go up and say a word to the patient.

'He's got a terrible headache, miss. And he won't take his medicine. He says *you've* got to give it to him.

Fiona tossed her tawny mane of hair.

'What nonsense, Wilkie!'

The Scots maid concealed a smile behind a discreet hand.

'Ay, he's a bonny lad, Miss Fiona. He's got a way with him, too.'

Fiona murmured an excuse to her aunt's guests, avoided her young sister's questioning gaze and went up to the sickroom. This time she found the patient very wide awake, feverish and restless. The table-lamp beside him flung up the gold lights in his thick hair which the bandages barely concealed. When he saw the girl, his eyes brightened.

'Ah. Now I'll take my dope,' he said, his tongue in his cheek.

Fiona stood looking down at him doubtfully.

She guessed he was 'ragging' her now. She was not used to being 'ragged', but to being treated like a princess. It half amused and half annoyed her. She said:

'You really must get as much sleep as you can.'

'Changed your dress again, I see,' murmured Bill. His gaze wandered over her. Quite honestly he thought she was a dream in that delicate velvet dinner-dress of palest green over which she wore a blue fox cape.

Fiona said haughtily:

'Do you mind?'

'No. Go ahead. I live on a merchant ship and wear a uniform and see little else but men in uniform. It's a change to see a lovely girl who puts on a different dress every hour.'

'Oh, you're impossible!'

His blue eyes gleamed at her derisively, but he said more gently:

'Don't let's quarrel again. I really want to bid you good night, Miss—er—Fiona—and to apologise for my bad manners. I'll be good now and take my medicine from Wilkie.'

Fiona seated herself at the bedside, lifted the little bottle and read the instructions. *One spoonful every four hours.* 'I'll give it to you now I'm here,' she said rather perversely.

As she guided the spoon to his lips, Bill smiled at her. He murmured:

'Thanks . . . Gorgeous . . .'

Her heart beat a degree faster. A feeling of

intense light-heartedness, almost merriment, seized her. She wanted to laugh with this man . . . and because of him. She did not wish to go downstairs and rejoin the sedate, conventional crowd, and listen to the usual fulsome flattery from the men who had dined her tonight. She wanted to stay and talk to Bill Lindsey. To learn more about him and his life which she felt sure must be utterly different from any life she had ever before encountered. He was so wholesome, so honest, so like the sea on which he sailed his ship. Fresh and unspoiled by the world.

In those blue eyes of his there were no subtleties, only truths. A simple man who liked simple things and who had the divine gift of laughter. He was grinning at her, lying there now like a drowsy schoolboy.

'You're rather a wonderful girl, menace or not,' he said.

Fiona, breathing fast, felt life and fun bubbling up in her throat. She said:

'And you're a strange, strange man. Tell me more about yourself. Tell me about your ship.'

Then she saw a wonderful look come into Bill Lindsey's eyes . . . a look that only two things in the world had power to bring there. The memory of his mother whom he had adored, and *The Falcon*, the ship in which he served.

Fiona sat there listening to him, but she only half heard his rhapsodies on clean shining decks, on the fine line from bow to stern, on the wonderful engines that throbbed in tune to the heart of the man who hoped to be 'Master' next time out to sea. She was thinking about *him*. She could see what his job meant to him; and she had never dreamed a career *could* mean so much, or that such tremendous enthusiasm for work could grip a man. (Philippe worked because his father forced him to. He put far more energy into his recreations.) Her father worked for one passion alone. Money. But Bill Lindsey's passion was for his ship and the sea.

She began to see that here was no ordinary man. She also found herself thinking, quite crazily:

'How wonderful for the girl he loves . . . if he loves *her* in the same way.'

CHAPTER FOUR

One week later, Fiona and Bill sat together on the deep-cushioned chesterfield at right angles to the fire in Lady Inverlaw's drawing-room.

It was a bitingly cold afternoon . . . and Thomas had just built up a big fire to please Miss Fiona. But neither the girl nor the man noticed the cold or the grey gloom of the typical Edinburgh day, for the atmosphere was full of enchantment, Bill Lindsey felt almost that he was under a spell, listening to the girl's sweet voice describing in detail her fairy-tale home in Casablanca. He who had sailed the Mediterranean could shut his eyes and see vividly those burning blue skies, the minarets and white walls and gorgeous glowing bowers. He was thinking:

'To see the moonlight there, with *her* . . . what an experience worth having!'

That morning the doctor had removed Bill's bandages. He had pronounced the patient fit enough to get up and come downstairs. Being strong and healthy, Bill had soon recovered. For one week he had been nursed devotedly by Wilkie, who had a soft corner for the handsome young officer. And every day, at some time or other, the girl whose car had knocked him down had been in to see him. Bill Lindsey, who used to say that all women were 'a menace', had now reached the surprising conclusion that he had no wish to continue his cycling tour, nor to leave this house wherein *she* lived. Nor miss one moment of her beauty and her charm. Never before had he met any girl who had created such a swift and deep impression.

He had also made an amazing discovery: that she was the daughter of Harry Rutherfield, head of the Anglia Shipping Co. . . . the shipping company that employed him. That was an amazing coincidence in itself. When they had first talked about it, Fiona had laughed and said:

'Ah! Now I know that Daddy can make or mar you, you had better be more respectful to me, Mr. Bill Lindsey.

And he had replied in his dry fashion:

'I'm not a social climber, Miss Fiona Rutherfield, and neither do I wish to gain any advantage through influence. If I get promoted I trust that it will be through my own efforts. But I shall never be anything but respectful to you, unless you try to smash up my bike and my leave again.'

Fiona admired him for that and had grown to look forward to the fleeting visits to his bedside, with her young sister looking on in shocked silence, and Aunt Jean turning up her nose.

This afternoon she realised that although she had told Bill Lindsey a great many things about her life in French Morocco, she had omitted to tell him the one salient fact—that she was engaged to be married to Philippe d'Auvergne. Bill had never seen her ring. She rarely wore during the day the huge valuable sapphire that Philippe had bought for her in Paris. And the one person who might have made haste to inform Mr. Lindsey of her betrothal . . . Aunt Jean . . . had retired to her bed with a 'flu-cold soon after Bill's arrival in the house and had not yet got out of it. So Fiona had done very much as she liked these last few days. And she more than liked her association with Bill Lindsey. She felt as though she had been living in a world of unreality, of dreams, until she met him. She felt that everything about him was so genuine—that with him there could be none of the affectations or veneer of her own exotic world. And when she contrasted him with her *fiancé* she had a sense of shock. Philippe was charming . . . but *he* was unreal . . . the thought of him was as nebulous and transient as the memory of her betrothal day. By French law she was his . . . by every other law within herself she belonged *only* to herself. And now she knew that she could never give that self utterly and completely to Philippe. Bill Lindsey, with his blue laughing eyes and his blunt direct manner, his frank and simple personality, had taken possession of her, although it was more than she dared to acknowledge even in the depths of her heart.

This morning she had had a letter from Philippe, written in his usual flowery fashion, and in his own language.

You will not care for Englishmen [he had said]. *They are dull and cold, like their country, although I admit they have integral character. But I shall not be jealous when I think of you meeting any of them. I know you are waiting for me and that your heart is mine alone,* ma petite fleur . . .

That was his favourite name for her. 'Little flower.' And looking back now, she could see that he had treated her always as a child—as something too delicate and lovely to be approached. He didn't know her. The real Fiona was just a flesh and blood, warm-hearted girl, who wanted someone to laugh with her, to take her at her face value . . . someone, in fact, like Bill.

He looked at her as they sat there together and, leaning forward, knocked the pipe he had been smoking against the fender.

'You've been wonderful to me, Fiona,' he said. 'I've had a week's holiday here that I shall never forget all my life. But I think now that I should go. In fact I *must* go tomorrow.'

She caught her breath and looked at him through the dark curtain of her sweeping lashes.

'Oh, must you, Bill?'

Bill Lindsey bit hard on his lower lip. There was an all-too-flattering suggestion in this girl's voice and eyes that she would be sorry when he departed. And when he looked at the maddening grace and beauty of her, his senses swam a little. But he admonished himself; he must keep his head. He couldn't make love to the daughter of his employer . . . a man so important that he had not even seen him. William Lindsey had been engaged by a subordinate.

And yet . . . if there was one thing Bill

Lindsey disliked it was the present social system . . . class hatred . . . distinction between the rich and poor. He had a clean record behind him and a promising future ahead. One day very soon he would be Captain Lindsey. He would have the right to propose to any girl in the world. But Fiona Rutherfield must have had a hundred proposals by now . . . many of rich important men wanting to marry her. Bill imagined he had summed her up, fairly accurately, once he got to know her better. He had decided that although she was spoiled and had led such a pampered and sheltered life, and knew nothing of struggle or poverty or the kind of devotion which made two people give up the world for each other, she had spirit and courage. And she was exquisitely sensitive . . . he, himself a sensitive man, was sure of that.

'Stay with us a little longer,' Fiona murmured.

Then Bill, ever straightforward, came to the point with a rapidity that shook her out of all complacency.

'My dear,' he said, 'if you want the truth, I don't dare stay. You are much too attractive.'

He saw the warm blood sweep her face and it made her look young and defenceless. He adored to see Fiona blush. And then to his horror he thought he saw two big tears come into her great green eyes . . . tears defeated him.

'Darling, what is it?' he asked. 'You aren't

unhappy, are you, Fiona?'

She looked at him dumbly. That 'darling' had robbed her of the power of speech. The idea that he was going tomorrow and that she would never see him again hurt her unimaginably. Of course it was wrong . . . she was going to marry Philippe . . . and she had no right whatever to feel this way. But she did and there was no denying it now.

Bill leaned forward. With a quick rough movement he took her hand and crushed it in both his and carried it to his lips.

'You're lovely . . . you're too lovely, my dear . . . I'm beginning to wish I had never met you . . . never!'

She looked at him and felt herself trembling. Nobody but Philippe had ever kissed her hand before and Philippe's kisses were light—almost ceremonial. But she could feel this man's lips burning against her palm. She felt now, for the first time in her young life, a suffocating sense of passionate desire . . . to be drawn into his arms . . . to be held close to him . . . to touch that bright thick hair of his, that brown strong face. Before she could re-strain the impulse, she had leaned towards him and said in a broken voice:

'Bill . . . Bill . . . don't leave me . . .!'

And then all resistance in the man seemed to snap and he caught the slim quivering figure against his heart.

Her arms went round his neck and for an

32

instant she looked up at him, her eyes magnificently beautiful, bright with tears.

Then he kissed her on the mouth. It was the first kiss of passion that she had ever given or received. She knew as she lay in his arms that this was the love that she had imagined and needed, and that this was the one man in the world to whom she could ever belong.

Bill Lindsey covered the lovely face with kisses. Between them she heard his vibrating voice:

'Darling, darling . . . *darling*! I love you. I am crazy about you. You've got to marry me, Fiona. You are the girl I've waited for all my life . . .'

Once more she remembered Philippe and slowly she drew back from Bill and looked at him in blind despair.

'What is it, Beautiful?' he asked her, and tried to take her into his arms again.

But she rose and moved to the fireplace and stood a moment with her face buried against her folded arms. She thought:

'How am I going to tell him? My engagement to Philippe is as binding as an English marriage. What am I going to do?'

33

CHAPTER FIVE

Fiona felt two arms slowly encircle her and knew that Bill was standing behind her now. She put her hands against both of his warm strong ones which encircled her waist, and turning her head, let her cheek rest against his for a moment. Her eyes closed. For a moment she gave herself up to the luxury, the delight of his embrace.

'Bill . . . my darling Bill,' she whispered brokenly.

'What's worrying you, Beautiful?' he asked her, and let his lips wander down the satin smoothness of the beautiful red-brown hair. She shivered a little in his arms and answered:

'I . . . I can't tell you . . . at least not today . . . I just can't.'

Bill's thick fair brows met in a frown of perplexity.

'What can't you tell me? My sweet, is there any reason why you shouldn't marry me . . . other than you are the daughter of Harry Rutherfield and I am only about to be Master of one of his minor ships?'

Then Fiona swung round, faced him, and placing both hands on his shoulders looked up into his very blue eyes.

'It's nothing to do with *that*. I swear I wouldn't mind whether you were captain of your ship or merely a steward or a stoker. I love you. I *know* that I love you, and I've never loved any other man in my life.'

He looked at her in silent wonder for a moment. Then he said:

'Gosh! It's hard for me to believe. Why should I be so lucky?'

Her magnificent eyes swam with tears. She said:

'I'm the one who is lucky. It's been the most wonderful revelation to me. I can't quite explain, but I do know that I've been waiting for this . . . for you . . . and that's why I haven't loved anybody before.'

He gathered her closer and touched her lips again with his in a swift ardent kiss.

'Then you mustn't be sad, Loveliest, and you must not be worried.'

She struggled with herself. She was tempted to tell him the truth, but had not the courage. She had only just discovered this wonderful new love. It would be too cruel to fling it away by telling Bill outright that she belonged to Philippe d'Auvergne, and therefore could not marry him. All kinds of wild ideas . . . wilder hopes . . . surged through her at this moment. She must see Philippe . . . she must tell him how she felt. She must find out if it was possible for her to break free. And yet, at the mere suggestion of such a thing, her heart failed her. When a marriage has been arranged between two families in France, there can be no backing out on either side. It was as though Philippe's wedding-ring were already on her finger.

And now she knew how wrong that arrangement had been . . . she resented bitterly her father's hand in it. He should never have sacrificed her on the altar of his financial ambition.

'I wish I knew what was troubling you, Fiona,' she heard Bill's anxious voice.

She could not tell him the truth . . . could not break his heart or her own. So she played for time. With the crazy hope in her heart that eventually she would find a way of defeating circumstances, she said:

'It's just that it . . . it is all so new. I'm dazed. I can't get my breath. And there are, of course, difficulties. I'll have to wait and ask Father's permission. He must see you and—' She broke off helplessly, her colour changing from red to white and from white to red again.

Then Bill laughed and gave her a little protective hug.

'You darling! You are such a child. I thought you were a sophisticated woman of the world, but I believe you are only a kid. That makes you all the sweeter. Of course you must get your father's permission and he must see me. I'm quite content to wait until then. If you love me and if you say I can do it, why, I'll just sail into Casablanca and walk right into your father's office and say: "Listen, sir, I'm a mighty lucky man. Your daughter loves me and I'd lay down my life for her. It's infernal impudence on my part but that's the way of it. And if you'll give the okay, I'll go out and buy the ring and the licence right now".'

Fiona laughed—a little broken laugh of love and happiness which bubbled up from deep down inside her. This was a man unlike any man she had ever met. Oh, how gloriously gay and vital and *real* he was. And how divinely simple. If only everything else were as simple. She tried not to think about Philippe or that sapphire engagement ring that sat in her jewel-box upstairs.

She remembered a conversation which she had had with her sister Louise last night as they were preparing for bed. Louise, with that little touch of primness . . . (Louise was *convenable* like their mother) . . . had fixed accusing blue eyes upon her sister and said:

'I think it is awful of you not to have told Mr. Lindsey that you are engaged.'

Fiona had replied:

'We've only got a little time in Scotland . . . a few weeks of freedom . . . why not make the most of it? Every man who knows that I am engaged treats me already as though I were a married woman, and I don't have any fun. Oh, Louise, I do want some fun before I settle down.'

Louise had looked at her half admiring, half accusing.

'It's very wrong to Philippe,' she had said.

And of course Louise was right, but then dear little Louise adored Philippe and it was a pity she had not been affianced to him instead of herself, Fiona. But now, as Fiona remembered that conversation, she regretted amongst other things the use of the word 'fun'. She didn't want fun any longer. She wanted serious, overwhelming love like this. She wanted Bill. Not for an hour but for always.

She surrendered herself to Bill's fervent kisses and then, flushed and breathless, drew back from him and said:

'We must be sensible . . . we must both think about it for a time. We hardly know each other. We mustn't rush blindly into anything, must we, Bill? I want you to know me better. I want to know *you*.'

The man, with his own pulses racing, body and soul on fire with love for this marvellous girl, took his pipe from his pocket and put it in his mouth. His pipe was Bill's refuge in difficult moments. He said:

'You're quite right, Sweet. You seem to be as sensible as you are glamorous. You're *perfectly* right. I wouldn't have any right to rush you into a serious affair with me. After all, you *are* Miss Rutherfield.'

That exasperated her.

'Oh, Bill, it's nothing to do with that.'

'Never mind, darling, the fact remains. You must get to know more about me. I'm so crazy for you that I'd like to shout my love from the housetops but I'm going to wait and see how you feel about me in a few weeks' time. I'm on leave and you are staying here with your aunt . . . we can meet, can't we? We must. You must make absolutely sure. Then when I go to sea again it will be first call Casablanca, and in the proper Victorian manner I shall approach your august father and ask for your hand in marriage.'

Fiona gave a helpless little laugh. She could just imagine her father's reactions if Bill walked into that big luxurious office—one of the most modern buildings in Casablanca in the Boulevarde de la Gare—and made such a request. She had a swift mental vision of her father. A big handsome man with a massive head, turning grey, and a ruddy skin. A cheerful man with some humour, but he had a harsh, almost frightening side to him. He was without softness or tolerance in business. He was a rich man and he had acquired his riches not only through brains but that flintlike hardness in his character. He had had an eye to the main chance when he had arranged the marriage between young Philippe and his elder daughter, possibly because he did not altogether trust the old d'Auvergne. Mr. Rutherfield had said one or two things in his time which had led Fiona to believe that. But with Philippe and Fiona married, there would be little chance of trouble in the firm.

Mr. Rutherfield had given Fiona and Louise everything that they wanted within reason, but Fiona was quite certain that this was one thing he would not give her . . . this chance of personal happiness at the price of breaking with Philippe. Never, never would he allow it.

She could not bear to think a moment longer. Body and brain were whirling. She said breathlessly:

'Then you'll go away tomorrow and we'll meet . . . meet outside this house, and get to know each other better.'

Bill was filling his pipe with a thoughtful air.

'Anything you say, Beautiful.'

'But you agree that it would be best?'

'In the circumstances, yes.'

'What are you going to do for the rest of your leave?'

He gave her the swift enchanting grin that made him look such a boy.

'Hang around Edinburgh and see you as often as I can.'

'Oh, Bill, I do love you,' Fiona said passionately, and throwing her arms round his neck reached up and kissed him on the mouth.

The pipe was laid aside. For a moment they clung together, then Fiona grew away from him.

'Somebody is coming,' she whispered.

Into the room came Louise. She had just been out. Hair and veil looked windswept and her blue eyes were peevish.

'I hate this Edinburgh wind,' she said. 'I shall be glad to get back to a decent climate.'

Fiona and Bill stood apart, neither of them meeting Louise's gaze. Fiona nervously lit a cigarette. Bill cleared his throat and looked at Fiona's sister with a smile. A pretty kid, he thought, but with none of Fiona's brilliance or fascination. He said:

'Don't you ever have too much sunshine and blue skies? I think this greyness is a pleasant change.'

Louise shrugged her shoulders.

'Oh, I love being in Scotland and I'm having a grand time, but I do hate the wind.'

Now she glanced with curiosity at her elder sister. Fiona looked a bit peculiar, she thought. And was there, or was there not, a trace of lipstick on Bill Lindsey's brown cheek? Louise felt shocked. What *was* Fiona thinking of? Really it was time this ship's officer left Aunt Jean's house. She had to admit he was wonderfully handsome, but she didn't care for fair men. Perhaps because she was so blonde herself. She thought the dark slender Philippe much more attractive. He was such a man of the world.

Bill met Fiona's gaze and looked hastily away again. He wasn't really very happy about this situation. With his innate honesty of purpose, he would have so liked to tell Louise here and now that he loved her sister and meant to marry her. But his conscience

41

forbade him to 'rush' Fiona. He must do as she wished and give her more time.

Murmuring the excuse that he must go out and buy some tobacco, he left the sisters alone.

Louise took off her hat and smoothed back her blonde curls.

'Fiona, I believe you have been *kissing* him. I'm sure I interrupted something . . . you must be out of your mind.'

'I am,' said Fiona, her eyes blazing, and suddenly she walked up to her young sister, seized her round the waist and embraced her. She added: 'Oh, Louise, Louise . . . I don't know what I'm going to do but I'm crazy about him, *crazy.* Out of my mind with love—yes—I admit it.'

Louise looked positively horrified.

'But *Philippe!*'

'I know. But I don't love Philippe. He's like my brother. Bill is the man I love. You can't believe what I feel like. Louise, what am I going to do?'

Louise sat down, blinking, blue eyes aghast. She looked at her sister as though she had done something criminal.

Fiona, flushed and excited, tossed her beautiful tawny head.

'I know what you are thinking and how you feel about it. But I've fallen in love with Bill Lindsey, and I just . . . can't help it.'

'Oh, Fiona,' exclaimed Louise. 'It is terrible.'

'Terrible and wonderful. Louise, wait till you fall in love . . . !'

Louise gulped. In her young mind she had been in love for a long time with Philippe d'Auvergne. She could not resist a very pleasurable thrill because her sister did not love him. And yet . . . like Fiona . . . she had been brought up to believe in the sanctity of a French betrothral, and she could see nothing ahead for any of them but tragedy. Two large tears welled into Louise's big blue eyes.

'What *will* Daddy say? Or M. d'Auvergne? Or Tante Marie? You'll have to get over this. You'll *have* to.'

Then Fiona flung herself down on the floor and put her head in her young sister's lap and whispered:

'I'm desperately, completely in love and I'll never get over it.'

'But why? I don't think Mr. Lindsey is nearly so elegant or clever as Philippe and—'

'It doesn't matter what you think,' broke in Fiona. 'Bill is the man I love. We understand each other. We laugh together. He knows the *real* me and Philippe doesn't. He can make a woman of me and Philippe couldn't. I just know it. It's fate, Louise. You can't escape your fate.'

'Oh, dear,' said Louise in a frightened voice, 'I wish we had never come to Scotland.'

'Thank heaven we did.'

'It is going to mean terrible trouble.'

'It will be worth it if Bill and I can be together eventually.'

'But you never can. You've got to marry Philippe.'

Fiona clenched her hands.

'Louise, I *can't*, now. Something must be done.'

'Does Mr. Lindsey know?'

'No,' said Fiona in a low voice. 'I've been a coward. I haven't dared tell him yet.'

Louse said primly:

'He'll have to know sooner or later, then I'm sure he will do the right thing and go away and leave you alone.'

Fiona's heart sank.

'I couldn't bear that. Oh, Louise, you don't know what this love is like. It would kill me if Bill went away from me now.'

'Oh, dear,' said Louise tremulously, 'I think I am going to faint.'

And then Fiona had to stop thinking about herself and put her sister on the sofa and ring for brandy. Louise was subject to fainting-fits. Poor little Louise who had never been very strong. Fiona knew that Louise would never give her away. She would be loyal to her sister even though she would never approve. But she had Philippe's interests at heart. She wouldn't help Fiona. Nobody would help her, thought Fiona desperately. Everybody would be against her.

On that cold April afternoon in Edinburgh,

she faced the fact that she would have to fight the whole world, including Philippe, her family, and perhaps Bill Lindsey himself, if she wanted to keep this wonderful new love in her life.

CHAPTER SIX

Twenty-four hours later Bill Lindsey left the Inverlaw mansion in Moray Place and betook himself to rooms in Heriot Row, which was a charming street of Georgian houses facing green gardens, where Mrs. Crombie, an obliging landlady, allotted him a large first-floor sitting-room with a small bedroom behind it. She volunteered to cook his meals and look after him like a mother, and since she was white-haired, enormously stout, and amiable, Bill was only too pleased for Mrs. Crombie to carry out whatever maternal obligations she felt towards him.

'It's a good deal nicer than living in a hotel, and after your aunt's house I shall need breaking in gradually,' Bill told Fiona with a smile.

Fiona, forced to let him leave Moray Place, had bidden him a tearful good-bye.

'Letting you go even as far as Heriot Row is awful to me now that I love you so much,' she had said.

To which he had answered gravely:

'My sweet, I can't bear the thought of being half a yard from you, let alone half a mile. But I can't stay in your aunt's house a day longer. I'm okay again and I must go. All I can say is, thank goodness for Mrs. Crombie. I've got a very pleasant sitting-room and maybe you'll come to see me one day. Or would that be asking too much?'

She had replied that she would come the very next day.

'Perhaps I oughtn't to suggest it,' Bill had added. But Fiona, flushed and reckless, had straightway assured him that it was a glorious suggestion and that she must see him alone for once. So Bill had driven away to his rooms a happy man and Fiona spent the rest of the day thinking about 'tomorrow'.

Luck favoured her even if it behaved in a contrary fashion to poor Aunt Jean, whose health was decidedly poor and had to remain in her bed. No one therefore to spy on her movements (not that dear Aunt Jean was the type to do much spying, but her Scottish conventionality would have forbidden her to allow her niece to visit any young man in his rooms even in broad daylight), but Louise watched her sister dress for this visit the next morning and questioned her closely.

'Where *are* you going? Why *must* it be alone? Are you lunching with Mr. Lindsey?' And so on, until Fiona grew impatient and

46

answered in quite a cross voice:

'Louise darling, can't I do anything without having to tell you about it?'

Louise reddened and her big blue eyes immediately grew liquid with tears.

'Oh!' she exclaimed. 'How unkind of you. I was only asking, and you used to tell me all your secrets.'

Fiona, penitent, dropped a kiss on her sister's head.

'Sorry, darling. I just hate being cross-questioned. And I haven't ever had any real secrets in the past. If I have now, it's because I've grown up. I've *found* myself. I'm not the ignorant child who left Casablanca with you.'

'Then you *are* going to Mr. Lindsey?'

'I'm lunching with him—yes,' said Fiona calmly. But her heart was far from calm and her eyes were like green jewels as she put the finishing touches to the sleek satin of her hair and perched upon it a delicious little blue felt hat which had a rim of grey astrakhan, matching the collar of her dark blue suit.

Louise stared at her fascinated. That was the special blue suit which had been bought in Paris by Tante Marie for Fiona to wear should she accompany Lady Inverlaw to any important functions in Edinburgh. So far Fiona had not worn it. Louise had to admit it suited Fiona perfectly. The little wide-shouldered coat was cut so as to make the small waist look even smaller, and the short skirt was full and pleated. On the slender feet were smart fur-rimmed boots—so suitable for a cold Edinburgh day and hard flint roads. Never had Louise seen her sister look so *chic*, so sophisticated. Somehow it frightened her. She stood staring at Fiona with such dismay in her childish eyes that Fiona came over to her and kissed her again.

'Louise, dearest, don't worry about me. Just let me manage my life in my own way. I'll be all right, and I assure you I have never been so happy—or unhappy,' she added the last two words with a little breathless laugh.

Louise shook her head.

'Unhappiness is bound to come of it. It is . . . you are being unfaithful . . . to Philippe . . .'

Fiona's lovely lips hardened.

'Why should I be faithful to a man whom I have never really loved or wanted to be faithful to? I'm not the meek, submissive child I used to be—ready to do exactly what Daddy or Tante Marie think best for me. I've grown up since I came to Scotland. I've found myself, I keep telling you, Louise.'

But the younger girl was still frightened and worried.

'I don't understand you, Fiona,' she said. 'You are under a spell and no good will come of it. Oh, I wish you wouldn't meet Mr. Lindsey. I wish you'd give him up.'

Fiona turned from her.

'No . . . not yet, anyhow,' she said under her

breath.

'What shall I tell Aunt Jean if she asks?'

'That I'm lunching out . . . with any of the young men whose names you remember . . . whom we met at the dance.'

'You are asking me to tell a lie,' said Louise severely.

'Then, darling, say you don't really know and I'll tell my own lie when I come home.'

Louise shook her head again.

'It can't be right to lie . . . that shows you are doing something very wrong, Fiona.'

Fiona was dabbing her throat with a few drops of scent and examining her flawless face in the mirror, as Louise said these words. For a moment, guiltily, she sat back and went on looking at herself. How she had changed, indeed, from the obedient, amenable Fiona who had been brought up in the Villa des Fleurs! She was a woman today . . . a woman wildly in love going to an assignation with her lover. And she was still, in fact, Philippe d'Auvergne's *fiancée*, and everybody who belonged to them would, like Louise, be horrified at the mere idea of her meeting Bill Lindsey . . . not only going to lunch with him, but (presumably) returning to his rooms to spend a long lovely afternoon by his fireside.

There was no actual harm in it. Bill would respect her . . . take care of her . . . it was just that they *must* see each other alone, instead of in the midst of a busy restaurant or a crowd of people in a hotel lounge. That was not very wicked. But she could not deny that Louise was right . . . she was, in a measure, being unfaithful to Philippe. At the same time, she had become bitterly resentful of that bond which had been made before she was of an age to discriminate or give her reasonable word. Coming to Scotland—meeting Bill—had opened her eyes to the glorious possibilities in this life. In no way could she visualise going back to the old bondage . . . or becoming Philippe's wife. Yet, how could she get out of it? That was the frail spot in the structure of her dreams and hopes. It was bound, she knew, to collapse one day and in the ruins she would be the most hurt. Bill would be hurt too. She could not bear that. Oh, what could she do? And how could she ever tell him? He, who meant to be so honourable, so correct, and to go to her father and ask for her hand in marriage.

Some of the ecstasy with which Fiona had started dressing for this big venture faded. Dejectedly she looked at herself in the mirror and over her shoulder at the prim, disapproving little face of her young sister. Then she stood up and deliberately sat on her doubts and fears.

'I won't be robbed of this happiness—I won't!' she cried. 'You can't say anything to make me stop meeting Bill today. You can give me away to Aunt, if you want.'

'Oh, Fiona,' broke in Louise in a stricken voice. 'You know I would never do that!'

Fiona melted and drew Louise into a quick embrace.

'Darling, sorry for even suggesting such a thing. I know you'll be loyal to me. Try to understand . . . oh, Louise, you don't know what it is to love anybody so much!'

Louise sighed. She thought she understood. She thought she loved Philippe . . . but not with this wild, passionate impetuosity. There was a crazy streak in Fiona from which Louise shrank because it was not really in her prim, virginal little soul to feel emotion with quite such a lack of restraint. She kissed Fiona back, however, and even wished her good luck.

'I'll never give you away,' were her last words. 'Although I'm sure you'll regret it, darling Fifi.'

But Fiona felt no regrets as she took a taxi to the North British Hotel where she was to meet Bill. And there he was, in the crowded lounge, waiting for her with as much impatience as she had driven to him.

Fiona felt a throb of pride as she saw him . . . her tall strong Englishman with the gold lights in his thick hair and that handsome tanned face. Even his accident and the long days in bed could not rob the sailor of his becoming bronze, the result of the salt sea and the tang of the winds.

Bill's whole face lit up when she advanced

51

toward him. How lovely she was in her smart blue suit with the grey fur collar framing her exquisite face and that adorable little hat on her tawny head. She was grace, perfection, from head to tiny, fur-booted feet. He took her hand in a warm grip and said:

'Sweet! It's heaven to see you.'

'Oh, Bill,' she said joyously. 'It's heaven for me, too. I missed you so last night. The house was like a vault. I passed your room several times and looked in and thought how awful it was that you were not there any more.'

He laughed and touched his head gingerly.

'Still bruised and knocked because a glamour girl drove her M.G. into my bike. But not ill enough to excuse me for staying as an invalid in your aunt's house, my dear. How is she, by the way?'

'Still laid up. I ought to be sorry but can't be,' said Fiona, echoing his laugh. 'Poor Aunt Jean. How shocked she would be if she knew I'd come to meet you like this. My sister is simply horrified.'

'Can't think why. You don't belong to them. You belong to yourself. Everyone in the world—men and women alike have a right to choose what they wish to do within reason once they pass the age of twenty,' said Bill stoutly. She bit her lip. Of course he didn't know about Philippe. Resolutely she drove the memory of Philippe away. It must not be allowed to spoil the memory of this day.

'Where shall we lunch?' asked Bill, taking her arm.

The contact with him sent a thrill through her and brought back the wild sweet thought of yesterday and their first long kiss. She murmured:

'Any where you wish, Bill.'

He mentioned the Aperitif. He had heard that one could get a good grill there. It was a smart little restaurant in Frederick Street. She at once assented. She and Louise had already been to the Aperitif. Everybody went there. Well, she didn't care who saw her with Bill. Let the world see. Let everybody who knew Aunt Jean tell her that her niece had been lunching there with a handsome, fair-haired young man. Today was Bill's day . . . *their* day. She had set her heart on it being so.

So they walked together, arm-in-arm, down Princes Street in the pale winter sunshine, with the grey old castle frowning from its battlements down upon them on one side, and the gay, handsome shops offering their wares on the other. All the well-known shops of Scotland's capital: Jenner's, the great stores; Mackie's, McVitae's, Crawford's, famous for shortbreads and buns and all the rich cakes made and beloved by the Scots for centuries.

Many a tall, brawny lad with a swinging kilt passed by: many a small boy proudly wearing his glengarry. The shop windows showed the gay scarlets, blues and greens of the tartans.

All the pride of the country was displayed here. And the east wind tore down the wide beautiful street, making Fiona shiver, used as she was to the languor and heat of her French Moroccan home. But she gloried in the cold, and that morning, so close to Bill, she fell in love with Princes Street and was aglow with the thought that she had Scottish blood in her veins.

'Up there, in that very castle, my grandmother was born,' she told Bill. 'Grandfather was in one of the Border Regiments stationed there. I like to think I come from that stock. There's something solid and good about it.'

'I agree,' said Bill, then, with a swift warm look at the lovely, sparkling face of the girl, added: 'But there is the French blood in you, too . . . to give you the sparkle, the grace, the wit that makes you such an enchanting creature. Mary Queen of Scots must have resembled you, Fiona.'

'Poor Mary . . . I hope I shall never be as unhappy as she was.'

'I hope not,' he echoed.

'Tell me about yourself . . . I want to know everything about you,' she said.

'I told you yesterday—what little there is. I'm a simple fellow and have led a simple life.'

'Oh no, you are not so simple. You are frank and honest but you've all your wits about you.'

'Is that your idea of me?'

'Yes,' she laughed up at him, loving his tallness.

'Maybe you're right. I know, for instance, that you are so lovely that I am a fool to think you can ever really belong to me. You were destined for greater things than life with a common sailor.'

She squeezed his arm almost in fear.

'Oh, Bill, don't say things like that. I don't want to be destined for great things . . . unless shared with you. And you are *not* a common sailor.'

'All right, darling, I give in,' he smiled. 'Now here we are . . . and you must eat a good lunch. It is the first lunch I've ever been able to give you.'

They walked into the restaurant. The narrow entrance was dark after the bright crisp day, but their eyes soon became accustomed to it, and then they were in the gaily lit bar at which a crowd of young people were already gathered drinking.

Fiona waited for Bill to leave his hat and coat. When he joined her, he asked what she would drink. She said that she never drank.

'That is . . . never cocktails,' she explained. 'Tante Marie did not like the idea of young girls drinking cocktails. But we always had wine—good vintage wines chosen by Daddy—on our table.'

'Then you shall have the best wine the Aperitif can supply with your lunch,' he said.

He refused to drink by himself and took her into the charming dining-room which had been decorated and painted by a leading Edinburgh artist. The pale green walls were delicately frescoed and there were little secluded sofa-tables, one of which the head waiter allotted to Bill and Fiona. He was a man of tact and he knew life. It was plain to his experienced eye that here were a young couple in love . . . wanting seclusion.

Bill ordered the lunch . . . everything that was 'special' for his lovely companion. The wine was chosen—an excellent hock which was at once put on ice for them.

They had *hors-d'oeuvre* and lobster and a rum sweet. Then coffee, although Fiona refused a liqueur. They sat there, lingering over the coffee. Nobody who knew Fiona was here today so she felt gloriously isolated with Bill. In a new, enchanted world . . . so different from the almost prison-like existence led in her home under the unrelaxing vigilance of parental authority.

She liked this English life . . . or Scottish if it must be called that since they were in Edinburgh. She could see that it was as conventional but not as strict in many respects as life in France for the *jeune-fille*. Here, girls were free to choose whom they wished to love and marry. Wistfully Fiona looked at Bill and he looked back into her melting eyes and felt his blood stir dangerously.

'Those lashes of yours . . . gosh, darling, they're a menace to any man,' he said softly. 'You'd better not look at me that way unless you want me to kiss you right here and now in front of all these people.'

Her heart beat fast.

'I wouldn't mind.'

'Oh, yes, you would, so I'm not going to do it,' he laughed, and set down his coffee-cup, and she thought how brown his wrists looked against his white cuffs. Brown and strong, with little gold hairs. There was something essentially clean-looking about him, and instinctively she compared him with Philippe, who was dark and pale and could almost be called effeminate beside this young ship's officer.

She was silent a moment and then glanced shyly, with tender longing, at the man.

'What are you thinking of, Bill?'

He poured out some more coffee for her from the glass cona-percolator which stood on their table.

'Only that you are much more beautiful than any other girl in the room—than in the world, if I may say so, without exaggeration.'

She bit her lip with nervous pleasure.

'Do you really think so?'

'Yes,' he said. 'Do you know, when I was at sea I used to keep a picture of Rita Hayworth in my cabin—just for fun. The fellows used to come in and ask me if it was my girl and I'd say "sure" just for fun. But I never thought I'd meet or fall genuinely in love with anyone half as beautiful. Lord knows she's alluring enough on the screen. But you . . . you're heavenly. More alluring than a dozen Ritas.'

'I've never seen her on the films. We don't go to films in Casablanca. My aunt thinks the cinemas there full of every kind of disease.'

'That might well be true. But how dull for you. You've been brought up in great wealth, great luxury, but you've had no fun, have you, my poor little Fiona?'

'None,' she admitted. '*This is* fun . . . being out to lunch alone with you. But oh, so much more than that.'

'I know, darling . . .' the endearment came from his lips so naturally, it enchanted her . . . but I can think of other things I'd so much rather be doing.'

'Such as?'

'Taking you over my ship.'

'Oh, your ship—I could almost be jealous—you love your ship so much,' she laughed.

'I love the sea, too.'

'"*Lover and Mother of men, the sea*",' she quoted.

'Who wrote such words? They're fine and true.'

'Swinburne. I was never allowed to read his poems because they were considered passionate and improper by Tante Marie, but I found a copy in Daddy's library and Louise

58

and I used to laugh over them. Now I don't laugh. I see what he means—about love. He has written marvellous poems about love.'

'I'd like to hear you read them to me,' he said, and for an instant passion burned in his own eyes as he touched her delicate slender hand with his brown fingers. Then he drew them back as though the contact with her unnerved him. He added: 'I can think of so many things I'd like to do with you, Fiona. Such as walking along the sea-shore at night, watching the moon silver that wonderful fiery hair of yours and making you look like a marble statue. Climbing mountains with you . . , reaching up for the stars. Strolling through a forest, picking violets. Drinking from crystal streams . . . making a cup out of those beautiful hands of yours. Sitting with you in some whitewashed, oak-beamed cottage before a roaring peat fire on a winter's night, roasting chestnuts. Taking you to Norway, down the fjords . . . sailing with you into some perfect sunset . . . everything I've done in my life as a sailor, and which as an ordinary man I'd like to do with you now.'

She listened breathlessly, her great eyes held by his, fascinated. When he had finished, she exclaimed:

'You're a poet, Bill, as well as a sailor. Oh, what glorious things you say . . . and think . . .'

His brown skin reddened a little and he gave a self-conscious laugh.

'I've never looked on myself as a poet. It must be your witchery. I'm really, as I said before, a very simple fellow. Oh, Fiona, my dear, I wonder if you could really be happy with me . . . sharing my life . . . a sailor's wife doesn't have too good a time. We'd be together sometimes, but often you'd be alone when I was at sea.'

'I wouldn't mind how long I had to wait if you came back,' she said fervently and with sincerity.

'You almost persuade me to believe you, darling,' he said with another laugh. 'But I've no right to ask it of you.'

She was silent again, crumbling a piece of roll in her long delicate fingers. *She* had no right to make him believe what she said. She was not free to become the wife of this dear brown, blue-eyed sailor. Yet she loved him as passionately as it was possible for her to love any man and she looked into the future with dread, with foreboding.

Lunch over, they walked out of the Aperitif and down Frederick Street, back into the broad sunlit thoroughfare of the most famous street in Edinburgh. Bill said:

'I now feel thoroughly happy, well-fed and lazy. But the wind is biting. I'd like to take you back to Heriot Row where Mrs. Crombie has lit a huge fire and will give us tea later on. Shall we go? Or would you rather I took you to a cinema?'

60

She swallowed nervously.

'I'd rather go with you to Heriot Row.'

'Shall we walk?'

'Yes. I love walking with you.'

'There's somethir I want to do first,' he said, and drew her into a big florist's which they had just approached. Despite her protests, he bought her a large bunch of red carnations.

'What shall I do with them? How can I explain them to my aunt and to Louise?'

'Give them to your aunt . . . anything you like,' said Bill. 'But I want you to have them.'

He liked to see her holding the great bunch of scarlet carnations. She was a girl who should be surrounded by flowers, by beauty, always, he thought. He spent more than he had ever before dreamed of spending on flowers for a girl—a generous portion of his week's pay—but did not care. This was his leave . . . the most wonderful leave in the world. He had discovered the most wonderful girl; and won her love. (That was a staggering thought!)

They walked over the hill and down into Heriot Row. Fiona fell in love with the row of lovely period houses, the grey façade was full of dignity and the houses were beautifully proportioned. There was nothing like them in Casablanca. She realised how tired she was of its artificial glamour, luxury bungalows, and the modern pretentious buildings in the town.

Wistfully she said:

'I think this would be a pleasant place to live

in. It's all so solid . . . and so full of the grace of a bygone age.'

'Wait till you see my sitting-room,' he smiled. 'It's an epic, really.'

She found it altogether delightful. A huge sunny room with long windows and a balcony. The furniture was massive and Victorian, but there was something very homely about it. In the middle of the room stood a table covered with a lace-edged cloth and on it was set a sumptuous tea. Scones and shortbread and Scotch buns. Enough food, as Bill said, to feed a whole family. That was Mrs. Crombie's welcome to the Lieutenant's 'young lady', as she called Fiona.

Fiona laughed and groaned.

'Why did I eat such a big lunch.'

'Well, you don't have to start on the tea yet,' he laughed back. 'Mrs. Crombie says she is going out on her messages . . . that's what they say in this country . . . it means shopping, but she'll be back to make our tea at four.'

Fiona glanced at her watch. A quarter to three. A whole hour and a quarter, alone here in this delicious, old-fashioned room with Bill. It was a fascinating thought.

She flung coat and hat on to a chair and looked at everything. Mrs. Crombie had a formidable array of china and pictures. The room was warm. A large fire burned in the black, Victorian grate. There was a big chesterfield at right angles to it.

Bill lit a pipe and said:

'Take a comfortable seat, darling.'

But she was peeping into his bedroom. It gave her a delicious thrill to see his things . . . his luggage by the window . . . his kit-bag, the plain sensible-looking brushes on the dressing-table, even the hair cream which he used. It was so domestic and so intimate. She looked back at him over her shoulder, her eyes dancing.

'A *jeune fille* intrudes upon a bachelor's privacy. Do you mind?'

'Not if you are the *jeune fille*,' he said.

His accent was atrocious, and very British, and she laughed at him. He grimaced at her.

'Oh, I know. But you're half French and live in a French city. No wonder you speak the lingo so well.'

'I'm not French this afternoon. I'm Scots. I'm just Fiona . . . your "young lady".'

He put down his pipe and held out his arms.

'My young lady, eh?'

With a swift, graceful movement that enchanted him, she sprang across the room and was clasped to his heart. He set his lips to her mouth in a kiss that robbed her of power to speak or move. Motionless, her slender body lay in that close embrace. Again and again he kissed her with deep passion.

At last he raised his head. He was pale and his breath was quickening.

'Fiona,' he said. 'You're too damned lovely,

63

darling. You go to my head . . . like the strongest wine.'

She sighed and opened her eyes.

'Oh, Bill, I love you,' she murmured.

'I love you . . . terrifically,' he said, and looked with a lover's ardent eager eyes at her every feature . . . then down to the lovely throat . . . the exquisite modelling of her breasts under the thin blue blouse. He bit hard at his lips.

'Darling,' he added, 'it's all going to my head . . . you and your love and your kisses. I'm not used to this crazy sort of feeling. I feel quite crazy when I hold you like this.'

She gave a low laugh of sheer happiness. In this moment, the shadow of Philippe slid entirely into the back-ground. She was all woman, proud of her own beauty and the effect which she had upon this man, insatiable for his kisses. All the voluptuousness in her intense nature was being awakened and developed under the caresses of his brown, hard hands. She trembled with delight and excitement as he continued to kiss and caress her. Then he let her go abruptly and picked up his pipe again.

'Let's sit down and talk, darling,' he said.

He drew her to the chesterfield and she sank down into the cushions. He sat beside her, holding one of her hands firmly while he smoked.

'I feel a bit of a cad,' he said.

64

'But, Bill—why?'

'Because this is all surreptitious and I'd far rather it was open and above-board.'

She liked him for that, but what he said brought back all the shattering realisation of her own invidious position. She wanted to speak of Philippe and her engagement, but could not bring herself to do so. She was being a coward and she knew it. Almost she despised herself for withholding the truth from this man who was so integral and above-board. Yet she so dreaded making her confession. To tell him about Philippe and see him go away from her . . . that would be too hard to bear. She had only just found him.

'I can't tell him . . . I can't!' she thought frenziedly.

He looked at her averted face.

'Do you think Mr. Rutherfield will dislike the idea of a marriage between us very much, Fiona? Hasn't he great ambitions for his lovely daughter?'

She admitted that he had. Bill sighed and, bending forward, knocked his pipe on the fender.

'That's what I fear.'

She said:

'Bill, even if Daddy forbade it, I wouldn't necessarily do what he wanted.'

'Darling,' he said, 'how sweet and dear of you. But I'd hardly have the right—'

'Would you give me up?' she broke in.

'Would you walk out and leave me just because my father disapproved?'

He looked into her swimming eyes. Her breast rose and fell quickly with her agitated breathing. She exuded love and innocent desire and the man would not have been human if he had not surrendered to her. He pulled her back into his arms almost roughly and put his lips against her pulsing throat.

'Beautiful, you tempt me. When you look at me—speak to me like that, I can't resist you. I'd take you away from your father . . . or anyone else.'

Her heart leaped.

'Would you . . . oh, Bill, would you really?'

'Anyone except a man you were legally bound to like a husband. I wouldn't want to play a dirty trick on any other fellow.'

Her heart sank again. She grew very pale and quiet. She was sure now that if Bill knew she was officially betrothed to Philippe he would say good-bye to her. She was so much in love with him that she could not tolerate that thought. Desperately she clung to him . . . to the love that was so new, so perilously exciting. He covered her face with kisses until it burned rose-red. Then gently he put her away from him and stood up.

'Darling,' he said, 'I mustn't kiss you any more. I'm only human.'

She looked at him questioningly. Bill Lindsey met the pure burning gaze of those large green eyes and adored her for her inexperience. He sensed rather than knew that Fiona Rutherfield was new to love and that love was new to her. She was born for love . . . her desire was there to match his own, but he had to protect her against her own emotions. And he thought:

'What a damned thing to do . . . to bring young girls up in 1938 to know nothing . . . to be so ignorant. Poor little darling. She's no modern glamour girl . . . she's unconsciously exciting enough to make a chap's brain reel . . . but she just doesn't realise it.'

He gave her a cigarette.

'Yes, go on . . . take one . . . smoke with me. It'll steady us both.'

'You do love me, Bill?'

'I'll never stop loving you,' he said. 'I've met the only girl on earth I'll ever love and if I don't marry you I'll marry no one.'

She sat smoking, watching him with her troubled gaze, and she thought:

'Somehow, I must get free . . . *somehow* . . .'

Then Mrs. Crombie came in with the tea and the tension lifted. They were gay companions again, gloriously happy . . . joking while they did justice to the tea, despite the big lunch. The hours seemed to Fiona to fly by on gilt-edged wings. Never, never before in her life had she been so deliriously happy. When it was time for her to go . . . when the blue twilight had covered Edinburgh like a chiffon veil . . . she felt almost panic-stricken. Supposing this was the last day she ever spent with Bill? Supposing something happened to separate them? She could not bear it.

She clung to him closely as he kissed her good-bye.

'You will meet me again. We will meet, even though you can't see my father or . . . or do anything about it yet?'

Of course, darling. I am only staying in Edinburgh in order to see you. You are my life now. You must know that.'

Her eyes filled with tears. She hated herself for her cowardice, for keeping the truth about Philippe from him. But still, in her inexperience of life, her almost childish desire to snatch the joy of the moment, she kept silent.

Once back in the big house in Moray Place she felt flat and depressed. She found Louise and one or two young people whom they had met the other night, drinking sherry in the library. Louise regarded her sister with some severity. How flushed she was, how guilty she looked, thought the young girl, and said:

'We've all been waiting for you, Fiona. Alison and Ian and Charles and all of us want to get up a party and go to de Guise. And, of course, you, too.'

'De Guise?' said Fiona, vaguely, and looked without interest at the tall young man in kilts, whose name was Charles, and his red-cheeked sister, Alison, and the others who were of no importance in her life . . . none at all.

'Yes, we want to dine and dance tomorrow. Will you come?' asked Ian Macdonald. (He had tried hard to flirt with Fiona at Lady Inverlaw's dance.)

She looked at him distantly.

'I . . . don't really know,' she murmured.

Louise answered for her.

'Of course Fiona will come. We'll have a lovely party. It is so good of you all to come along and suggest us joining you.'

Ian Macdonald brought Fiona a glass of sherry. Mechanically she sipped it. It was warm and elegant here in the big library. It spelt good taste and security. These young Scots were all of good families; approved by Lady Inverlaw. There would be no harm in going with them to a dance in a big party tomorrow. Daddy wouldn't mind, nor Tante Marie. Not even Philippe would question the propriety of it. But Fiona's thoughts were winging to an old-fashioned apartment in Heriot Row; she was reliving this afternoon, that stolen tea-party with Bill Lindsey . . . his passionate, disturbing embraces. She felt almost a sense of despair. How could she ever get away from her old life . . . all its restrictions . . . and claim a right to enter that new, enchanted life with Bill?

After the guests had gone, Louise looked with some rancour at her sister.

'Really, Fiona darling. you were so strange—almost rude to our friends. What has come over you? What *have* you been doing? You've been out for *hours.*'

Fiona took off her hat. She felt chilled, unhappy. After her lovely day with Bill, reaction was setting in. She remembered suddenly that she had left her gorgeous bunch of red carnations in his bedroom . . . she had thrust them into water in a basin. She had meant to take them away. Now he would find them and be disappointed because she had not got them here tonight. She felt suddenly exhausted. When Louise started to reproach her again, she lost control of herself and burst into tears.

'Oh, leave me alone!' she cried. 'I'm so unhappy. Leave me alone . . .'

And she ran past the astonished and disturbed Louise, out of the library and up to her room. She refused to come down again that night.

CHAPTER SEVEN

One week went by. A memorable week for Fiona because her whole world, which had been so ordered, so comparatively peaceful, before, seemed to have turned upside down.

Louise had little to say on the subject of Bill

70

since Fiona's outburst that night. She maintained an attitude of silent disapproval. Lady Inverlaw was up and about again. She had seen nothing of Mr. Lindsey since his departure and was thankful he had gone, because although she had nothing definite to go on she was quite sure that her eldest niece had become far too interested in the handsome young officer.

Every day of that week Fiona met Bill somewhere . . . if only for an hour or two. But never again at Heriot Row. Bill thought it better not. They walked and they talked . . . talked unendingly, and Fiona had lived for their meetings, restless and dissatisfied when she had to dance attendance on her aunt or the friends who came to the house; totally disinterested in any of the parties or dances arranged for her benefit.

She was now heart and soul absorbed in Bill. And he seemed equally absorbed in her.

The last time they met . . . walking together through Princes Street Gardens, looking at the flowers, where so many other couples in love had walked before them . . . Bill had said:

'You've done something I wouldn't have thought possible a few weeks ago, my dear. You've become as dear and necessary to me as the ship in which I sail. And don't think it a poor compliment if I compare you with an abstract object like a ship. For years *The Falcon* has been my one and only love and I've served her with the devotion of my being. Now I want to serve you with an equal but different devotion. My ship and my woman—my two predominant passions.'

Fiona had laughed and said:

'Put me first, darling, or I *will* be jealous.'

'You *are* first,' he had said, with that deep look in his brilliant blue eyes which never failed to stir her. 'I only long for the day when I can ask your father's permission to marry you.'

'And supposing he doesn't give it?' she had ventured to say.

'Then,' said Bill, 'I shall marry you just the same.'

For hours afterwards she remembered those words with exquisite pleasure and pain. He was a man, indeed. A man not to be denied. And she knew that she would not, in any ordinary circumstances, have waited for her father's permission. She would have gone with Bill Lindsey to the ends of the earth no matter what anybody said. It was only Philippe, that *mariage de convenance* which stood like a flaming sword, barring her way to paradise.

Soon she would have to tell Bill—she would *have* to.

Meanwhile she had not even dared to sit down and write to Philippe to tell him what had happened. Soon she would have to pay for her lack of courage and she knew it. But today was so sweet. Today which belonged to Bill and to Bill alone.

She reached a pitch where she could no longer bear hurried stolen meetings. Bill was growing impatient too. He wanted much more of her. Whole evenings . . . long days . . .

It was queer how closely they had become knit, Fiona thought, even in this short time of their abbreviated meetings.

She had told him every detail about her life in French Morocco. He had told her about his own life . . . less glamorous, much harder and more lonely than hers, for he had been orphaned as a small boy, both parents having died in a railway disaster in Canada where the family had lived for some years. A good deal of Bill's boyhood Fiona learned, had been spent in Vancouver. Then at the age of fourteen he had returned to England to live with an uncle who was a seafaring man. Then the young Bill had trained for the sea.

This uncle, Luke Finnigan, and his wife Mary were now retired and living on a pension in their little house in Golder's Green. Bill contributed to their meagre income. Fiona had learned that generosity was one of Bill Lindsey's many nice qualities. He was grateful to the old couple who had been kind to him in his boyhood. But it had been a hard boyhood and a stiff training at sea where he had started at the very bottom of the ladder.

All the more credit to him, Fiona thought, that he should now at such a young age have

73

attained his Master's ticket. She was beginning to learn all the nautical terms from him. She wanted to know them; to know all about that 'other passion' in his life. She learned, too, about simple humble people who work for their living . . . the thrill of achievement, as opposed to the boredom of riches acquired through inheritance. She and her sister had known nothing but luxury from the cradle onwards. As Philippe d'Auvergne's wife that luxury would have continued. If she married Bill Lindsey she would have to face a very different kind of existence, and she *wanted* to. With all her heart and soul she wanted that new life, no matter what sacrifices it entailed. But there remained . . . Philippe. She knew that she could not continue much longer with this dissembling . . . this putting off of the evil day when Bill must be told about the barrier between them. Sometimes when Bill fancied he saw a tragic, almost hunted look in those large lovely eyes of hers, it troubled him and he questioned her. But she would say nothing except that she loved him, and for him that was enough.

Louise confessed herself unhappy and afraid whenever Fiona slipped out of the house to meet Bill Lindsey. But it never entered her head to betray Fiona to her aunt. Lady Inverlaw, however, became suspicious of the hours which Fiona spent without the rest of the family. It wasn't normal or natural for the girl to like to go shopping or walking so often alone. Besides, Jean Inverlaw was no fool and she rather suspected some kind of an affair was going on between her beautiful impulsive niece and the attractive ship's officer who had spent a week in this house.

One day she questioned Fiona outright.

'Are you seeing this man, William Lindsey?' she asked.

Fiona, pink and defiant, answered:

'Yes, Aunt Jean.'

Lady Inverlaw clicked her tongue.

'Fiona, I am surprised and disappointed in you. You—an engaged girl . . . stealing out to an assignation with a common ship's officer like one of my tablemaids . . .'

Then Fiona exclaimed:

'Bill isn't a common ship's officer. He may not have had a public-school education or have money and background like the men who come to this house, but he is intelligent and he has read heaps of books and there is little he doesn't know. He is the most wonderful man I have ever met in my life.'

'Oh, dear,' said her ladyship, 'have you fallen in love with hint?'

'Yes, Aunt Jean. I have, and oh, Aunt *Jean*, I don't know what I'm going to do—I love him so much. And he loves me.'

'But, my dear child, your *father.*'

'I know, he would have a fit. And there is Philippe. You needn't remind me. I know it all and it is driving me mad. Daddy had no right to arrange my marriage when I was still a child. It is out of date . . . it's . . . *wicked. I* ought to be allowed to choose my own husband.'

Jean Inverlaw passed a handkerchief nervously over her delicate face. In her heart she agreed with her niece. She had always thought Harry's action in tying this child down most reprehensible. But it was done and could not be undone. And she had to be loyal to her brother. Besides, even if it were not Philippe d'Auvergne, this bewitching girl who had set all Edinburgh talking about her beauty and charm could have made a better choice than First-Officer William Lindsey of *The Falcon.* Lady Inverlaw was a snob, and because of that she found it easier to go against the other instincts which might have persuaded her to sympathise with Fiona.

'I quite see all that, my dear child,' she said hurriedly. 'But under no circumstances can you break your engagement, and the sooner you and this young man realise the fact the better.'

Fiona went white . . . so white that Lady Inverlaw was quite worried. Really, the girl was too emotional, she thought.

'I can't give him up, Aunt Jean. I can't even tell him about Philippe. It would kill me.'

An argument ensued . . . an argument in which Fiona fought for her love and Lady

Inverlaw for what she considered 'the best thing'. The result was negative. Lady Inverlaw retired to her room wondering whether she ought not to make some excuse to send both the girls straight back to Casablanca, and Fiona rushed up to her room in floods of tears. This state of affairs continued for yet another week during which everybody concerned in the affair seemed loth to take definite action. Jean Inverlaw, sorry for her niece, and unwilling to start trouble, did not write to her brother. Fiona, unbelievably happy in the presence of the man she loved, and unbelievably miserable when away from him, could not bring herself to tell Bill about Philippe.

Disaster came on the day before Bill was due to return to his ship. That very morning, Fiona had looked at her face in the mirror and seen a change in herself . . . the unawakened girl who had led such a sheltered life in the past and merely skimmed over the surface of romance had become a woman. It was written in her eyes—and in the new, passionate and tender curve of her mouth.

Inside her cigarette-case Fiona had a snapshot of Bill which someone had taken of him at sea, leaning over the rails, looking back, as he had told her, towards the coast of French Morocco, her own home. She brought out this snapshot and with burning emotion glanced closely at the strong handsome face of the man. He wore white tropical uniform and a peaked cap at a rakish angle on his head. Oh, how she loved him! It was growing impossible for her to write to Philippe as a young girl should write to her future husband. Bill was the one, the only man in the world she could ever love.

Today she must tell Bill the truth. She *must.* They were meeting for tea at the Caledonia Hotel. During that meal, her confession must be made. Together they must find some method of securing her freedom.

But for all her good intentions, Fiona was not destined to break that news to Bill, herself. He was fated to hear it in a much less attractive way.

It was at lunch-time that the cable came from Philippe—came like a thunderbolt into the quiet and dignified atmosphere of the Inverlaw house. Louise saw her sister's face change colour when she read it and heard the sharp intake of her breath. Louise said anxiously:

'It isn't bad news, is it, Fiona?'

Without a word, Fiona handed the cable to her sister, then rose and walked out of the room, a handkerchief pressed to her quivering lips.

Louise read the cable aloud to her aunt:

'Arriving Britain by Clipper first week May stop join you Edinburgh stop we will return to

Casablanca together for our marriage stop tout a toi—Philippe.'

'Oh, goodness!' said Louise, her heart beating fast, her cheeks pink and hot.

'Oh, dear!' said Jean Inverlaw. '*Now* there is going to be trouble.'

'Oh, there mustn't be,' broke in Louise. 'Philippe is so sweet. Fiona mustn't hurt him. She must be made to forget that Bill.'

'Run up to your sister, Louise,' murmured Lady Inverlaw. 'Try to talk some sense into her.'

Louise sped out of the room. If only that cable had been sent to her, she thought wistfully, how wildly happy she would have been. Foolish Fiona to prefer Mr. Lindsey. But poor Fiona! Louise could imagine what a state of mind she must have been flung into by this unexpected cable. Philippe was coming to claim his bride.

On top of that bombshell came yet another. For Mr. William Lindsey himself had just received an urgent summons to interview his skipper, and although he had never done such a thing before, he was forced to telephone the Inverlaw residence and cancel his tea appointment with Fiona. Thomas took the call—and Thomas, who had always rather resented the Mercantile Marine officer being brought into this house, gave that message to her ladyship instead of Miss Fiona. It was then that Jean Inverlaw decided that she must act, and act for the best.

She spoke to Bill Lindsey from the library.

He said:

'It is imperative that I should speak to Miss Rutherfield.'

'Mr. Lindsey, for your own good . . . and for Fiona's . . . I must ask you not to see her again,' said Lady Inverlaw. A moment's pause, then came Bill's voice (charming, she had to admit): 'I'm awfully sorry, Lady Inverlaw, and all that, but, you see, I want to marry Fiona.'

'I'm sorry too,' said Lady Inverlaw. 'But my niece happens to be already engaged and she has just had a cable from her *fiancé* in New York to say he is flying home to arrange their wedding.'

CHAPTER EIGHT

A moment's silence greeted Jean Inverlaw's words. She had to admit that her conscience pricked her when she reflected that this must have been a blow of no small dimensions to the young man. Quickly she said:

'I really am sorry, Mr. Lindsey, but—'

'Please don't bother to say any more,' came Bill Lindsey's voice. It cut like ice. 'Good-bye.'

'Now, just a moment,' began Lady Inverlaw, flustered. But all that she heard was the purr of the dialling tone. Mr. Lindsey had rung off.

Lady Inverlaw was a good woman, and at heart a kindly one, and almost as soon as she had done this thing she regretted it. She did not like to hurt anybody. She was also a little afraid that she should have minded her own business and allowed her niece to manage this thing her own way. In order to make up for her delinquency, she hastened to Fiona's bedroom and walked in.

She found Fiona in a high state of nerves and emotion. With a cigarette between her slender fingers she was pacing up and down the room, cheeks scarlet, eyes glittering. When she turned to face her aunt, there was a wild look in the big greenish eyes which startled her ladyship. Fiona was the first to speak.

'Aunt Jean!' she said breathlessly. 'I can't marry Philippe. I *can't*. I must send a cable. I must do something. I love Bill. I know I do. It's no ordinary love. There is something between us that . . . oh, you wouldn't understand. You're so calm and practical . . . you think that money and position matter. But I know they don't. Nothing matters except love in the way that Bill and I have found it and—'

She broke off, choking, flung her cigarette-end into the fireplace and looked with a trapped expression round the handsome spacious bedroom. Its very dignity, all the correctness of its Edinburgh atmosphere, seemed to mock her turbulent spirit and to say: 'Now, now! Young ladies like yourself must learn to be controlled and to do the *right thing*...

But the right thing in Fiona's mind was to give way to this love which had blossomed in her heart for a young ship's officer, who, even when he became a captain, might only earn £20 a month. (Half as much as her father gave her and Louise for a dress allowance!)

That cable from Philippe telling her that he was coming home to claim his bride had shaken Fiona to the foundations. It had brought him so perilously close and for so long now Philippe had seemed a far-off dream ... something that she had accepted before she left her Paris school because she had been told that this 'arranged' marriage was the best thing for her. She had met no other young men and had no other experience. Since her arrival in Edinburgh, she had tasted the sweets of freedom. She had learned so much more about life and men. And now she had met Bill and knew that to marry a man whom she did not love as she loved him would be nothing short of a tragedy.

She flung out a hand in appeal to Lady Inverlaw.

'Help me, Aunt Jean . . . don't let them force me to marry Philippe.'

Louise came through from the adjoining room. She had obviously been crying. She added her appeals to those of her sister.

'If poor darling Fiona really feels like this, can't we do something, Aunt Jean? Up to now I've thought it Fiona's duty to marry Philippe, but perhaps if she really cares so much for Mr. Lindsey she ought to marry *him*. Only you can't get out of a betrothal in France easily, can you? I've been telling Fiona. *I know* it is a sort of legal arrangement between our father and Philippe's.'

'It's monstrous!' exclaimed Fiona, her magnificent eyes flashing. 'I was young and ignorant when it was all done. Oh, Aunt Jean . . .'

Lady Inverlaw sat down and put a handkerchief to lips which were trembling. She felt faint. She had to admit that this thing was getting too much for her to handle. She also felt it was time she confessed to Fiona what she had done.

Having done so, she was staggered by the effect which it had. For Fiona turned milk-white and such a heartrending look came into her eyes that Jean Inverlaw turned away her gaze. Dear me, she thought, why was the girl so *dramatic!* And yet this wasn't acting. It was obviously genuine emotion. Fiona had none of her father's cool or calculating side. She was excitable, acutely sensitive and highly strung like her Parisian mother. The sooner Philippe d'Auvergne reached this country the better. It was up to him to tackle this problem.

Then she heard Fiona's voice, low and

passionate.

'I'll never forgive you . . . never, *never!* I can't bear to think of what you've done to Bill. That he should hear of my engagement in such a way! Oh, Bill, Bill, how terrible! He'll think the very worst of me. He won't understand. I could have made him understand. I was going to tell him, myself, this afternoon. Now you've ruined everything.'

Louise began to cry again.

'Oh, Fiona!' she moaned.

Fiona swung round, darted to her bed and picked up her short fur jacket and little fur hat which were lying upon it.

'Where are you going?' gasped Lady Inverlaw.

'I'm going to find Bill. I must! Things can't be left like this. It would kill me. I've got to see him and make him understand that I haven't just been amusing myself. I shall tell him the truth about my engagement to Philippe.'

'But I don't know where Mr. Lindsey is,' said Lady Inverlaw weakly. 'All that he said was that he had had a summons to his ship and—'

'Very well,' broke in Fiona, 'I shall go to the ship.'

Louise stared at her sister.

'But you can't! Fiona, it would be most *infra dig.*'

Fiona turned round on Louise.

'Don't use that word to me. I am sick of all

84

these words—what is *convenable* or *propre* or *comme il faut* and all the other things Tante Marie says all day long. I want to be like other girls. I want to be free to live and love as I wish. Nothing, *nothing* shall part me from Bill.'

With this she rushed out of the room. Lady Inverlaw and Louise stared at each other. They heard the front door slam. Louise said in a weak voice:

'Oh, dear, Aunt Jean, I know Fiona. When she is in a mood like this, she generally gets her own way. She'll go to the ship and see Mr. Lindsey, and I can't *think* what will happen.'

'There, there, my dear,' said Lady Inverlaw. 'Don't upset yourself. You know you aren't strong . . .'

Louise continued to weep, mainly because she loved her sister and was upset for Fiona's sake. But in her heart there was a little flutter of excitement. Supposing Fiona *didn't* marry Philippe. The handsome, the charming Philippe might turn to *her* on the rebound! That was an idea which little Louise hardly dared enlarge upon.

Meanwhile, Fiona was driving as quickly as she dared (even at this crucial moment she didn't forget Bill's warning to her to keep within the speed limit) on her way to Leith. It was not a particularly nice afternoon. Since lunchtime a *haar* had settled over Edinburgh. It was misty and raw, and several times Fiona had to slacken speed down Leith Walk. The tram-lines were wet and the flints on the Edinburgh streets looked slippery. Several times, too, she had to stop to ask her way. She was filled with the most frantic desire to get to Bill. She *must* see him. If part they must, then it could not be in this way. He must at least be made to believe that she loved him. She could imagine all the awful things he must be thinking about her by now.

At last she reached her destination. A more dreary, forbidding place than Leith Docks she thought she had never seen. She got out of the car and stood looking around her. The sight of the wet, oily-looking streets, the dismal wharves and the brown dirty water lapping against the walls, filled her with depression. There were few people in sight except some workmen in overalls, one or two sailors and a policeman. Fiona, shivering with cold and nerves, drew her fur jacket tighter around her and let her gaze wander from one boat to another. Grey sooty tugs . . . dredgers . . . merchant ships . . . coaling boats. Amongst them was *The Falcon*. She *must* find *The Falcon*.

She hurried up to the policeman. It took her several moments to understand his broad Scots dialect when he answered, but finally she deduced that *The Falcon* was lying alongside the dock about five hundred yards down the quayside.

Fiona hurried through the mist, conscious that her teeth were chattering. The policeman looked after her with raised brows. One seldom saw so beautiful and richly dressed young ladies in these parts. Better keep an eye on that smart-looking little car of hers, he thought.

Then Fiona found the ship. And despite her intense anxiety and the misery of the moment, a thrill went through her at the sight of *The Falcon* . . . Bill's 'second passion'. Not a very big ship—2000 tons, he had told her—grey and white, with two slim masts and one funnel. Even on a day like this Fiona could see that the decks were clean and shining. She was in process of being repainted. Fiona, standing on tip-toe, peering anxiously at the ship, could see one or two navvies at work but not a sign of an officer.

How was she to get on to the ship? How was she to get a message to First-Officer Lindsey? And supposing Thomas had taken the message all wrong and Bill was not on board at all?

Suddenly she saw a boy wearing blue trousers and jersey, sea-boots and a peaked cap on the back on his curly head, come down the gangplank. Quickly she ran up to him.

'Oh, please, can you tell me if First-Officer Lindsey is on board?' she asked breathlessly.

The boy, a stoker, looked at her with some surprise, and wondered whether one of his favourite film stars had come to life in front of his very nose. He was from London and answered Fiona in pure Cockney:

'Yaas . . . 'e's on board all right, is 'is nibs, having a couple with the skipper when I last saw 'im, miss.'

Joy radiated from Fiona's face and inspired the young stoker to even greater admiration. Fiona said:

'Oh, please, will you go and tell him that I am here?'

The boy whistled and grinned.

'Strike me pink . . . break in on the skipper and the first officer like that? Not me!'

'Oh, you must,' exclaimed Fiona breathlessly. 'It's most urgent. Tell him that Miss Rutherfield is here, or else take me on board yourself.'

'Not me, miss. That would be more than me job's worth.'

'Then go and tell Mr. Lindsey that I'm here. Please, *please*!'

The stoker surrendered. As he said to a pal that night over a glass of ale, 'I could 'ave tripped over 'er eyelashes, they was that long, mate, and w'en she sez, "Please, please," to me in that there cooing sort of voice, I'd 'ave walked in on the King at Buckingham Palace to satisfy 'er.'

And so the stoker delivered Fiona's message. A little dubiously he put his head into the skipper's cabin and announced that a Miss Rutherfield was waiting to see Mr.

Lindsey. The first officer's face turned crimson as he heard the message. The captain, a short, fat little man with a grey beard, gave a hearty laugh. He was a kindly soul and fond of his first officer.

'Chased by a lassie, eh, laddie? Dark horse you are. Thought you never had any truck with womenfolk!'

Bill stood up. Two hard lines had carved themselves on either side of his lips. His colour had faded.

'If you'll excuse me, sir,' he said stiffly. 'I'll be back directly, but I'd better just let the lady know that I can't get away.'

The skipper chuckled.

'Nonsense, Bill. You go along and take her out for a cup of tea. We've finished our talk. See you tomorrow, eh?'

Bill hesitated. The stoker's announcement that Miss Rutherfield was here at the docks and wished to see him had flabbergasted him, but in no way did it take off the edge of the pain he had been feeling ever since Lady Inverlaw's revelation of what Bill considered 'sheer duplicity' on Fiona's part. The shock he had received had staggered Bill's little world about him. Not only had he loved her as he had never thought it possible to love a woman, but he had believed in her. He had taken it for granted that she must have had admirers, but never for a single instant had he imagined she was engaged. He had seen no ring and she had

89

never mentioned the *fiancé* in the background. There could be only one explanation. She was amused with him, Bill, for the time being, but that was all.

Bill had decided that he would never trust another girl's word, neither would he give his heart to another woman to break. He was finished with Fiona and he was finished with love. He was going back to his old, his first, love—his ship.

The last thing he wanted to do was to see Fiona. But even though she had hurt him so profoundly he could not send her a curt message by a stoker.

He walked down the gangplank. Fiona watched him coming, her heart throbbing wildly. It was the first time she had seen Bill in uniform. She thought how well the neat blue, and that peaked cap on the fair bright head, suited him.

'Oh, Bill!' she said tremulously, and held out her hand. 'Bill, thank goodness I've found you.'

He did not take the little hand and there was no answering smile on his face. It was granite hard. If, deep inside the man, he was torn with the old love and desire at the sight of her exquisite face and figure, he did not show it. He said:

'Why have you come?'

'Bill, I had to explain.'

'There is no explanation possible,' he cut in

roughly. 'You're engaged to be married. Better not waste time in a place like this, Miss Rutherfield. Stay at home and write to the man you are going to marry. That would be more suitable.'

She went scarlet and then white. Such a wounded look came into the big brilliant eyes that he turned his head quickly away. Damn it, the girl must be a consummate actress. Anyone would think she really cared about him. Sheer misery made him snap at her.

'For lord's sake, get into your car—drive home and leave me alone.'

Then Fiona said passionately:

'I won't. I won't go until you've heard me. You don't understand and you have got to be made to. You've got to hear my story.'

'Look here,' began Bill, 'if all you wanted was an affair with me because you were bored while your future husband was away, why didn't you say so? That would have put a different light on the whole show and it wouldn't have been so dishonest. You—'

'Oh, be quiet, Bill!' Fiona interrupted again in a frenzied voice, 'I know what you're thinking and feeling and I don't blame you, but give me a chance. Why in heaven's name do you think I've taken the trouble to come down here if I don't really love you?'

That floored him. He felt himself out of his depth. He was torn between the desire to snatch her in his arms and kiss that lovely sorrowful mouth and to take her by the shoulders and shake her as he would a child who was exasperating him.

'You must come with me,' said Fiona. 'I'll drive you somewhere where we can talk. Only don't look at me like that—give me a chance, *please.*'

Bill drew in his breath. He shoved the peaked cap a little farther back from his brow and shook his head as though bewildered. He didn't know what to think.

'Oh, all right,' he said wearily, 'I'll come with you. What's it matter now? I really don't care.'

She could not bear to hear him speak like that. She could not bear his accusing gaze or the awful gulf that seemed to be widening between them every moment. She only knew that she must make him understand that she hadn't meant to hurt him and that she had never, *never* loved Philippe d'Auvergne.

She took his arm. Despite himself he allowed her to do so, and walked with her along the quayside to her car.

CHAPTER NINE

The story was told. Bill Lindsey knew everything at last. He sat in the car beside Fiona, smoking his pipe, brooding over it.

They had driven away from the docks, up Leith Walk and on to the Crags that overlooked the City of Edinburgh. The *haar* still hung over the landscape, but they could see the dim shape of chimneys and housetops and the wreathing smoke which had earned for the historic city the name of 'Auld Reekie'.

Immediately below them lay the stately, sombre buildings and grounds of Holyrood Palace, where the ill-fated Mary Queen of Scots had spent so many bitter and tragic days. Up here on the Crags the wind blew cold and the air was raw. There were no people in sight. They were quite alone. And Fiona sat with her face buried in her hands, silent, tears trickling slowly through her slender fingers.

For a long time Bill could not bring himself to speak. He had so much to work out in his mind. But not a single word of the explanation which Fiona had given had escaped him. At least he knew now that she had spoken the truth. He would stake his life on that. If she had been only playing with him she would never have sunk her pride and come in pursuit of him. And if she had erred in not telling him right from the start about her engagement, he could see now that she had a genuine excuse. She had been attracted by him as swiftly and as strongly as he had been attracted by her, and she had not wanted to spoil it all. Later, when her feelings toward him had become serious, she had shrunk from hurting both him and herself. It would all have been unforgivable had her case been an ordinary one. If, for instance, hers had been a normal engagement. But this *mariage de convenance* which was being forced upon her was, in Bill's opinion, both abnormal and a crime. He knew that such things went on in France, but this was the first case which he had ever had to consider at all seriously. And it involved the one girl in the world whom he, himself, wished to marry.

At last he took his pipe from his mouth and spoke to Fiona.

'Look here, I don't want to criticise your father. I am only an employee of his and he is a big important man. But I must say here and now that I think it was criminal of him to bind you down when you were only sixteen. In no circumstances has anybody any right to make you go through with this marriage.'

Fiona's head shot up. Her lovely face was smudged with tears but her eyes were radiant.

'Oh, Bill, then you understand and you *do* forgive me. You won't stop loving me?'

He put his pipe in his pocket and turned to her. All the pain, the harshness that had seemed a few hours ago to dry up the very springs of his emotion, fell away from him like a cloak at the sight of her sweet tear-stained face and her touching humility. He had never been more in love with her than in this moment when he drew her into an impassioned embrace and kissed her.

94

'My darling, my darling,' he said huskily. 'What a brute I have been to doubt you. Forgive me for what I said to you at the docks. Don't ask *me* to forgive *you*. I understand everything now.'

She clung to him, burying her face against his warm neck.

'Oh, Bill, I couldn't have borne it if you'd gone on hating me.'

'I never hated you.'

'Oh, you did. I saw it when you looked at me.'

'My sweet, it was only because I loved you so much and thought you'd played a dirty trick on me and didn't really care.'

'I've done nothing but care,' she sobbed. 'It's been getting me down for days. Every single day I've tried to steel myself to tell you about Philippe and couldn't. But I was going to tell you today and Aunt Jean ruined it all.'

'Arcot Jean hit me a knockout blow,' said Bill grimly. 'I walked out of that call-box punch-drunk, I can tell you.'

Fiona laughed. Midway between laughter and tears she surrendered to the blessed comfort of his arms. There were still grave difficulties ahead of them, but nothing mattered so long as Bill continued to love her.

Bill was talking again about her betrothal to Philippe. He had nothing good to say about it. If, as Fiona said, it was a case of legal documents and signatures between the two

95

families, it was all the more monstrous.

Fiona said:

'But you won't stop loving me . . . you won't let this drive you away from me, will you?'

'My darling,' he said gravely, 'I'll never stop loving you now. And if I can see some way of helping you get out of this tangle so that I marry you, you can be certain I shall do it.'

'I'll tell Philippe everything the moment he arrives,' she said feverishly. 'He is coming to Edinburgh. I'll *have* to tell him.'

'And your father?'

'Heaven knows. He has set his heart on my marriage to Philippe and these engagements are so binding in France, Bill. It is simply *awful.*'

'You poor little thing!' he said, and lifted one of her hands to his lips and let it stay there a moment.

'Something must he done, whatever Father or Philippe have to say.'

'Well, until this fellow Philippe gets over here, I suppose we are at a standstill,' said Bill gloomily.

'I suppose we are,' she sighed.

'And I've got to go to sea in a week's time.'

'Oh, Bill!'

'What's more,' said Bill, in the same dejected voice, 'I've had a disappointment about the command of the ship. The Company has signed the skipper on for another month or two for various reasons. But I hope to take

96

his place in June or July.'

'Everything seems to have gone wrong,' said Fiona.

'The whole thing is that I ought not to have come into your life,' said Bill in a bitter voice. 'I've no right to ask Rutherfield's daughter and heiress to throw up a wealthy *fiancé*, and—'

But Fiona interrupted him. She flung herself back into his arms and kissed his lips to stifle the words.

'You're the only man I shall ever love or ever marry,' she exclaimed.

For an hour they sat there talking, planning, hoping. But the moment of separation had to come again. Fiona knew that her aunt and sister would be frantically worried about her. There was to be a sherry party at six o'clock to which Aunt Jean had invited several of her important Edinburgh friends to meet her nieces. Life had to go on . . . such silly trivial affairs as this must be attended to. One could not behave without any consideration for others, no matter how much one was in love, Fiona told herself. But an impenetrable gloom seemed to envelop her whole being when she drove the M.G. down from the Crags and along the narrow streets of old Edinburgh leading back to the West End. She could hardly bear to say good-bye to Bill. But good-bye it had to be and it was agreed between them that they had best not meet again until Philippe arrived.

'After all, you are engaged to the fellow, I suppose,' Bill said reluctantly. 'And until you are free, I've no right to be with you.'

Much as Fiona deplored this, she had to admit that Bill was right.

Formality forbade that they should do more than clasp hands when they parted. Full of depression and foreboding, Fiona garaged the car and walked into her aunt's house.

She had planned to go straight up to her room and have a long talk with little Louise. But Louise must have seen Fiona coming and was already in the hall to greet her. Her big blue eyes were bright with excitement.

'Fiona, Fiona! What a good thing you've come home. Aunt Jean and I have been praying you would. There is a terrific surprise waiting for you. Go into the study and see who is there.'

'Not Philippe!' gasped Fiona, her heart missing a beat,

'No, not Philippe.'

Fiona breathed again.

'Who, then?'

'Go and see,' said Louise.

Fiona took off her fur hat, shook back her long lovely hair and walked into the study. She saw a large portly familiar figure standing before the fire. A man with a grey head, and a big square face burned to a reddish tan.

'Daddy!' she exclaimed.

Harry Rutherfield came forward with both

hands outstretched.

'Well, well, my little Fiona!' he said heartily. She ran into his arms and kissed him. She was glad to see him. She was very fond of her father. But there was a horrid little feeling of doubt which chilled that pleasure as his lips brushed her cheek. She had always been a little afraid of him—afraid of the cold hard streak which she knew to be somewhere in his nature. To her he had been a loving and indulgent parent, but there had been one or two occasions out in Casablanca which had marked themselves on the sensitive girl's memory. Once when one of the native servants had disobeyed him, she had heard her father curse the man in his own language and turn him ruthlessly out of his service. Another more important affair was when a head clerk of the Anglia Shipping Line had put himself at the head of a movement amongst the employees of the Line to get higher wages and better hours. When Rutherfield had refused the appeal, this man had organised a strike. And Harry Rutherfield broke him. Fiona knew none of the details, but she had heard the matter being discussed between her father and his friends and Tante Marie. She must have been about fifteen at the time. She had also heard through gossip that the wretched man not only lost his job but that her father had seen to it that he did not get another. One day the miserable fellow had come to the Villa des

Fleurs begging for another chance for the sake of his starving wife and family. Harry Rutherfield had refused that chance. Fiona could remember vividly going, herself, to her father and imploring him to reconsider his decision. She could remember also the cold ruthless look in his eyes when he had answered:

'You must never interfere in business, my dear, and you had better learn at once that it is unwise for anybody to try to get the better of me. That man made a bargain and he broke it. He enticed others in my firm to break theirs. I have no mercy on people who do not stick to their contracts . . .'

It was queer, but somehow today, when she walked into Aunt Jean's study and saw her father, she remembered that very incident and those very words. And something inside her quivered. For *she* had made a bargain with Philippe d'Auvergne and she knew that her father would never permit her to break it.

His next words informed her that neither her aunt nor her sister had mentioned Bill Lindsey to him.

He drew her towards the fire, beaming at her.

'Come and tell me all that you have been doing, my dear. I hear great news. Philippe is on his way home and so there will be a wedding in Casablanca soon, eh? Tante Marie will have to take you and Louise to Paris and get you a trousseau, eh, eh?'

Fiona's heart sank to the lowest depths. But with Bill's kisses still warm on her lips, her courage did not fail her. White, taut, she put back her head and faced her father.

'It is just as well you've come, Daddy,' she said tersely. 'I'd better tell you at once that I've met somebody else . . . over here . . . somebody I've fallen in love with. I want you to let me break my engagement to Philippe. I can never marry him now—never!'

CHAPTER TEN

While Fiona spoke those brave words, she kept her gaze fixed on her father's face. She fancied that a little of the ruddiness left the full cheeks and that the lips under the iron-grey moustache tightened. He continued to smile but the pupils of his eyes became mere pinpricks. Then he said in a jocular way:

'Goodness gracious me! What a lot of nonsense! What a baby you are, to be sure. I can see that I've spoilt my pretty Fiona. Fallen in love with some young man over here . . .? What would Philippe say?'

Fiona swallowed hard.

'I don't know. That's what I want to discuss with him . . . and you, Daddy.'

Harry Rutherfield moved to a table on

which stood an ivory box . . . a box of exquisite Moorish workmanship which he, himself, had sent to his sister with one of his generous cheques enclosed in it. He opened it and extracted a cigarette.

With his face averted from his daughter now, he said:

'You will never discuss it with Philippe, my dear. That would be . . . shall we say a tactical error . . . which I would never allow my little girl to commit.'

Fiona, her heart pounding, broke out passionately:

'Daddy, do stop all this "little girl" business. I am not such an innocent baby. If I was ignorant when I came to Scotland, then I think that you and Tante Marie are greatly to blame. Both Louise and I have been kept far too much out of the world. I have learned what it is to be free . . . to think and act for myself. And I know that it wasn't right that my marriage should have been arranged for me before I knew what it all meant.'

Mr. Rutherfeld lifted his head and gave Fiona the coldest look she had ever received from him. That smile of his made her uncomfortable and apprehensive. It was two-edged.

'And do you know what marriage means now, my dearest Fifi?' he asked softly.

'Not exactly,' she said with crimson cheeks. 'But I know what it is to *love* someone—really love him.'

'I can see,' said Mr. Rutherfield, 'that Tante Marie was right when she deplored my action in sending you and Louise alone to Scotland. It was one of my few blunders. I thought it right that you should get to know more of your Aunt Jean, for whom I have the highest regard, and that you should also learn something of this country. But I imagined you would be sensible and, indeed, I counted upon you behaving honourably, Fiona.'

An anguished look came into Fiona's eyes.

'Oh, Daddy!' she exclaimed. 'I haven't wanted to be dishonourable. The thought of Philippe has worried me terribly. But you must try to understand. My marriage with him was *arranged* by you and M. d'Auvergne. I accepted it because I thought I had to. But I don't think so any more. I love Bill and I want to marry *him*.'

'And who is—Bill?'

Fiona clasped both hands behind her back. It was infuriating, but her father made her feel like a guilty schoolgirl. The palms of those small hands were damp, and her slim body was trembling with nerves. Of course, she might have known that she would get neither help nor sympathy from Daddy.

In past years, while she had been entirely under his direction . . . the beautiful dutiful daughter . . . all had been well. But once again she could hear his harsh voice after the dismissal of his clerk, telling her that it was unwise for anybody to try to get the better of him. She wished that Bill were here so that she could hold on to him and have his moral support. She said bravely:

'Bill is First-Officer William Lindsey.'

Mr. Rutherfield examined the point of his cigarette. 'First-Officer William Lindsey,' he echoed. 'A sailor, eh?'

'Yes, in the Merchant Service; and he is expecting to command his ship very soon,' said Fiona eagerly.

'And what ship is that, may I ask?'

'*The Falcon*, Daddy.'

'*The Falcon*,' repeated Mr. Rutherfield slowly, and looked at his daughter hard. 'That name sounds familiar. Isn't it one of my own ships?'

Fiona licked her dry lips.

'Yes, Daddy, it is. Bill is an employee of the Anglia Shipping Company. It is a coincidence, isn't it?'

The man took no notice of that eager and rather pitiful young voice, neither did it move him a fraction of an inch that his young daughter was trembling, sick with nerves, before him. In his fashion he loved Fiona, just as he loved Louise. Of the two girls, Fiona, who was strong and brilliant and beautiful, was his favourite. That only made it all the more necessary in his estimation that she should live her life according to his ideas. His own thirst for power and money was now, as it had always been insatiable. He wanted Fiona, too, to have power and money. He knew perfectly well that after his death, if he was still the prosperous man he was today, that both his daughters need never want for money. But he was hale and hearty and had no intention of dying for another twenty years . . . perhaps thirty. And he had a partner. A clever and cunning man, Gaston d'Auvergne. A man whom Harry Rutherfield, personally, disliked, although he admired his business ability. Harry had watched Gaston all these years and he was convinced that d'Auvergne was open to corruption; too fond of women and wine like others of his nationality.

There was a certain widow, a Madame Brizaque, in Paris—a clever, designing woman of great physical charm. Philippe's mother was dead and d'Auvergne was contemplating putting Yvonne Brizaque in her place. Harry disliked and feared Yvonne more than his partner. Once she became Gaston d'Auvergne's wife, these two might plot together to steal from him, Harry Rutherfield, interests in the firm which were his by right. He had recognised this fact during the last five years and meantime Madame Brizaque had been gaining more and more of a hold on d'Auvergne.

It was this factor which had persuaded Rutherfield that the best thing to do was to unite his eldest daughter with d'Auvergne's son. Whatever his weaknesses, the Frenchman adored his son Philippe. For Fiona to break that betrothal now would, in Harry's estimation, be nothing short of a major calamity. The unity of the two houses of Rutherfield and d'Auvergne *must* be cemented by personal as well as business ties. On that Fiona's father was determined. In addition to this, Philippe was a good match, and for Fiona to throw herself away on an officer of a small merchant ship would be sheer lunacy.

When Rutherfield spoke again, he did so quite gently, but even Fiona in her distraught state of mind was quick to recognise the imperturbability of the man.

'My dear child . . . my *dearest* Fifi . . .' (that was his pet name for her) 'of course this the most absurd thing I have ever heard. You, Fiona Rutherfield . . . you, whom Philippe is coming home to marry almost at once . . . to have fallen in love with one of my penniless employees and—'

She broke in, frantic with her love and her fear:

But I don't care how penniless he is. I love him. Oh, if you could see him, Daddy! He is quite out of the ordinary. A marvellous officer . . . one of the most devoted and efficient men in your Line. Oh, if you knew him you wouldn't be so derogatory.'

'My dear,' said Mr. Rutherfield, 'you

surprise me. This young man appears to have influenced you very considerably in a short space of time.'

'He has. I admit it. It is because I know we were born to love each other.'

Rutherfield shook his head. He pitched his half-smoked cigarette into the fire, then walked up to the girl and put both his hands on her shoulders.

'My poor little Fifi. I'm afraid this is going to be very painful both for you and for me. I have no wish to hurt you. You know that from the time you were born I have wanted you and your sister to be happy. If you have become infatuated with this young man, I am very sorry, because it will upset you to say good-bye to him. But it must be good-bye, Fiona. You must realise that. You have an obligation not only to yourself and me but to Philippe—' He paused and lifted her left hand, adding regretfully: 'Whose ring, I see, you are not wearing. Run along and find it, darling, and put it on at once. Let us hear no more about this—First-Officer William Lindsey.'

Fiona moved back from her father. Breathlessly she said:

'No! I can't. I won't. I must tell Philippe that I'm not going to marry him. And I shall never say good-bye to Bill. Whatever you do, I shall make Philippe release me. He has always been kind and sweet to me. When I tell him about Bill he will understand and let me go.'

Even as she spoke those words, her heart quailed a little. Her father's face was so pale now that it was almost livid. There was a terrible pause. Then he said:

'Do you mean to defy me?'

'I love Bill,' she half-sobbed the words. 'Please, please, Daddy, don't ask me to give him up.'

Another pause. At length Rutherfield said very quietly:

'You said just now that this young man is a very loyal and efficient officer, and that he is about to get command of *The Falcon.*'

'Yes,' she nodded, 'he is.'

I see,' said Mr. Rutherfield, and proceeded to take out a diary and a slim gold pencil and jot down a few words.

Fiona watched him, her brows contracted. Somehow she sensed that there was some sinister meaning behind those words which he was writing. Her knees began to tremble under her. She had never felt more afraid of her father. Indeed, this was the first time that she, personally, had ever been afraid of him. She gasped:

'Daddy, what are you going to do?'

He looked at her with a smile which she was never able to forget. A cold and heartless smile which robbed her there and then of any natural affection for him which she had felt since her childhood. His next words merely proved that she had foundation for her dread.

'Fiona, my dear, you may forget that I am not only your father but the head of the Anglia Shipping Company . . . that no appointment is made in that Line without my approval and that no matter how highly this young man of yours was recommended for the command of one of my ships, unless I approved, he would never get it.'

She gasped again.

'But you wouldn't stop Bill from getting it? You wouldn't do anything to *him*?'

'In the ordinary course of events, no. I have nothing whatsoever against him, and if he is efficient he will go far . . . in fact, if he is as good as you say—and you are as sensible as I hope you will be—he may even be given a better command. I have bigger and better ships than *The Falcon*.'

An instant's silence. It did not take very long for Fiona to realise the significance of her father's quiet words. He did not intend to sanction any attempt on her part to ask Philippe for her release. If she said good-bye to Bill, Bill would get a bigger and better job. But if she defied her father and went to Bill, he would never get his command. In other words, this was a hideous form of blackmail. So hideous that Fiona felt sick with hatred for her father despite the close kinship between them. It roused all her deepest emotions. Panting, she blazed at him:

'Oh, how despicable of you . . . how simply

despicable! You'd rather ruin an innocent, faithful man and break my heart than lose whatever you hope to gain by marrying me off to Philippe. That's what it is. I see it all now.'

Mr. Rutherfield shrugged his shoulders and put his diary back into his pocket.

'All this will not get you very far, my child,' he said. 'And no amount of abuse of me will alter my decision. Unless you say good-bye to this young man immediately, the Anglia Shipping Company will have no further need for his services. We have too many applicants for the command, and of course if he is dismissed my service and he kicks up a fuss or tries to get into some other line, he will find himself a marked and ruined man. A word from me and nobody will listen to what First-Officer Lindsey has to say.'

Fiona stared at her father as though not able to credit her hearing. It was terrible to her to think that her own father could be so cruel. She broke out:

'It's what you did to that clerk of yours . . . you let him starve . . . him and his wife and children . . . because he offended you. Oh, how *unspeakable!*'

'Stop shouting at me,' said Rutherfield calmly. 'I don't wish to hurt this young man in the least. In fact, I'll see that he gets everything that the most ambitious ship's officer could want—if you will co-operate with me. But for reasons best known to myself, as well as the fact that you are in honour bound to Philippe, you *must* marry Philippe as soon as he comes home.'

The half-hour that followed seemed like a nightmare to the girl. For a short while she stormed, argued, pleaded, alternating between reproaches and tears. Louise came in and was turned away. The *haar* that had hung over Edinburgh all the afternoon turned to rain . . . pitiless rain that drenched against the windows of Moray Place. It grew dark and cold. In Fiona's heart the chill of death itself settled, and left her without a vestige of hope. Her love-dream receded far, far out of her reach. Harry Rutherheld won. He had known from the beginning that he would win. And he had to admit even to himself that it was because Fiona's love for this young man was real . . . and real love means total sacrifice . . . that his was the victory.

She would not ruin Bill. He loved her and he wanted her. But she was woman enough to realise that if he lost his job and could not ge it back again it would almost break his heart. His job meant so much to him. He had looked forward so ardently to being master of his ship. Robbed of that, financially ruined, how could he marry Harry Rutherfield's daughter? He would feel he had no right even to ask her. His hurt would be so great that it might even come between them. And that Fiona could not bear. Oh no! She loved Bill far too much to be the

111

cause of his losing all that he had so far lived for. Better that he should lose her, Fiona, and go back to sea . . . gain his ambitions and forget her (no, he would not forget but in time he would be resigned), and she . . . well, she dared not even think what she would feel, carrying out her contract to marry Philippe d'Auvergne.

She had no choice now. Love had made it for her. She promised Mr. Rutherfield that she would write to Bill and tell him that she would never see him again. She could not, of course, tell him why, so he would have to place his own construction upon her decision.

Fiona sat in a chair with her face buried on her arm. She was not even crying. She was mute, taut with pain. Out of the mists of that indescribable pain she heard her father's voice again:

'My poor little Fifi. I pity you, my child. Indeed I do. But one day you will thank me for this. You will get over your infatuation, and when you are Madame d'Auvergne you will be grateful to me, I assure you.'

Then Fiona lifted her head, and out of those great eyes of hers gave her father a look which made Harry Rutherfield feel more uncomfortable than he had ever felt in his life. It was a look of hatred and of an implacability which might have been his own.

'I'll never be grateful to you,' she said between her teeth, 'I'll never thank you and I'll

112

never love you again. You've ruined my whole life.'

He raised his brows and then gave a short laugh.

'Ah, but remember, my dear, that if you'd gone to your Mr. Lindsey, his life would have been ruined as well as yours.'

With a gesture of despair Fiona sprang up and rushed out of the room.

CHAPTER ELEVEN

It was Louise who came to her sister's rescue that night. Hitherto the younger girl, delicate from birth, had been so spoiled and pampered that she had never really faced trouble of any kind. But she was truly devoted to Fiona and even though jealous of her at times—especially where Philippe d'Auvergne was concerned—and a little inclined to be smug, Louise had a warm heart. She was horrified by Fiona's complete despair following upon that stormy interview with their father.

Fiona lay face downwards on her bed, denied still the relief of tears although she shuddered as she lay there, and now and again a great gasping sigh came from her. She would not admit her aunt. She took no notice of the various messages which her father sent up, begging her to come downstairs and be sensible. She would see no one but Louise, and to Louise's little hand she clung, drenched with suffering.

'I've got to give him up, Louise . . . I've got to send him away! I can't bear it!' she kept moaning.

Louise was the one who wept. Her eyes were swollen with tears of sympathy. This was what her sister should be feeling for Philippe—this anguish of love. It seemed terrible that it should be so misdirected. Louise, under Lady Inverlaw's influence, was quite sure that Mr. Lindsey was beneath Fiona's regard and that the whole affair was shocking. She could not get Fiona to tell her what had passed between her and their father. On that subject Fiona's lips were sealed. Deep in her heart the girl knew that the man whom she called 'Daddy' had proved himself no kindly father but a monster of cold calculating cruelty. But that she must keep to herself. She hated him now. But let Louise go on thinking that he was wonderful. Why should poor little Louise also taste the bitterness of disillusion?

In answer to Louise's repeated questions, Fiona said:

'Never mind why . . . I've just got to send him away. I daren't see him again. I might tell him the truth, and then he would perhaps wish to ruin himself for my sake.'

'Oh, what are you talking about, darling?' wailed Louise.

'Never mind. Let me lie here a moment . . . let me think . . .'

But the hours went by and Fiona was no nearer to reaching a solution to her problem. She just did not know how to tell Bill that he must go away and never see her again. How could she, when with every passionate impulse in her body and soul she yearned for him? She lay there, drowned in grief, remembering every contour of his face, his touch, his kiss, the unspeakable ecstasy of that moment when he had taken her in his arms up there on the Crags and told her that he would love her for ever.

What would he think if she sent him away now? What could he think except that her courage had failed her and that she preferred peace and security to a struggle with and for him?

Finally Louise hit on a plan. She, herself, would go to Mr. Lindsey's rooms. She would tell him that he must not see Fiona again. She would try to soften the blow.

'I promise you I will do everything I can, because I am so dreadfully sorry for you both,' Louise assured Fiona.

Fiona sat up. Louise was shocked at the sight of the changed white face of her sister.

'Yes,' she said dully, 'perhaps that would be a good idea. You go to him, Louise . . . he is at Heriot Row . . . Take a taxi. You can slip out without Daddy or Aunt Jean seeing you. Just tell him that it is all impossible, and that I can't see him again. But tell him . . .'—her voice broke—'tell him I love him.'

Louise, hastily putting on a fur coat and tying a scarf around her head, nodded.

'I promise. I'll do everything I can to make it easy. Oh, I know you'll be thankful when it is all over, Fiona. When Philippe comes back he will make you forget Mr. Lindsey.'

But Fiona did not hear this. She had turned and flung herself down on the pillows again. Now the tears came, wild and bitter, raining down her face. Louise, biting her lips to keep back her own tears, hurried out of the room.

About a quarter of an hour later, Louise stood in the sitting-room of the house in which Bill Lindsey was staying, talking to this man who had so vitally affected her sister. She had seen little of him when he had been staying in her aunt's house. This was the first time, perhaps, that she had ever really spoken more than a few chance words to him. She had to admit afterwards that he made a deep impression upon her. In spite of her childish adoration for Philippe d'Auvergne she could not deny that First-Officer William Lindsey was an extraordinarily handsome young man and that there was something strong and magnetic about him which would make any feminine heart flutter. When she told him that she had come here on Fiona's behalf to ask him to go away and not see her again, she watched that handsome face tauten and grow white under the bronze. A look of mortal hurt clouded those blue and candid eyes of his. Louise's tender heart was touched, but she believed that it was for Fiona's good that she should do this thing.

'Fiona is terribly sorry, and so am I,' she said naïvely. 'But, Mr. Lindsey, really it could never have come to anything . . . my sister has *got* to marry M. d'Auvergne.'

Bill's hands clenched at his sides.

'Is this Fiona's own decision?'

'Yes, I'm afraid it is.'

'I don't believe it,' he broke out harshly. 'After what she said to me a few hours ago, I can't believe it.'

'Oh, but it's true . . . you see, my father has come . . . when she got back from her meeting with you, he was there and he talked to her and made her see how impossible it was for her to break her engagement.'

Bill stood mute. So that was it! The great Mr. Rutherfield had arrived and talked Fiona into seeing that any continuation of her affair with him, Bill, was out of the question.

'You can go and telephone Fiona . . . speak to her yourself . . . if you don't believe me,' added Louise. 'Only I think it will give her much more pain. It has hurt her terribly having to say good-bye to you. I really think she *is* awfully fond of you, Mr. Lindsay.'

The man's soul was in torment, but the

ghost of a smile lifted the corners of his lips as he looked down at the fair-haired Louise, with her large tearful blue eyes. A weak, pretty creature, this girl, with none of Fiona's brilliant charm, and yet there was something in the delicate contour of her brow and chin . . . something in her voice, which reminded Bill all too painfully of Fiona. He said between clenched teeth:

'Oh, how *damnable*! . . . If two people love each other . . . were meant for each other . . . *why* should fate separate them like this? Oh, I know I was crazy ever to think she would leave everything for me, and I oughtn't to have asked her. But I did . . . because I thought she wanted to, and that we could have made something of life together.'

Louise sighed.

'I must go back before they find out that I have gone,' she said. 'Try not to be too upset. I'm sure Fiona will recover once Philippe comes home.'

'I dare say,' said Bill Lindsey bitterly.

'May I take my sister a message from you?'

'Yes. Tell her that I *quite* understand.'

'Is that all?'

'What else is there for me to say?' came from Bill, and there was such a look of strain on his fine young face that even Louise, young though she was, felt a desire to put her arms around him and comfort him. She concealed this desire, however, and hurried away.

At home she found that Fiona had pulled herself together, dressed, and made up her face. There were no traces of tears left. She looked ill and haggard and she had put on too much rouge which Louise implored her to remove.

But Fiona, her eyes glittering, gave a hard laugh.

'Oh no, leave it on. Let Daddy and Aunt Jean think I am flushed with happiness because Philippe is coming home. Now tell me . . . did you see *him*?'

Louise recounted her meeting with Bill. Fiona listened intently.

'And that is all he said? Just that he . . . understood?'

'Yes, darling.'

'How did he look?'

'Pretty awful,' said Louise glumly. 'Obviously he does care a lot for you.'

A moment's silence. Fiona put a hand to her throat. She did not intend to break down again. But the most bitter pain devastated her whole being. She knew exactly what had happened. She could picture it all. Bill had said that he understood. But of course in his imagination she had failed him. Tomorrow or the next day he would go to sea, carrying with him only the memory of a love which appeared too weak to stand on its own feet. And she would willingly have died for him. That's what she was doing . . . mentally dying . . . in order to save him from ruin.

Suddenly she said:

'Don't mention his name to me again . . . never, Louise . . . *never.* Do you hear?'

'I hear,' said Louise.

The two sisters stared at each other miserably. Somehow in that moment, like a psychic flash, there passed between them the irrefutable knowledge that one day they would both hear that name again . . . that Mr. William Lindsey had by no means gone out of their lives.

But for the moment that was how it appeared to be.

That night Fiona and Louise sat with their father and aunt and two charming young officers . . . Cameron Highlanders . . . at a dinner-party which had been hastily arranged by her ladyship. One of these officers made every attempt to interest and amuse Fiona Rutherfield, and she laughed and talked to him. But her eyes were stricken and her heart heavy with pain. Mr. Rutherfield, believing that he had won the day without any loss to himself, planned to go out in the morning and buy his elder daughter a handsome present. Somehow he would win back the affection he knew he had lost.

When he said good night to her, he told her (with what he thought great generosity) that he had already written to the authorities concerned and told them to give Mr. Lindsey immediate command of a new ship . . . 3000 tons . . . which had been launched not long ago at Liverpool.

'It is one of the biggest merchant ships we have built and a beauty. Captain Lindsey will be proud of it. You've done well, my dear.'

Fiona did not even thank him. She avoided his goodnight kiss and went to her room. Long after her sister was sleeping, she lay awake, the hot tears trickling through her fingers. Captain Lindsey! That sounded fine, and it would make Bill happy to get command of such a fine new ship. But he wouldn't have her, his beloved, and she wouldn't have him.

'Oh, Bill, Bill,' she whispered in the silence of the night, 'I do love you so!'

*   *   *

Two days later First-Officer William Lindsey was hastily summoned by his skipper and acquainted with the astonishing news that a telegram had been received from the company's head offices in Liverpool, offering him command of *The Albatross*, which had just completed its maiden voyage and was shortly leaving for the Mediterranean.

Bill was frankly staggered by this. He had expected to be master of *The Falcon* but *The Albatross*! Why, it was one of the most prized commands in the Anglia Line. It was stupendous news. The skipper smacked him on the back and congratulated him.

'Always knew you would go far, my boy. If I were ten years younger, I would be jealous.'

Bill remained silent. There was no particular excitement in his breast. He was thinking bitterly: 'It has come too late. If Fiona had loved me enough to stand by me, how proud and pleased I would have been.'

The thrill had lost its savour. It was a dead world for Bill Lindsey. He packed up and went to Liverpool, leaving all that was gay and bright and enthusiastic behind him in Edinburgh where he had first loved, and then lost, the only girl in the world for him.

Fiona knew that he had gone. It was not that anybody told her. She just knew . . . And Edinburgh had become for her the grave of all her hopes and dreams. She wanted nothing better now than to leave it. Perhaps back in Casablanca, in the warmth and beauty of the Villa des Fleurs, she might regain some peace of mind, some modicum of happiness.

Meanwhile, there hung over her the dread shadow of Philippe's return. All too soon May Day came and, twenty-four hours afterwards, Philippe's arrival in the country. He telephoned to her late at night from London, speaking to her in French.

'I am flying up to Glasgow tomorrow morning, and shall then motor to Edinburgh and to you, *ma très chère*,' he said eagerly (her heart was like a stone as she listened to that familiar, charming voice). 'We will have so much to talk about.'

'Yes, Philippe,' she said dully.

'It is as well that we are going to be married at once. You will have heard all the rumours of war. Heaven alone knows what may happen at the end of this summer if that man Hitler continues with his madness.'

Fiona did not answer. She did not interest herself in war or politics. In any case, her father had always said there would never be another war with Germany.

Came Philippe's voice again:

'I long to see you, *petite fleur*, and you . . . do you long for me?'

She hesitated. She did not visualise Philippe's pale aristocratic face. She only saw Bill's brown tender one. Somehow, she told herself, she must remember that it was Philippe whom she would marry when she returned to Casablanca. *Somehow*, tonight, she must give him a suitable reply.

CHAPTER TWELVE

'Are you there, Fifi?'

She pulled herself together.

'Yes, I am here, and of course I am longing to see you.' Somehow she forced the words.

That seemed to satisfy Philippe. He went on

talking to her. The three minutes became a quarter of an hour but still he spoke—an expensive trunk call meant nothing to the son of Gaston d'Auvergne. He was always extravagant. At length he rang off and Fiona lay back in her bed and covered her face with her hands, trying to figure out how she was going to go through with the sacrifice which she had made for Bill's sake. It was not that she hated Philippe. She could only think of him with affection and the most friendly feelings. Philippe in the past had meant so little. Now as a future husband he had become a very real figure. And he was actually in this country waiting to see her, travel back with her to Casablanca and there lead her to the altar. Because she had learned to love Bill Lindsey, the mere idea of this marriage terrified her.

She heard Louise's excited voice.

'Was that Philippe on the 'phone? I'm sure it was!'

Fiona looked at her sister. Louise was sweet, she thought, in her pink satin-quilted dressing-gown, open at the neck showing the milk-white throat, around which hung a gold chain and little gold cross. Louise was very devotional. What a tragedy that *she* was not the one betrothed to Philippe, mused Fiona. They would have been so well suited in every way, and she so obviously adored him.

'Yes, it was Philippe,' said Fiona. 'He is flying to Glasgow tomorrow and will be here during the afternoon.'

Louise's fair young face flushed with pleasure.

'How simply thrilling.'

Fiona made no answer but turned over in the bed and hid her pale face in the pillow. Louise heaved a sigh. She sat down on her sister's bed and putting out a hand touched the beautiful tawny hair which lay like a cloud of red-brown silk on the pillow.

'Oh, Fiona,' she said sorrowfully, 'do try to forget *him* and give Philippe a real welcome. He will be so disappointed if you don't.'

Silence. Then from Fiona:

'I'll try, Louise. Now go to bed, darling. It's late.'

'I would like to think that you'll do everything to make Philippe happy,' persisted Louise.

Once again Fiona turned and looked at her sister. Then her lips twisted into the ghost of a smile. Leaning upwards she clasped Louise's thin young figure in a warm embrace.

'You're rather a pet, sister mine. So kind and good. I wish I were half as good. You'd do your duty no matter what it cost you. Even though you love him yourself, you'd gladly see Philippe happy with me, because you think it right that we should marry. I wish I had your outlook, but I haven't. I just can't face the future philosophically. I only know that I want Bill and that it is *killing* me.'

Louise, easily moved to tears, was soon weeping for Fiona . . . (and a little for herself because she did love Philippe very dearly and he was not for her). She did what she could to comfort the other girl.

'I think you're wonderful, Fiona darling . . . you're much better than I am. You've done your duty and given up Mr. Lindsey. And you're always thinking of me. I'm the one who is selfish and I get tired and cross easily too. I love you, darling Fiona. We all do. Don't be miserable.'

'Go back to bed,' said Fiona brokenly.

Louise touched the little gold cross at her throat.

'I'll pray for you,' she said, in her prim little way, and the words reminded Fiona with faint and sweet regret of the days spent in the convent school in Casablanca where the good nuns had taught them both when she and Louise were small children.

'Yes, Louise, pray for me,' she whispered. 'I shall need all your prayers.'

'Oh, I'm sure you'll feel differently when you see Philippe tomorrow,' said Louise on a more hopeful note.

But on the morrow Fiona felt no differently. From the hour that she awoke it was to the same persistent hear-ache for Bill. She wondered where he was . . . if he was in his new ship now . . . at sea . . . or still on shore. Oh, if she could only see him—or even hear

126

from him! He had come so suddenly into her life, and with equal suddenness he had left it. But that her feeling for him was real she knew beyond doubt, because she could not stop missing and wanting him.

The meeting between Fiona and her *fiancé* took place just before tea, alone in Lady Inverlaw's handsome library, where a fire had been lit—for the May day was cold. The family had discreetly arranged that nobody should be there to disturb them.

Fiona had a fit of nerves as soon as she heard the doorbell ring, and later Thomas came into the library and announced: 'M. Philippe d'Auvergne.'

She saw Philippe walk across the room toward her with the quick light tread which she remembered. He was an extremely graceful young man of slim build. He looked pale and tired after his long journey, but his almond-shaped dark eyes were alight with eagerness as he reached the girl's side. He seized both her hands and carried them, each in turn, to his lips.

'Fifi! My beloved Fifi!' he said, in a voice full of emotion. He had the easy emotionalism of his race, but behind the sentimental façade Philippe d'Auvergne was well controlled and had a slight tough of hauteur which gave him distinction. Everything about Philippe was very well-bred. He had carefully kept hands, exquisitely oiled and brushed hair, black as a raven's wing, and faultless clothes. He boasted a Savile Row tailor but had the Frenchman's love of somewhat colourful socks and ties.

'My beloved Fifi,' he repeated, and kissed her hands again, 'what heaven to see you after our long separation.'

He spoke in French. It was the language in which they usually conversed in French Morocco. Fiona heard herself murmur a suitable reply, but the hands which he kissed were ice-cold and her whole body was quivering.

She knew him well . . . as boy and girl they had seen much of each other. They had played tennis . . . danced . . . corresponded, first as friends and later as an engaged couple. But never had they really been lovers. And never until today had he seemed such a complete stranger. She did not even feel at ease with his language, which she spoke like a native. She knew that there was something utterly English in her . . . something which had responded to Bill Lindsey. He alone was real . . . dear, strong, brown, blue-eyed Bill, her sailor who had teased and kissed her in the same breath.

Weakly Fiona sat down on the arm of a chair. She was glad that Philippe had made no attempt to do more than give her the customary kiss on her brow. Then he stepped back a pace, staring at her.

'I think you have changed . . . yes, you've grown more beautiful and more mature, my little Fifi.'

'Have I?' she said, and her lashes drooped nervously.

'More mature,' he repeated. The thought seemed to give him pleasure. He took a silk handkerchief from his pocket and dabbed his lips with it. Fiona could catch the strong odour of eau de Cologne which emanated from that handkerchief. It made him seem to her a little effeminate. Perhaps it was because she had got to know and love a thoroughly masculine being like Bill that Philippe should appear effeminate today. She tried desperately to give him the welcome which Louise had wanted her to give.

'It is wonderful to see you back, *mon cher.* Tell me about your journey.'

But he was not thinking about the journey. He continued to look intently at his *fiancée.* When he had last seen her in Casablanca months ago she had seemed a radiant child untouched by life or love. What had altered her so completely? he wondered. Today she appeared aloof, and, he had to admit, less spontaneously affectionate in her attitude toward him. He was sensitive and could feel the new embarrassment and restraint in her manner. Her eyes had a deep secretive look. There was a strangeness about her.

'You are truly a most beautiful woman, Fiona,' he said at length. 'I am a very lucky man.'

To hide her nervousness, she turned and walked to the sofa and sat down. Philippe followed and sat beside her. For a moment they exchanged news. He told her a little about his life in New York, the long flight which he had just made by Clipper, and then by 'plane to Scotland. He said how cold it was up here in May. He did not like Scotland and he did not think he was going to like this big gloomy house, he said. He wanted to make immediate arrangements for their return to Casablanca where it was so warm and beautiful.

Fiona agreed to everything. Her father was there, too, she informed him. They could all travel home together.

'And Louise? My little sister-to-be. Is she well?'

'Very well and looking forward to seeing you.'

She could feel his bright dark eyes probing hers, and she could not conquer the uncomfortable sensation that it caused her.

'Let us see if Daddy and Louise are in,' she murmured, and would have risen but he pulled her back.

'I want you alone a little longer. I can't stop looking at you. You have grown lovelier than a dream.'

She tried to laugh, but the laughter died as Philippe pulled her into his arms. Passion was stirring in him. He held her closer than he had ever done before. His lips travelled slowly

130

down her cheek towards her mouth, while he murmured words of intense admiration and love. Yes. Philippe was playing the lover today in all seriousness, and under his caresses her face grew paler and her heart sank like a stone.

'Kiss me, my Fiona,' he murmured against her ear. 'Kiss me, my exquisite wife-to-be.'

Mute, helpless, she hung in his embrace. Every instinct in her rebelled against this thing. She had not dreamed until now what torture this sacrifice would be. Here, in this very room, Bill Lindsey had first taught her the meaning of passionate love. His ghost was here now, coming between her and the young man she was being forced to marry.

Then Philippe's lips claimed hers and she broke away from him, panting, scarlet.

'Oh no, *please* don't!'

Immediately Philippe regained his composure. Releasing her he stood up and walked to the fireplace, pulling a cigarette-case from his pocket.

'I am sorry if I have offended you,' he said haughtily.

She looked at him with despair.

'Of course you haven't. I . . . there is no question of offence. I . . . it's just that we have been apart so long and I—'

'*Soyez tranquille*,' broke in Philippe with a cold smile, 'I can see that I have been too hasty. My apologies, *ma chère*. I am afraid my absence from you has not made your feelings toward me any more ardent.'

She felt cornered . . . trapped. She knew that unless she made an effort Philippe would realise that something really serious had transpired while he had been away. He might even guess that there was another man. With all her heart she wanted to tell him about Bill. She wanted to be frank. But for the moment she dared not. She must give herself time . . . give this thing a chance. After all, she had made the sacrifice for Bill and she must abide by it.

Courage came to her rescue. Quickly she sprang to her feet, and of her own accord went to Philippe and put her arms round his neck.

'You must forgive me . . . it is because I haven't seen you for so long . . .' she said, stumbling over the words. 'Don't be angry with me, dear Philippe. Be patient.'

At once he melted and caught her back in his arms. She ravished his senses with the beauty of her great green eyes and the red-brown satin of the hair that curved so alluringly down to her neck. In America he had thought of her as she had thought of him, in a rather nebulous way. He had grown to manhood knowing that this marriage had been arranged for him, and like a good Frenchman had accepted the fact without question. But this afternoon for the first time he fell seriously in love with his future wife.

CHAPTER THIRTEEN

The Rutherfield family, accompanied by Philippe d'Auvergne, left Scotland and returned to French Morocco a few days after Philippe's arrival in Edinburgh.

Mr. Rutherfield was in good spirits, for, as far as he could see, his elder daughter had accepted her fate, and although he had to admit that she was cool and changed toward him, he told himself optimistically that that would alter again once her marriage had been celebrated and she found herself an adored and happy wife.

Philippe alternated between ecstatic happiness because of his newly developed passion for his bride-to-be and disappointment because he could see plainly that she was not in love with him. Many women had loved Philippe d'Auvergne—charming Parisians, smart Americans, and English girls. He knew exactly how soft and yielding a woman could be in a man's arms . . . the look that should come into her eyes just before he kissed her . . . the way those eyes would close in ecstasy during the kiss . . . the desire to match his own. But Fiona in his arms was a creature of ice rather than fire. She was always sweet to him and not nearly as wayward and dominant as she used to be. But he knew perfectly well that her heart did not beat one fraction faster for love of him. He had questioned both her and the family as to the men she had met n his absence. In his own mind he was positive that this lovely girl who had been affianced to him since her schooldays was now in love with another man. That alone would account for her present psychology. But he could find out nothing. The name of Bill Lindsey and that brief tempestuous episode in Fiona's life was kept a deadly secret by everybody concerned.

So Philippe continued to hope that he would win Fiona's love before their wedding day. He told himself that Scotland had been too cold and stark for her. In the sunshine, the glamour of her own home, she would melt toward him. Philippe was a believer in the correct 'setting' for love. But Fiona, anxious though she was to leave Edinburgh (so full of bitter-sweet memories for her), equally dreaded the return to Casablanca. Her father harped on the fact that her wedding must take place within a month at the latest.

Flying by Air France from Toulouse to Casablanca, she experienced a sense of captivity, of frustration, such as must, she told herself ruefully, have been felt by many a young Moorish girl hundreds of years ago when she was to be sold in the slave market to the highest bidder.

Philippe was her friend. He was kind and charming. Nevertheless she knew that she was as helpless as that that slave. She had been sold by her father to his partner's son and heir. There had been no actual money transaction beyond the usual gifts and deeds between the two families. But the essential fact remained.

So, one brilliant day, Fiona came home. No longer the radiant childlike Fiona who had left the Villa des Fleurs with her sister, full of excitement at the thought of a visit to Edinburgh, but a woman who had loved and suffered. And she knew, even as she drove with her family and *fiancé* from the airport to her home, that the ghost of Bill Lindsey came with her. He was always with her. She thought of him unceasingly.

It was a glorious hot afternoon. Both she and Louise were used to the heat and loved it. They both wore thin dresses and large hats and carried sunshades. Through smoked glasses Fiona looked out upon the golden beauty of the familiar scene. The white buildings with their flat roofs and painted shutters. The narrow winding streets. The intense blue of the shimmering sea and sky, and in the distance the fierce desolate mountains.

Many people recognised the wealthy Rutherfield family who had lived here like princes for half a century. The Arab women, in their long embroidered robes and black yashmaks, eyed the party inquisitively out of their long painted eyes. Frenchmen saluted.

Arabs, Negroes, Chleuhs, salaamed as the shadow of the great shipowner's Rolls-Royce fell upon them.

Then as they turned through the beautiful gates into the grounds of the Villa des Fleurs, there came upon Fiona the hopeless feeling that she would no more be able to forget Bill here than she had done in Scotland. The very glamour of the place enhanced her longing for him.

It was all so lovely . . . the magnificent harbour, the modern town, the centuries-old native quarters, and the magnificent feathery palms and delicate green of eucalyptus that threw welcome shadows against the harsh whiteness of the buildings.

And now they came to the Villa des Fleurs—long, low, exquisitely designed. (It lived up to its name. The native gardeners made sure there were always flowers in its shady garden. Violet-coloured morning glories, sweet-smelling rose geraniums and the more violent passionate hue of the bougainvillaea which rioted over the walls.)

Louise leaned out of the car and exclaimed:
'Isn't it marvellous to be back?'

Philippe, with an eye upon Fiona, said:
'Truly marvellous.'

Mr. Rutherfield, with a smug expression, put in: 'And what a setting for your wedding, eh, my little Fifi?'

She turned and gave him that long cold look

which never failed to make Harry Rutherfield feel uncomfortable. Then she smiled at Philippe. Not even he, who loved her, could know that her heart was breaking as she answered:

'A wonderful setting.'

But to herself she whispered: *'Bill, Bill, why couldn't it have been you? Oh, my darling beloved, where are you now?'*

The car drew up before the front verandah. Two Senegalese menservants, wearing the scarlet and white livery of the Rutherfield household, came running out to take the luggage.

But no Tante Marie as they had all expected. And five minutes later Fiona knew that her aunt had been taken seriously ill that morning, and already a specialist had been wired for and was flying over from Paris.

At once the family pleasure in the return home evaporated and gave place to grave anxiety. Tante Marie was a great favourite with everybody, and strict though she was with the girls, Fiona and Louise had looked upon her as both mother and aunt for many years.

Philippe, having made sure that he could do nothing here, left the family and drove to his own home. The sisters hurried to their aunt's bedroom.

They were both shocked at Tante Marie's appearance. She was a *petite* woman in her early fifties and always smart and immaculate like so many Parisians. But her face was shrunken and yellow and she looked desperately ill. There was a terrible pain, she said, in her side, and she admitted now that she had been feeling bad since Christmas but had told them nothing.

'*Chère petite tante*,' said Fiona, 'we must get you well now we are home.'

'Indeed, yes,' said Madame Duronde. 'There is your wedding to prepare for.'

'Yes,' said Fiona quietly, and Louise avoided her sister's gaze.

But Destiny made a move in Fiona's favour this time. That wedding which Mr. Rutherfield desired so enthusiastically, and wished to hasten on, did not take place in June. Nor, in fact, could the union between the two young people be effected at all that summer. For Tante Marie's illness turned out to be even graver than she, herself, feared. The specialist from Paris said she must be taken to the French hospital in Casablanca at once and operated upon. Although Tante Marie was not told, the doctor admitted to Mr. Rutherfield and his daughters that there was not much chance of Madame Duronde surviving. Her illness was incurable.

So for the next two or three months the grim shadow of Tante Marie's impending death hung over the Villa des Fleurs. Mr. Rutherfield chafed against this stroke of misfortune, but he had to agree with the d'Auvergne family that it would not be seemly for a wedding to take place while Tante Marie lay at death's door. And the poor woman took a long time in dying. After her operation she lingered for several weeks. Fiona was deeply depressed, but at least her poor aunt's fatal illness had given her unexpected respite. There was no talk of buying a trousseau and no immediate fear of a wedding just now.

Philippe, himself, when he and Fiona were sitting together on the verandah one afternoon drinking tea in the English custom, confessed that he was not really sorry for the delay.

'Passionately though I love you, my little Fifi, I know that you are not really in love with me,' he said. 'Only time can change your feelings. Soon I shall have to return to New York. I cannot neglect our business over there any longer. But I will be back at the end of the summer and perhaps by then . . . you will have grown to care as you should for your husband.'

Fiona coloured. It was the first direct allusion that Philippe had ever made to her lack of passion for him. She concealed her thankfulness that he would soon be going away again and that her freedom would be pro-longed. Giving him her hand, she said:

'I am deeply grateful for your patience and consideration, *mon cher Philippe.*'

He gave her a long searching look. She was exquisite in her white linen dress, pearls around her neck and his huge sapphire ring on her finger. But she had grown pale and thin and so much too serious these days. Naturally she was shaken by the thought of her aunt's impending end, but he was confident that there was something else . . . something much more serious . . . inwardly grieving Fiona.

'Fiona,' he said suddenly, 'you love another man, don't you?'

The shock of that unexpected question confused Fiona. She flushed violently and rose to her feet.

'I . . . oh, really, Philippe! . .

'Don't worry to tell me, *mignon*,' he said almost angrily, 'I know. I will not even ask you questions. I shall continue to expect that once you are my wife you will give me your entire devotion.'

She wanted to speak to him, to tell him about Bill, but she could not. But her great eyes swam with tears. He lifted the hand that wore his ring, kissed it and walked away from her. And she knew that nowadays Philippe was torn with jealousy.

That next week Tante Marie was still alive, and much against Harry Rutherfield's will Philippe d'Auvergne returned to New York and all plans for the wedding had once more to be cancelled.

In that same week Hitler's army marched into Poland, and before they all knew where they were England and France had declared war against Germany.

Personal matters had to be laid aside. In the interests of their two countries, Harry Rutherfield and his partner worked day and night. 'The Anglia Shipping Line was now in process of being taken over by the Government.

Fast and furious the black clouds of war blew up and clouded the horizon, but Casablanca remained as peaceful and lovely as ever. The sun shone just as brightly and there seemed little change in the daily life led by Fiona and her young sister. But Tante Marie had breathed her last and lay buried in the little Catholic churchyard and an old Scottish governess, Miss Macdonald, had come back at Mr. Rutherfield's request to chaperone his daughters. He had so often to be away these chaotic days.

Louise did not like Miss Macdonald. And she hated all the war talk, and . . . incidentally . . . fretted for Philippe, who was still the idol of her heart. But Fiona, in some strange way, found her spirit uplifted in the midst of the convulsions which were shaking Europe. She was still free . . . Philippe had cabled that he was coming home as soon as he could get a seat on the Clipper. But he had not come yet, and she would not allow herself to think about her wedding. She worked for the Red Cross. And the work occupied her mind and her time. Although Miss Macdonald, who was a dry, unsympathetic woman, had never been a favourite of hers, the woman had a new charm for her. Leith was her birthplace and of Leith she often talked, and Fiona found herself listening hungrily, ridiculously moved by the very mention of the word. Would she ever forget how she had rushed to Leith Docks in that agony of longing to see Bill?

The long-drawn-out anguish of this summer had not dimmed his memory or lessened her desire for him. And now she fell to wondering what would happen to him in this war. There were dangers at sea. The U-boat menace . . . the horror of mines. No ship would be safe.

One day there came upon her such a passionate longing to get news of him that Fiona waited for a day when she knew her father to be in Gibraltar, then went down to the Anglia Shipping Company offices in the *Boulevard de la Gare* and asked one of the clerks for the latest movements of *The Albatross.*

The man told her respectfully that no shipping movements could now be disclosed for reasons of security. Fiona said:

'Oh, *please*, can't you tell me *anything* about it?'

Few men were ever able to resist Fiona when she looked and spoke like that. And after all, she was Miss Rutherfield, thought the clerk. There could be no harm in telling her what he knew. It was little enough. Just that *The Albatross*, commanded by Captain

Lindsey, had recently returned from a trip round the Cape and was actually due :here in Casablanca some time this month. He felt sure, he said, that Miss Rutherfield would not ask for dates as he must not give them.

Fiona thanked him and left the office, conscious that her heart was beating like a sledge-hammer. An excitement teemed through her blood such as had been absent within her for many a long weary month. *The Albatross* was coming to Casablanca! Captain Lindsey in command! Bill . . . *Bill* would be here some time this month. She might see him! She *must* see him.

And then, with a feeling of terror, she remembered the submarines and the mines, and she knew that now there would be no rest for her, no peace of mind, until she actually saw with her own eyes that Bill's ship was safely anchored off Casablanca.

CHAPTER FOURTEEN

That next morning, Harry Rutherfield returned from Gibraltar only to tell his two daughters that he must shortly leave them for a longer period. He was a tired and somewhat disgruntled man, these days, working at high pressure. Gaston d'Auvergne was in Paris where the political situation was none too good, although the spirit of the people was high and there was a great deal of talk throughout the country about the invincibility of the Maginot Line.

Young Philippe was dealing with things in New York. A great deal of new responsibility had fallen on to the shoulders of Fiona's father. His next journey was to be Portugal. He was flying to Lisbon in another twenty-four hours.

Before he left he had a long talk alone with his eldest daughter. It was the first time since their memorable scene together in Edinburgh that they had discussed things alone. Fiona had studiously avoided talks with her father.

She froze as soon as her father began talking to her today. She felt not the slightest affection or respect for him. And he was feeling the fact. For the first time in his life his approach to her was a little timid, even appealing.

'You are happy these days, aren't you, Fifi?' he asked her. 'I mean, my dear'—he cleared his throat—'there is no longer any doubt in your mind about your marriage . . . it will be celebrated as soon as Philippe can get back to Europe?'

'If you say so,' was Fiona's icy rejoinder.

Harry Rutherfield lit a cigar and puffed at it for a moment in silence, his brows contracted. They were sitting in the long low drawing-room—the most English room in this villa. It was furnished with Queen Anne walnut, which had been specially brought over from London, and fresh English-looking rose-and-white chintzes.

The rainy season in Casablanca had set in. Today the white buildings of the town were obscured by a mist, and in here the servants had lit a wood fire in the big open Spanish grate. Fiona stood with her hands spread out to the blaze. She looked calm and poised. Mr. Rutherfield felt irritated because he could not probe beneath that calm exterior. Even Louise, whom he questioned now and again, could not tell him whether or not Fiona was still thinking about that fellow Lindsey. She never appeared to mention him to her sister.

It was sheer desperation to discover the truth that made Harry Rutherfield himself bring up that forbidden name.

'Fiona, you surely must realise after all these months where your duty lies, and how wrong it would have been to throw Philippe up for that fellow Lindsey.'

The sudden bright scarlet that touched Fiona's high cheekbones gave away to her father the unpleasant truth that the name still had power to stir her.

'I'd rather not discuss it,' she said.

Mr. Rutherfield cleared his throat again.

'Now, now, Fiona, there is no need for you to keep up this unfriendly attitude between us.'

She fixed her large clear eyes upon him steadily.

'I can never be friends with you again,' she said. 'I shall never forgive what you did to me—never.'

'But, Fiona, my child, it was for your own good—'

'I see no object in discussing it,' she broke in, and her breath came fast.

Rutherfield chewed the end of his cigar. He knew . . . and Fiona was perfectly well aware that he knew . . . that *The Albatross* was due at Casablanca. *He* could not stop the ship putting in here, whatever his personal feelings or desires. He could not so completely interfere with the sailings on his Line. Now less than ever, for since the war Bill was serving under the Government as well as the Anglia Line. But Bill had done well. The reports that Rutherfield had received of the new captain . . . the youngest in the Line . . . had all been excellent.

Rutherfield said:

'I carried out my share of the bargain. Lindsey is climbing to the top of the tree and—'

'Why do you keep talking about him?' interrupted Fiona, her eyes blazing at her father. 'I don't want to hear. I've carried out my share of the bargain, too. I've told Philippe that I'll marry him when he comes back.'

That was all that Mr. Rutherfield wanted to

know. He sighed with relief. Now he could go to Lisbon without undue anxiety. He was quite sure that Fiona was a girl of her word. And if she saw Lindsey when he was here . . . well, it would be too bad, but their meeting would have no far-reaching results. All the same, Rutherfield wished he were not leaving Casablanca at this moment.

He thought:

There was a certain Spaniard living in this town, a Senor Miguel Cortez. A small business man, mad for money, a despicable, whining upstart who always licked the great Harry Rutherfield's boots. It might be as well. thought Fiona's father, if before leaving home he went to see Cortez. The man would spy on young Lindsey here with the greatest of pleasure, if it meant a fat cheque for him. And after all there were ways of spoiling things for Lindsey (just in case his head should be swelled from a sense of his own importance). Ways which, if they took effect, could never be blamed upon him, Fiona's father.

He murmured a few more words to his daughter and then left her.

Fiona walked to the window. She stared out at the mist, down to the harbour which could be seen from this window, for the Villa des Fleurs stood on the crest of the hill. The Mediterranean looked grey and stormy. Out there somewhere, thought Fiona, *The Albatross* was approaching the French

Moroccan coast. Nothing could stop It coming—except a torpedo or a mine. Fiona knew that her own father could not stop it and her mind exulted. She whispered the dear, forbidden name painfully:

'Bill, oh, *Bill!*'

Before Mr. Rutherfield set out for Lisbon, he called the little family together and made a new suggestion. There was a war on, he said . . . a war which had not to any great extent affected Casablanca at the moment; but in England and Scotland girls were joining the Forces, wearing uniform, doing their bit. Mr. Rutherfield considered himself a patriot and he wished his daughters also to do *their* bit. Rolling bandages at the local hospital was not enough. The name of Rutherfield must be kept before the public eye. (That, Fiona thought with sarcasm, was her father's main reason for wanting his family to serve the country . . . he loved to be noticed by authorities higher than himself.) He suggested that as the Villa des Fleurs had many empty rooms . . . far too many (they gave no parties these days since Tante Marie's death) . . . it should be turned into a Red Cross Hospital for naval officers, both French and English. He would put it under the auspices of the *Croix Rouge* in Casablanca. Miss Macdonald could run the domestic side. He would finance the equipping of the place and the building of a small operating-theatre. The house was beautifully planned and could soon be adapted to the purpose. Fiona and Louise would, of course, serve here on the nursing staff as V.A.D.s.

Miss Macdonald considered the idea an excellent one. In her thrifty Scots mind she felt that the Rutherfield fortune should be expended in a cause like this rather than wasted on mere extravagances. Louise was thrilled and embraced her father, for whom she had a warm regard.

'What a wonderful idea, Daddy. We must start at once.'

Then they all looked at Fiona. She nodded in her quiet way. She was always so quiet these days. The vivid excitable girl of the past had changed indeed.

But she approved of the plans. She wanted something to do . . . something *real*. It seemed only right that her beautiful home and her father's money should be offered for the good of France and Britain.

After that there was no longer peace or quiet in the famous villa. The *Croix Rouge* accepted Mr. Rutherfield's generous offer with alacrity. There were many voluntary workers and plenty of native labour, and Miss Macdonald and the two Miss Rutherfields gave unstinted service. It did not take many days to transform the luxurious villa into a small but efficient private hospital. There were ten single bedrooms and the ballroom and large billiard-room, which made wards of ten beds each. There remained nothing now but the installation of the operating-theatre.

One wing overlooking the harbour was left as it used to be for the Rutherfield family.

As the day of completion drew nearer, Louise grew more and more thrilled. In these days when a major catastrophe had overtaken the world, she was fast forgetting her own delicacies and assured both her sister and Miss Macdonald that she was strong enough to be a nurse. She looked enchanting in her new uniform and knew it. And she was looking forward to the first convoy of wounded to arrive.

Fiona, too, looked lovely in her V.A.D. uniform. Somehow it added to her glamour even with that tawny hair half-concealed by the crisp white veil. But she shared none of Louise's excitement. There were too many things on her mind. Nearly every day she heard from Philippe, and every letter expressed his ardent desire to get back and marry her.

In his last note he had said:

I know that I am going to find you changed again, my beloved Fifi, and that you will have a real welcome for me this time. You will make me the happiest man in the world . . .

Such a letter could only distress her. For

absence from Philippe had done nothing toward increasing her warmth of feeling for him. She could still think of him only as a charming brother, and these days, during the hectic activity in the villa, she could only think of *The Albatross* and the man who commanded the ship.

Every morning, as soon as she woke, she rushed to her window and looked down at the harbour to see if she could discern a new merchant ship. Once or twice she imagined that she did and raced down in her car to the waterfront, only to find that she had made a mistake.

She even wondered, sometimes, if her ruthless father had arranged that the course of *The Albatross* should be diverted, and so Bill would never come at all.

Day after day went by. The first batch of wounded arrived at the villa, over which now waved the flag of the *Croix Rouge*. The little operating-theatre was finished. Matron and nurses had been installed. One or two girls whom Fiona and Louise knew in the district came daily as V.A.D.s and Louise flung herself into the work wholeheartedly.

The officers all adored Louise. They found her youthful sweetness, her big blue eyes and blonde curls a refreshing sight. But it was admitted that the elder Miss Rutherfield was the more fascinating of the two. They raved about her beauty and her grace. But they could not get near her . . . she was unapproachable. They took it for granted that she was wrapped up in her *fiancé*, Philippe d'Auvergne.

The weeks flew by. Harry Rutherfield was detained in Portugal, and instead of coming straight home was making a tour of the Spanish seaports.

Still *The Albatross* did not come to Casablanca and Fiona gradually lost hope. The wild longing which had surged into her heart when she heard that Bill's ship was due here died down into a dull ache. She felt as though that heart were breaking all over again.

Then, one evening, Louise, in all innocence, came off duty, joined her sister for tea in the drawing room and broke some devastating news to her.

'Have you heard, Fiona? One of Daddy's ships was torpedoed just off here this afternoon. Isn't it awful?'

Fiona looked quickly at the younger girl. Her heart gave a queer lurch and the colour left her cheeks.

'What ship, Louise? Do you happen to know?'

'We are not *supposed* to know,' said Louise. 'But one of the girls told me that she had heard her brother say that he heard in the club it was *The Albatross.*'

Dead silence. Louise, looking up from the tea which she had been about to drink, saw that Fiona's face was twisted with agony. She put down her tea and sprang up.

'Darling, what is it? Are you ill?'

'I knew it,' Fiona said in a hollow tone, 'I *knew* it would happen.'

'What, darling? Fiona, what is it?'

Fiona put two clenched hands against her cheeks. She said in a strangled voice:

'Bill Lindsey is captain of *The Albatross.*'

Louise blinked. It was the first time she had heard that name from her sister for long months.

'Oh, dear!' she said weakly. 'How do you know?'

'I know,' said Fiona, and burst into wild tears.

It was as well that Miss Macdonald was busy in the hospital wing. Louise was aghast. She had been under the impression that Fiona had more or less forgotten Bill and settled down to the thought of her marriage with Philippe. It was terrible to hear her cry like this. Louise said what she could to comfort her. Nobody yet knew what had happened to the crew of *The Albatross*, she said. Perhaps they were all saved. Perhaps Captain Lindsey would be brought into this very hospital.

'Although, of course,' added Louise, with a touch of her old primness, 'that would not be at all wise.'

Then Fiona, eyes glittering with tears, and lips distorted, said passionately:

'I don't care. I only want to know that he is

153

alive. I only want to hear his voice again. Oh, this cruel awful war!'

'Oh, dear!' said Louise. You mustn't let Mac know how you feel. She'd be *shocked.*'

'A lot of people would he shocked if they knew how I feel,' said Fiona, and, rising, went to the long french windows and looked out. It had been a day of brilliant sunshine. In another moment there would be that swift transition from light to darkness. No twilight in Casablanca. At the moment the sea was a gorgeous purple-blue and the sky a blaze of orange colour. Fiona looked with swollen eyes at the harbour. Her mind was full of terror. She thought she could see a picture of Bill going down with his ship. He would be the last to leave it. He would stand on the bridge calm and immovable, in his blue uniform, that peaked cap at a rakish angle on his head. Perhaps he would try to swim. But gradually the waves would defeat him. They would close for ever over that bright handsome head. Or perhaps having been injured by the explosion . . . but, oh, no! Fiona's thoughts could carry her no farther. She covered her face with her hands. He could not be dead . . . he *mustn't* die! A heartrending sob shook her body.

Louise thought:

'Poor Captain Lindsey! And yet perhaps it would be better for us all if he—'

It was at that moment that the drawing-room door opened and Miss Macdonald put in her head.

'Sister Le Mesurier wants all help possible in the wards, girls. Can you both come? There's a new convoy in . . . one of your father's ships was torpedoed a few hours ago.'

Fiona and Louise turned and faced their old governess. Fiona felt as though she could hardly breathe.

'Oh,' she whispered, 'were there many saved?'

'I could not tell you,' said Miss Macdonald.

Fiona picked up her cap, fixed it on her red-brown head, her fingers trembling so that she could scarcely adjust the pin, and rushed into the hospital wing.

CHAPTER FIFTEEN

The Albatross had been torpedoed within sight of Casablanca.

When the explosion had occurred, the captain of the ship had been as Fiona had pictured him—standing on his bridge. Just before the U-boat sighted them, Bill was looking at the distant line of the coast with mixed feelings. This was not the first time he had sailed into Casablanca. But never before had he known such a storm of emotion to shake him. For the word 'Casablanca' held such meaning for him now. *She* lived there.

That lovely feckless creature who, in far-away Scotland, had torn the heart out of his body and left him utterly destitute. Through these long months at sea he had tried to fling himself whole-heartedly into his job and on the surface he had done all and more than was expected of him. He had received more than one word of praise from his superiors. *The Albatross* was a grand ship and he was devoted to it and to his crew. But never for an instant had he stopped thinking about Fiona Rutherfield, never had he recovered from the shock, first of loving, then of losing her.

He had tried to make things better for himself by dwelling on the thought that she was weak and unworthy . . . that her father had persuaded her all too easily to leave him, the penniless young officer, and carry out her contract with the wealthy Frenchman. But he had not succeeded. He could remember only the beauty and sweetness of her in his arms and that last long kiss which they had exchanged up there on the Crags above Edinburgh. A kiss in which he had felt that she had given him her soul as well as her lips.

Wherever he had sailed . . . India, Africa, Aden, Port Said, Malta . . . he had carried with him the memory of her. The outbreak of war had given him something new to think about . . . fresh responsibility and unaccustomed hazards at sea. But the thought of Fiona haunted him remorselessly.

He took it for granted that she was now Philippe d'Auvergne's wife. As he approached the French Moroccan coast he shrank from the very idea of landing. He might meet her . . . see her with her husband . . . that would be too painful. He almost made up his mind not to go ashore. Anything rather than see her as another man's wife. Then the torpedo struck . . . and Bill Lindsey came nearer to death than he had ever been in his life before.

The explosion almost ripped the gallant beautiful ship, which was the pride of his heart, in two. There was little time for the captain to give orders. All too soon he shouted the final one: '*Abandon ship.*' The U-boat had made off without offering any help. Bill, struggling in the cold rough water, had the bitterness of seeing many of his faithful crew drown before his eyes. His left arm was a dead weight. His shoulder was injured in that first explosion. Just before he fainted from loss of blood and exposure, he murmured Fiona's name. He seemed to see her lovely vivid face bending over his. He heard her sweet husky voice. It said:

'Bill . . . Bill, I still love you. *Bill, speak to me . . . look at me . . .*'

And those were the words he actually heard when, three hours later, he first opened his eyes to find himself in bed. He had been picked up unconscious, taken into Casablanca on a gunboat, brought to the Villa des Fleurs where his arm had been dressed . . . and he had known nothing about any of it. It was as though he passed from one shock to another . . . one world to another.

He struggled back to his senses and was amazed to see that what he had thought to be a vision in his dying moments was reality and fact. It *was* Fiona's face. It was her voice.

'Bill, speak to me,' she kept saying.

But he could not speak to her at that moment. No words came. His eyes, drugged and heavy, looked past her round the small white unfamiliar room, then back to her. He stared at the Red Cross uniform . . . the nun-like veil, and deep into the brilliance of her imploring eyes.

'Bill,' she repeated his name brokenly. 'Oh, dear, dear, Bill.'

Then the words struggled from him:

'Where . . . am I?'

'In the Villa des Fleurs, my home. It is now a hospital.'

He laughed a little, stupidly, like a drunken man.

'Gosh! That's comic.'

Fiona alternated between a stab of pain and of keenest joy. It was so like Bill to make a jest of things. It seemed so long since she had heard that sort of language. *'Gosh, that's comic!'* Nobody else but Bill could have described the situation like that.

'It's been too awful,' she said. 'When I

158

heard that *The Albatross* had been torpedoed, I was afraid you were dead. I went through hell. I stood by and watched while stretchers were lifted out of the ambulance. When I saw you lying there, looking so white and helpless, I thought you might be dying. But Sister says it is only your arm that is hurt and it will soon be well again. It is a wonderful escape.'

'Who else is here?'

'Your second officer and the surgeon lieutenant.'

'What about First-Officer Roddy?'

'No . . . he isn't here.'

'Poor chap!' said Bill gloomily. 'Poor chap!'

'But many of your crew are safe. They have been taken to the other hospital. You mustn't worry, Bill.'

'My poor old ship,' he said, his eyes full of pain.

'Oh, Bill,' said Fiona, 'don't be too upset. Just thank God *you* are still alive.'

Then he gave her a profoundly cynical look.

'What reason have *I* to be glad to be alive? Death is sometimes kinder than life—kinder than the love of women. The sooner you get me transferred to another hospital the better.'

She winced.

'Do you hate nee so much?'

'I don't hate you at all. I try not to think about you.'

'But you do . . . just as I think about *you*,' she said feverishly. 'Things aren't any different. They can never be between us. Oh, Bill, say so!'

'For God's sake, leave me alone and play fair by your husband,' he said thickly. Every nerve in his body was wide awake and quivering now. Now that he saw her again . . . now that she was close to him . . . he was seized with the old wild desire to drag her head down and press his lips to her mouth.

Then Fiona said:

'I'm not married, Bill. I'm still . . . free.'

He caught his breath. 'Why?'

'My aunt died. Philippe had to go back to America. Many reasons.'

Bill gave a short laugh.

'I see.'

She looked at him intently. The sight of him lying there was so inexpressibly wonderful to her. After the months since their parting in Edinburgh, it was nothing short of a miracle to be in contact with him again. His face looked dark mahogany brown against the white linen pillow. His hair was thick and bright as she remembered it. She felt an almost uncontrollable longing to thread her fingers through its brightness. Once before, she had sat beside his bed . . . in her aunt's house in that faraway northern city . . . But then he had teased her and they had laughed together. Something warm and electric had sparked between them, culminating in unimagined delight. But now that spark seemed to

160

emanate only from her. He spoke to her, looked at her as though he held her in contempt. In a heart-breaking voice she said:

'Do you think hardly of me, Bill?'

'I repeat that I try not to think of you at all,' he said between his teeth. 'And now do go away and leave me alone.'

Her breath came hard and fast.

'Then you do think—'

'Oh, what's the use?' he broke in wearily. 'I understand the whole show. I realise I hadn't the right to ask you to chuck your family and *fiancé* and money for me, and you had every right to give me the air. Well, there we are. But I think you had better not try to start anything again. It may be amusing for you, but it isn't for me, and you are still engaged. Get someone else to do the nursing and let me transfer, and the quicker the better.'

He spoke harshly, even brutally, because of the very force of his desire for her. But his words and his attitude wounded her to the quick. She wanted to explain, to tell him how her hand had been forced, how she had been blackmailed into what he called 'giving him the air', but she could not. That part of her bargain with her father she must keep or it would all be useless. With a choked sound she turned and walked out of the room. And Captain William Lindsey turned his face to the pillow, feeling mentally and physically sick.

'Oh God,' he kept saying to himself, 'oh

God.'

Fiona walked into the hall and met Sister Le Mesurier, a *petite* French nurse, who wore medals of the last war. She beamed at the young lady of the house.

'You have found an old friend from England, eh?' she said in her own language. *'C'est très bon!'*

'Yes,' said Fiona, with a bitter smile. 'But I don't think I wish to be put in charge of the case. I suggest that the American girl, Nurse Wilson, looks after Captain Lindsey.'

'As you wish, *ma petite*,' said the Sister, and looked with some surprise after the young V.A.D. Mademoiselle Rutherfield must have had a quarrel with her English friend. How white the girl looked, to be sure.

Fiona was on duty until ten o'clock that night. She hardly knew how to get through with it. Her head ached, and she felt in a state of nervous tension. She was even more miserable than she had been before Bill Lindsey came back into her life. Every time she passed the door of his room she experienced a sense of sharpest anguish. Lee Wilson was in charge of that room now. After she had helped Sister dress the arm and prepare him for sleep, the American girl came out and raved to Fiona about Captain Lindsey.

'Gee! What a stunner! I reckon he's the best looker little me has seen this side of the Herring Pond. I'm darned glad now I can't get

162

a passage back to America for the moment. What blue eyes! And he's not married. Watch me make a pass in that quarter!'

Fiona smiled. Lee was pretty and amusing. Usually she liked Lee, but this evening she hated her. She felt madly jealous. (She, who was Philippe d'Auvergne's future wife, and could never be anything to that man who was lying in there!) She wondered how she could tolerate the situation. Perhaps it would be best to do as Bill suggested and get him transferred. As soon as he was up and about she would suggest sending him to the French Naval Convalescent Home in Marakesh.

At half past nine Lee Wilson went off duty. Just before ten it was Fiona's last duty to take a drink round to the patients.

With her heart knocking against her ribs she entered Captain Lindsey's room, carrying a glass of hot milk on a tray.

Bill was feverish and not so well this evening. As Fiona approached his bed, he looked at her with hot blue eyes. She was as beautiful as an angel in that white uniform, he thought. He wished she would keep away from him, and his expression as good as said so.

Fiona set the glass down on his table.

'I'm sorry . . . Nurse Wilson is off duty and I had to come,' she said stonily.

'It is very kind of you to wait on me, Miss Rutherfield.'

She blushed scarlet and her great eyes

suddenly flashed at him.

'There is no need to treat me like this . . .' she stammered.

'Don't let it upset you,' said Bill in a satirical voice.

She battled with herself and tried to appear unconcerned.

'Is there anything more you want?'

'Nothing more, thanks.'

Her professional eye noticed that his bandage had slipped a little. She put a hand out and manoeuvred it gently back into place. As she bent over him he caught the familiar scent that had so intrigued him in Edinburgh, and it nearly sent him mad.

He said under his breath:

'You look so damned beautiful . . . so angelic . . . I wish to heaven I had never set eyes on you again.'

'Oh, please!' she protested.

But Captain William Lindsey was weak with fever and the shock of the torpedoing, and he was certainly not himself. All mental strength seemed to have deserted him. There flowed in his body nothing but the undeniable longing to take this girl into his embrace.

Before he could control himself he had put out his right arm and pulled her down to him.

'Damn you, Fiona, you still drive me crazy, *absolutely* crazy!' he said. And the next moment she was lying on his breast, yielding to an impulse as mad and passionate as his own,

164

her lips against his, in a long, and so-much-longed-for kiss.

CHAPTER SIXTEEN

It seemed to Fiona that life for her had held no meaning until this moment and during that kiss. She made one involuntary little effort to draw back, but Bill's arm tightened and then she yielded utterly. All was very quiet in that tiny hospital room. The rain had ceased. The silence of the Mediterranean night embraced the Villa des Fleurs. Outside, the world was bathed in white moonlight. There is no moonlight in the world so strong, so intense and clear, as that in Casablanca.

Fiona, with her lips pressed to Bill's, and her eyes shut, felt as though there were a kind of delirium in her veins. A delirium of love for this man which had been fired in her months ago in the cold conventional atmosphere of her aunt's Scottish home—and which had consumed her ever since.

From the bazaars came the faint plaintive drone of a native song. The long sad '*Aie . . . ee . . . ee*' of the Arab. Shrill, unmusical, yet poignant, like an everlasting cry for happiness denied, for hope abandoned.

Fiona heard that cry. She had heard it all her childhood, here in Casablanca. She had

165

passed so many times through the bazaars and seen the squalor and the suffering and the sadness which existed under the glamour of the glittering town. She could not have lived here so long and not known the cruelty, the sheer misery that lies behind all the burning colour, the picturesque beauty and the beckoning smile. But it had never affected her. Her life had been too sheltered, too content.

But now everything had changed. She loved . . . she had suffered . . . she was mortally afraid of losing that love and she had learned that life can be brutal and implacable to the young who love—that it is the quickest thing in the world to step from sunshine into shadow.

That long-drawn native song of passion and despair filled her tonight with a sense of foreboding, and all the sharpness of the grief which she had first experienced after Bill had gone out of her life.

Wildly she clung to him, sobbing his name, meeting the hungry demand of his lips with all the response in her generous young heart.

'Darling, I love you . . . darling, darling, don't send me away from you again. I love you,' she kept repeating crazily.

'Fiona,' he whispered, and ran his fingers through the red-brown silk of her hair which he had done only in his dreams for so many hard and lonely months. 'Fiona . . . my sweet . . . my sweetest . . .

At length the sound of footsteps in the hall

outside made them draw apart. Tense and white they looked into each other's eyes. Then with trembling fingers Fiona picked up the veil which had fallen from her head. She was speechless . . . shaken to the core of her being.

Bill said:

'Why did you kiss me like that? Why? *Why?* After what you did to me in Edinburgh.'

She said:

'You don't understand . , . and I can't tell you. But I love you. That's all I know.'

The man lay breathing hard and fast. He burned with a fever that was not merely physical but mental. A fever of passionate love for this girl which seemed to drive all sanity from him. In vain he tried to bring back a note of humour into the situation.

'Gosh, honey, it will take more than a glass of hot milk and two aspirins to send this patient to sleep. I want to get up and dress. I want to go down to the sea and take you with me, and sail with you to the world's end.'

Fiona shook her head, trying not to cry.

'Don't make a jest of it now. I couldn't bear it.'

'Darling, I've got to joke or tell you to get out of my life and stay out of it. I can't stand much of this sort of thing. Do you get a kick out of making a lunatic of me? Do you enjoy being first of all disloyal to the man you are going to marry and then disloyal to me . . . the man you are afraid to marry?'

She drew back as though he had hit her a blow, and the colour suffused her face and throat.

'Oh!' she gasped.

He gave a hard laugh.

'Take away the hot milk and for the love of Mike give me a cigarette. I need something to steady my nerves.' She looked at him wildly.

'You can't say things like that to me—you can't.'

'And you can't kiss Bill Lindsey the way you did just now and then calmly walk up the aisle with your Frenchman. I just don't reconcile the two facts. Either you are the most heartless, scheming little—'

'Don't,' she interrupted. 'I tell you I won't let you say things like that. Bill, *Bill*, if you only understood . . . if I could only tell you.'

'Tell me what?'

She hid her face in her hands. He was torturing her. It was all she could do to restrain the human honest impulse to confess what her father had done. But she couldn't bring herself to do it. It would vindicate her . . . it would even make her a heroine in his eyes, perhaps, but it might also have far-reaching and disastrous effects. To begin with, he would so loathe the thought that she suffered for him. And he would loathe her father and might do something mad and foolish. She was beginning to know her Bill. He was a strong, resolute young man with a deep pride in

168

himself and his work. To be informed that it was only through her sacrifice that he had gained his promotion and sailed as captain of *The Albatross* would be a bitter pill for him to swallow. No, she could not do that to him. Nor could she cheat. Her father had carried out his share of the ignoble bargain. She must carry out hers, and, war or no war, she was still petrified that Harry Rutherfield could break an employee if he chose.

She had only one loophole left to her now: to tell Philippe the truth and see how he reacted. Yes, when Philippe came back to Casablanca, she would ask for her freedom. And if he was the man she thought him, he would not allow an innocent man like Bill to be made a victim.

Bill Lindsey looked at the girl, wondering what was in her mind and why she sat there so silently with her face hidden in her hands. He had said cruel hard things to her, but only because his love for her was so very great. The passion was dying down . . . and dull despair had replaced it. He put out a hand and touched hers.

'Never mind, Fiona. Go away and forget about this. We seem to have a had effect upon each other. Perhaps I am to blame as much as you. And if you want to marry this other bloke, why the hell shouldn't you?'

She raised her head quickly and looked at him, and he was shocked by the agony in her eyes.

'But I don't want to, Bill. I love you.'

That baffled him, and he stared at her, frowning.

'But listen—'

'No, it's no good,' she broke in. 'You'll never understand and I can't explain; but I *do* love you, and I don't want to marry Philippe.'

'I give up,' said Bill Lindsey.

'I know it must seem incomprehensible to you. I know you must have thought me weak and that my love was worth nothing when I broke with you in Edinburgh, but I *had* to do it, Bill.'

His blue eyes, bright with pain and fever, scrutinised her.

'Is it still because of the French arrangement . . . this engagement that is so hard to get out of?'

'That—and other things.'

A long silence. Through the night there came again that long cry of an Arab song, and more than ever it affected Fiona with its note of unbearable pain.

'Oh, I wish I were dead!' she said, in a voice of such feeling that Bill was shocked. All his own perplexities and doubts in her receded. He put out his uninjured arm and tried to draw her near him again.

'Don't talk like that,' he said huskily. 'Nothing can be as bad as that. Surely there must be some way out.'

She caught his hand and put it against her cheek with a touching gesture of humility which somehow embarrassed him.

He said, 'I believe you really do care . . .'

'I care so much that it is killing me,' she said.

'I think it looks like killing me, too,' said Bill Lindsey, with a brief laugh.

Then Fiona dragged her hand away from his and stood up.

'I mustn't stay. I mustn't go on talking. It is awful of me to have allowed all this. You aren't fit. I'm a poor nurse, I must say.'

'Nurse be blowed! Come back and kiss me again. darling, darling.'

'No. There mustn't be any more kisses. Not now, anyhow. Philippe is coming back soon. I'll see him . . . talk to him.'

'Oh, what's the good?'

'It may be all right,' she said in a high-pitched nervous voice. 'It must be.'

'What's the good of us loving each other?' said Bill. 'You are Rutherfield's daughter and I—'

'I beg you to believe that has nothing to do with it—nothing!' she broke in.

He passed a hand across his forehead. It was wet. He felt as cold now as he had been hot. And the room was beginning to revolve a little. He watched Fiona pin on her veil . . saw the compunction in those large lovely eyes of hers as she bent over him.

171

'Oh, Bill darling, you're ill and I've made you worse. Bill, I'll send Sister to you. I must. I can't stay myself. But, please, please believe that I love you, whatever happens.'

He knew then that he was too tired to argue. He knew also how profoundly he wanted to believe in her. He gave her a crooked smile. His head was going round and round. 'Okay . . . I'll remember that.'

And it was, indeed, the last thing he remembered that night. For then he fainted. A scared, white-faced V.A.D. rushed to find Sister Le Mesurier, and when Captain Lindsey came back to his senses the young V.A.D. had gone. Sister was at his side and he was being bathed from head to foot in order to bring down the fever.

At the other side of the villa, Fiona, avoiding questions from her sister and Miss Macdonald, went straight to her bedroom and locked herself in.

Without switching on the lights she walked across the dark room and pulled back the curtains. Opening the windows she went out on to the balcony and stood there in the cool night air, drenched in moonlight. Moonlight that showed up the white flat-roofed houses of Casablanca from one end of the city to the other. Moonlight that silvered the dark waters of the Mediterranean.

'*Aie . . . ee . . . ee . . .*' came the old familiar cry from the native quarter, and the distant lilt

172

of music echoing through the night. Tonight the town was filled with French troops back on leave from the desert. All the hotels and cafés were full and there was dancing and singing everywhere.

A strong scent from the orange trees reached the listening, watching girl. The gardens of the Villa des Fleurs, drenched from the heavy rain of the day, threw up a rich penetrating odour.

Fiona cupped her burning cheeks in both hands and looked through her lashes at a scene which she had looked upon hundreds of times in her young life, but which, tonight, seemed to have a new significance for her. Here in this villa, injured, ill, lay the man she loved and who loved her. So close to her and yet removed from her by so many barriers. She could feel the pressure of his strong right arm and the burning fever of his kiss. Through her mind chased the echo of all the things he had said . . . harsh . . . cruel . . . tender . . . passionate. The wild hot tears pricked her eyelids and she looked up at the sky, blazing with stars, and whispered:

'Oh, stars, help me . . . help us both.'

Beside her bed, on the table (as convention demanded), stood her photograph of Philippe d'Auvergne. His handsome and aristocratic face looked at her possessively, she thought, even smugly. It was as though he said:

'You belong to me.'

173

She ran to the bedside and turned the photograph face downward on the table with a childish gesture.

'I can't marry you, Philippe—*I can't. Oh, what am going to do?*'

She flung herself across the bed and buried her face in the pillows, shaken by a storm of weeping.

CHAPTER SEVENTEEN

Two days later Harry Rutherfield returned to his Casablanca residence.

He knew, of course, that *The Albatross* had been torpedoed. But he did not know that the officer commanding it had been saved and brought to his own home as a patient. He learned that only when his spy, Miguel Cortez, met him with that information as soon as he landed at the Casablanca airport.

Harry Rutherford raised his brows. It was a pity. A great pity that the man who was such a menace to his Fifi's future happiness should not be in the list of those lost at sea. Drat this young man! He seemed to he destined to cross Fiona's pathway first through one coincidence, then another.

Harry Rutherfield dealt with the matter in his own determined fashion.

As soon as he reached home he sent for his

elder daughter and told her that he knew that Captain Lindsey was here.

Fiona, who was in uniform, and just going on duty, looked at her father. She was very pale, he thought, and obviously in a highly nervous condition.

'Yes,' she said, 'Bill is here. He has been very ill for the last forty-eight hours, suffering from shock and exposure. As soon as Sister Le Mesurier thinks it safe, I am having him transferred to the official hospital. For the moment we think that the wisest thing.'

Mr. Rutherfield eyed her with some surprise and relief.

'That is very sensible of you, my dear Fifi. *Very* sensible indeed.'

'It is best for all of us under the circumstances,' she said coldly. 'It makes things too awkward for us being under the same roof. Especially as Philippe is coming back at the end of this week.'

'Ah! You've heard?'

'Yes, I had a cable from him this morning. He is coming by air.'

Mr. Rutherfield rubbed his hands together.

'And no doubt you will make all the arrangements for your immediate wedding, eh? I am very pleased with you, Fifi, and I will, of course, see that Captain Lindsey gets another command.'

Fiona clenched her hands. She felt that it was terrible that a girl should grow to hate her own father as much as she hated this man today. He stood like a ruthless giant barring her from Bill. She wanted to let him know how she really felt—to wipe that pleased look from his face—to tell him that when Philippe came back she intended to unfold the whole story to him and throw herself on his pity. But for the moment she kept quiet, as she saw no object in rousing her father's anger.

She had seen Bill once or twice since that night of the passionate scene between them, but only for a short time. He was a sick man and his injured arm was troubling him. Sister said it was imperative that he should be kept very quiet. But Fiona was happier than she had been for months. Early this morning, before she came off night duty, she had stolen in to see him. He had lifted her hand to his lips and whispered:

'You're so beautiful. I love you so much . . . whatever happens.'

And she had run her fingers through his thick bright hair and whispered back:

'I love you too, darling . . . whatever happens,' and knew that this time he believed her.

Now she was waiting for Philippe. If he would release her nothing that her father could do would hold her back. She had at last reached the conclusion that for a man with Captain William Lindsey's reputation in a war like this there would always he a job. If she could secure her freedom, she would go to Bill next time, against the wish of her family, without a penny, without anything. To be with *him* was enough. It was only the legal engagement to Philippe d'Auvergne that was still binding her, and still deterring her from her purpose.

Harry Rutherfield looked uneasily at his daughter, but he could get nothing more out of her.

That same day he sent for the matron who was in charge of the little hospital and informed her that it was his wish that the English Mercantile Marine officer, Captain Lindsey, should be transferred to the Naval and Military Hospital here as soon as possible. When the matron started to be inquisitive Mr. Rutherfield shut her up with that cold determination of which only he was capable.

'I have my private and personal reasons, Matron, and you will oblige me by not mentioning this to any of the other staff, and in particular to neither of my daughters.'

The matron, a Frenchwoman who had spent most of her nursing career in Morocco, and who knew that Harry Rutherfield's wishes must be respected—he was an all-powerful factor on this coast—made haste to say:

'*Oui, oui, monsieur,* I will arrange at once for the transfer.'

And so it happened that before Bill was really ready to be moved he found himself being put on a stretcher, taken into an ambulance and driven away from the Villa des Fleurs. He did not see Fiona in order to say good-bye to her. When he asked the matron, who saw him off, the reason for this sudden departure, she gave him the answer which had been prompted by Mr. Rutherfield.

'We have not the electrical apparatus here which is necessary for your shoulder, Captain. You are ready now for such treatment and you will be better in the big hospital.'

Bill's thoughts and feelings were mixed as he made that short journey down the hill and out to the big white hospital which stood midway between Casablanca and Bousbir— about a mile from the town.

It was a wrench leaving the villa . . . *her* home. He had grown to look forward with passionate eagerness to the moments when his door opened and the loveliest of all women would steal to his bedside and for a moment touch his hand, let him drown in the green depths of those wonderful eyes of hers.

Why had he been sent away so abruptly and without warning? He and Fiona had agreed that it might be best for him to leave the Villa des Fleurs, but now that he was actually going it was the last thing in the world that he wanted to do.

'She might have said good-bye to me,' he thought gloomily. And he knew, indubitably, that he was more in love with her than ever.

He wondered what would be the end of it, what could happen when her *fiancé* returned from New York. Perhaps he had already returned and that was why he, Bill, had been hurried away; to avoid undue embarrassments all round.

And now Bill Lindsey experienced a new emotion . . . jealousy. Supposing Fiona changed her mind again . . . yes, d'Auvergne might persuade her into thinking it her duty to marry him.

Bill could not altogether wipe out the memory of what had happened in Edinburgh. There was still a lingering doubt in his mind as to the strength of Fiona's love for him and he was still only half satisfied with his own part in the affair. For after all he *was* only an impecunious employee of the Anglia Shipping Company, and she was Rutherfield's daughter. That was a bitter fact that could never wholly be forgotten or denied.

The American V.A.D., Lee Wilson, who had been given the privilege of accompanying Captain Lindsey in the ambulance, fluttered her lashes at him.

'Gee! I'm darned sorry you're leaving us, Captain,' she said, and left him in no two doubts as to her particular feelings toward him.

Lee was a smart, pretty girl, but Bill could not get up even a vestige of warmth toward her. He smiled feebly and tried to joke. But all the time the ambulance was moving swiftly down the white dusty road toward Bousbir, the voice of his heart was crying: *'Fiona! Fiona! Fiona!'*

Meanwhile, on the sunlit verandah, Fiona and her sister were having a few short sharp words.

'I wasn't told that Bill was to go. I was sent down to the town to get bandages while they moved him. Obviously it has been a conspiracy,' Fiona was saying furiously, and she *was* furious . . . white and shaking. Of course she knew more than she could tell Louise. She was confident that her father had done this and she could not control her resentment.

A little while ago she had gone into Bill's room with a bunch of carnations which she had bought for him in the town, only to find his bed empty. The disappointment had been shattering. And all that nonsense about needing electrical treatment—of course it was only a blind. The horrid little matron was in league with her father.

Louise, at her most prim and disapproving, admonished her sister.

'You really oughtn't to go on like this, Fiona. It isn't fair to Philippe. It isn't worthy of you . . .'

'Oh, be quiet—you don't know what you're talking about,' said Fiona with burning cheeks. 'You know perfectly well that I love Bill and I can't help it. I'm not *going* to help it any more.'

'Fiona!'

'You can say what you like and I know you adore Philippe. Well, I wish to heaven he'd been affianced to you and not to me.'

It was the first time that Fiona had ever said anything quite so frank and revealing to little Louise. The girl turned quite white and stared at her sister almost in horror.

'Fiona, you're saying awful things!'

'Perhaps, but you don't understand, Louise, and I can't tell you what has happened.'

'I think, as I thought in Edinburgh, that you are mad,' said Louise in a shocked voice.

'All right—love is a madness,' said Fiona with a short laugh. 'And as it is, I agree I am right off my head.'

'Oh, dear!' began Louise, but her sister swung round on her exclaiming:

'Now don't start to cry, Louise. I can't stand it today. I can't stand any more at all, and if they think they are going to keep me from Bill they are wrong. I'm a free agent. I can go down to the other hospital to see him any time I like, and I shall go.'

'The sooner Philippe comes home the better,' said Louise faintly.

Fiona tilted that magnificent tawny head of hers and laughed again in a manner which quite convinced the younger girl that her sister was not quite sane.

'I agree,' said Fiona. 'And when he comes

181

back this time I am going to ask him to release me from our engagement.'

'I think Daddy ought to know,' began Louise.

Then Fiona interrupted her. She gripped her sister's hand so hard that Louise winced. She said under her breath:

'If you ever discuss my affairs with Daddy, I'll never forgive you—never. I warn you, Louise, don't interfere. There has been too much interference already. Leave me to manage this affair in my own way. Do you hear?'

'Yes,' whispered Louise, and then added in a choked voice: 'Oh, Fiona, how can you be so cruel and beastly to me?'

Immediately Fiona melted and took Louise's sobbing figure into her arms.

'Darling, I'm sorry. Don't cry, Louise. Forgive me. I really don't think I know what I am doing or saying. You can't think what it means to love a man so much and to be tied to another. Don't judge me too harshly, Louise. You may think me crazy, but don't turn against me. You are my sister and we've always loved each other. Whatever happens, stand by me, Louise.'

And then Louise, who despite her passion for Philippe secretly thought her sister the most wonderful being in the world, made haste to kiss and reassure her. So for the moment the two girls clung together, weeping.

It was this domestic little scene that Harry Rutherfield himself interrupted. Outside the door he had heard most of the conversation between the sisters, and he had registered a mental vow that before long he would get Captain William Lindsey not only out of this house but out of Casablanca. But now he had news which he hoped would act as a further deterrent to any of Fiona's plans.

'I have a real thrill for you, my dear,' he said brightly, addressing his elder daughter. 'I have just received a telephone call from my old friend Gaston. Philippe is already in Paris. He arrived there by air yesterday and is now on his way to Casablanca. His father is coming with him, also his aunt, Thérèse, and her husband, Henri Concours. We must give a dinner-party for them here tomorrow night.'

Louise said nothing. She felt weak and a little frightened after the scene with Fiona. Fiona, making no effort to wipe the tearstains from her face, looked hard at her father.

'Why the family party?' she asked:

He beamed at her.

'My dear, Gaston thought that at a time like this it would be senseless to delay your wedding a moment longer, and has suggested that your marriage takes place the day after tomorrow. Philippe has the necessary papers and naturally he wishes his aunt and uncle, who are the most important members of his family, to attend.'

183

Fiona's heart missed a beat. She turned very pale.

'Why such a sudden arrangement for my wedding? I haven't even a trousseau prepared.'

Her father continued to smile at her. She felt that it was a two-edged smile . . . certainly it held a warning in it.

'I'm sure you have enough, my dearest Fifi. In wartime, a large trousseau can neither be purchased nor expected. Madame Concours is bringing you over some things that she thought you would like, and you have, of course, your dear mother's bridal dress and veil.'

Fiona's hands clenched.

'Philippe said nothing to me about this.'

Mr. Rutherfield's smile was then positively freezing.

'Philippe is a dutiful son, my dear. It is his father's wish that this marriage should be solemnised without further delay and he has not argued the point. There have been too many postponements already.'

Fiona stood very still. She trembled from head to foot and her mind was whirling. It was as though she felt the net closing in around her. The old sensation of the trapped and imprisoned slave came over her again. Of course she could see what had happened. This was her father's doing again . . . approved, no doubt, by Gaston d'Auvergne. She could picture the two men . . . her father hinting that

184

the engagement had been too long, and that she, Fiona, was young and impressionable and that in a war like this it would be good for her to have a husband to look after her, etc., etc.

Louise drifted out of the room. Agonised, Fiona looked at her father and for the first time since their quarrel in Edinburgh she melted into an appeal to him.

'Daddy,' she said huskily, 'don't make me go through with this. Give me a chance. Don't rush me into marriage, I beg you.'

He avoided her gaze.

'You've had quite enough breathing space, my dear,' he said, 'and you must not lose sight of the fact that this is no ordinary engagement. *You are as good as married to Philippe already.* It would be a terrible disgrace if you made any attempt to break with Philippe now. Things have gone too far. Besides, there are other reasons, Fiona, which make it imperative that our two families should be united.'

Speechlessly Fiona stared at him, then she turned and rushed out of the room. A moment later Harry Rutherfield saw her leave the villa. She was not in uniform, but wore a light blue dress and coat and one of the big shady hats that she so often put on to shield her from the sunshine, for despite the fact that this was November the afternoon was as bright and warm as a summer's day in England.

Rutherfield smothered an oath. He knew perfectly well where Fiona was going. She was off to the hospital to see that fellow Lindsey. Well, if he could stop *that* meeting, so much the better. Anything to gain time until the d'Auvergne family arrived and Philippe could take charge of his bride.

Rutherfield knew the M.O. in charge of the hospital. He put a telephone call through without delay. He thought perhaps he could say something which would satisfy that gentleman that it might be best for Captain Lindsey not to receive any visitors this afternoon.

CHAPTER EIGHTEEN

As Fiona sped down the white dusty roadway that led to Bousbir she had no coherent idea of what she meant to do—or what she wished Bill to do. She knew that she was not really free like Louise would have been, for instance—to defy her father, run away from home and just say to Bill, 'Take me . . . marry me . . . nothing else matters.' Something *did* matter . . . her bond with Philippe. Fiona, for all her British blood and instincts, was half French and had been reared in the strict conventional manner of a French family. *She could not, in all conscience, marry Bill Lindsey until Philippe set her free.* Besides, no priest, no registrar in Casablanca or anywhere else,

186

conversant with her family history, would perform the ceremony.

She felt, too, that she at least owed it to Philippe to be honest with him before she took any drastic step. This headlong flight to Bill today was born of the crazy wish to see and speak to him and make him understand that never now, although she died, would she belong to any other man. Let Philippe and his people arrive tomorrow. Let her father do what he could to enforce the marriage. She would never willingly place her hand in Philippe's and utter the final binding words of the marriage service.

Under all her defiance, her courage, she was little more than a frightened girl—heart almost bursting with emotion. The future appeared to her so formidable. There were so many barriers between her and her Bill. Her father loomed, a powerful, menacing figure, before her. Defy him she might, but he was Harry Rutherfield of the Anglia Shipping Line, and Bill's chief. Bill was under Government orders, but Rutherfield could still put a finger in the pie and help or hinder that precious career. Fiona shuddered to think what he might not do out of sheer spite if his daughter ever slipped out of her commitments to the d'Auvergnes and became Mrs. William Lindsey.

Fiona put a hand up to shield her eyes. In her hurry she had forgotten her dark glasses and the winter sun in Casablanca can be strong. It was a brilliant day. She could see a rim of blue silken sea to the left. To the right lay the dark outline of the mountains. Along the road were many little white houses with flat roofs, on the *terrasses* hung washing . . . gay, coloured flags of domesticity. The pale blue-green of the pepper trees threw their shadows against the white walls and the bright enamelled doorways of the houses.

Fiona had been down this road many times, but never before on foot and alone. How shocked poor Tante Marie would have been—she mused—Miss Rutherfield walking along the Bousbir Road . . . *alone*—she who had never been allowed out without one of her family, and a servant in attendance.

Two or three Arab women, heavily veiled, padded along on their leather-slippered feet, and glanced curiously at the English girl in her smart clothes. An old Riff peasant riding a donkey—a small, patient grey creature, far too heavily burdened—made an obeisance to her. Fiona returned his greeting. One or two big American cars shot past her, raising a cloud of dust. A small company of French soldiers, good-looking, impudent, smiling, made open remarks about the beauty of Mademoiselle's figure and slender ankles and left Fiona blushing scarlet. She even began to wish she had asked Louise to accompany her.

She left the town behind her. The road grew

188

more lonely. The country around was flat and uninteresting. Little to be seen but dwarf palms and Barbary figs, borders of blue-green aloes, and pale prickly pears.

Fiona, in spite of her troubles, realised suddenly how little she had ever seen the details of the countryside, always driving a car. One had to travel on foot like this to see everything.

Bousbir lay yet a mile away, but she was within sight of the huge white building which was the Naval and Military Hospital. Hot, footsore, apprehensive, she hurried on. And she thought: *'Bousbir . . . they call it the "City of Kisses" . . . Oh, Bill, my darling . . . all the romance and colour and passion of this country means so much more to me now that I know you and have experienced the heaven of your love.'*

Her first real setback was when she reached the hospital and in the cool waiting-room, dimmed by sun-blinds, was informed that Captain Lindsey could not see visitors.

Fiona uttered an exclamation:

'But I must see him. it is very urgent.'

The Army sister, who had been especially chosen by the Chief Medical Officer to interview Miss Rutherfield, eyed the lovely, excited girl coldly. She was a dried-up stick of a woman, London-born, but had nursed out on the French Moroccan coast for the last twenty years. She was bad-tempered and had missed the marriage market entirely. It seemed now that the warm sap of human understanding had been dried up in her, both by the fierce sunlight and disappointment in her sex-life. She had not the least sympathy for this girl or any other beautiful young woman. 'A bold creature, this one,' she decided, 'running after wounded officers.'

'I'm sorry, but it is impossible. The doctor's orders are that nobody may see Captain Lindsey.'

Fiona gasped.

'Sister, I am Miss Rutherfield, of the Villa des Fleurs, and—'

'I am quite aware of that, Miss Rutherfield,' interrupted the woman. 'I am also aware of my orders and the doctor has forbidden Captain Lindsey to receive visitors.'

'Is he worse then . . . is he ill?'

'He is going on quite well, thank you,' was the acid reply, and the woman thought: 'What eyelashes . . . they might be stuck on . . . and that complexion . . . no need for beauty treatments. I couldn't look like that if *I lived* in a beauty parlour . . . *I hate* her and her melting eyes. . . .

Fiona, breathing quickly, made another appeal:

'Sister, can't you please stretch a point . . . it really is a vital matter?'

'You must excuse me. We are very busy today,' said the Sister coldly, and moved to the door.

Fiona followed her, her throat dry.

'I beg you. Let me see the M.O.'

'He is not in.' (That was a lie.)

'But this is ludicrous. I *must* see Captain Lindsey. Tell him I am here. He will want to see me.'

'I am sorry, Miss Rutherfield, but you must conform to our rules. This is a properly run hospital,' said the woman. '*Good* afternoon.'

Fiona was defeated. Her sense of misery and disappointment almost choked her. To come all this way . . . then to be forbidden to see him. It was intolerable.

She lingered in the well-kept grounds of the hospital for a moment or two, trying not to cry with chagrin. She looked wretchedly at the building, there were many wards . . . all on the ground floor, with wide verandahs facing the south. Tomorrow, alone, she would have to cope with Philippe and his family. But she must see Bill this afternoon. She *must*.

Suddenly she saw a youthful figure in V.A.D. uniform. Eagerly she watched this girl approach. And hope revived in her as she recognised an old friend—Yolande Deuchars, daughter of a one-time Consul here, and a girl who had been many times to the Villa des Fleurs and in turn had entertained the young Rutherfields.

Fiona hailed her joyfully.

'Oh, Yolande!' she exclaimed.

'Fiona . . . *comment ça va, chérie?*' returned

191

the French girl with surprise and pleasure. Yolande was a great admirer of the eldest Rutherfield sister. She, herself, was a thin, plain girl with glasses and a long pointed nose. She was, however, incurably romantic and by nature the antithesis of the Sister who had just taken such malicious delight in thwarting Fiona. Yolande adored beauty in her sex and Fiona had often been especially kind to her and given her some lovely presents.

Swiftly Fiona explained the reason for her visit to the hospital.

'You see, Yolande,' she finished, the tears glistening on her lashes, 'that I must see him . . . I *must* . . .'

'*Mon dieu!*' gasped Yolande, and considered the matter seriously for the moment, one arm around her friend's trembling figure. Then, looking round and about, she said: 'I know! I know which ward he is in. My cousin Jeanne is the ward-sister. I will take the *Capitaine* a message. I, myself.'

Fiona embraced her.

'Oh! You saint . . . you angel! . . .'

Yolande rolled her eyes heavenwards, her theatrical French soul delighting in this secret love-affair. It was awful . . . when Fiona was engaged to Philippe d'Avergne . . . Deliciously wicked. It must be fostered, certainly.

'Do you know how he is?' asked Fiona anxiously.

'No, but I will find out. Wait here, *chérie.*

Behind these palm-trees, so that old cat Sister Leonard cannot see you. I will be back . . . *toute-suite . . . soyez tranquille, chère amie.'*

Fiona felt better. Excited and hopeful, she watched the little French nurse speed up the drive to the hospital. She waited for her return on tenterhooks . . . madly impatient. It seemed a long time, although it was in fact only ten minutes, before Yolande returned and then Fiona ran to meet her.

'Well . . . well . . . have you seen him?'

Yolande, breathless, beaming, drew her friend back into the seclusion of the palm-trees. Yes, she had seen the *Capitaine.* But how handsome . . . what a Viking of a man with his blue eyes and tanned face and curly hair. His lashes were tipped with gold . . . *dieu* . . . he was fascinating, etc., etc. (Fiona cut short these rhapsodies, although they pleased her. What message had Bill sent her?) Bill had sent all his love and told her that he was much better; in fact quite strong enough to walk. Tomorrow morning he would put on his clothes and escape from his room and meet her in Casablanca. Could she come for him in a car and wait outside the hospital gates? First he would see the doctors. Then, when they were all busy elsewhere, he would slip away. About noon.

Fiona breathed hard and fast.

'But, Yolande, is he strong enough?'

'He says so.'

'Oh, but no harm must come to him.'

'He can stay in the car with you. He need not get out of it,' suggested the resourceful Yolande.

'Oh, tell him I'll be here, no matter what it costs me,' said Fiona, swallowing hard. 'Give him my dearest love. Tell him I will come for him, Yolande.'

'I will, *chèrie*, have no fear.'

And with that much grace, Fiona was forced to be content. The two friends kissed. Fiona turned back along the road to Casablanca. Tomorrow . . . at noon. Philippe would be here by then, of course. But she would get away. There would be no immediate wedding, however deeply she shocked Philippe's relatives. On that point she was determined.

God bless dear little Yolande. (Lucky Yolande, who could see and speak to her 'Viking of a man'. How well she had described Bill!) Fiona burned with emotion at the memory of that tanned face and the lashes 'tipped with gold'. She longed unbearably for the touch of his lips against her mouth.

She reached her home worn out, feet blistered from the unaccustomed walking. But her spirits were high. She was to see Bill tomorrow, and he had sent her all his love. That was enough . . . for the moment.

She stepped into the hall. Louise, who had seen her from an upstairs window, was calling:

'Fiona . . . Fiona . . . come up . . . it's time

194

you were changed. Philippe may be here any moment. He is flying from Toulouse.'

Fiona came face to face with her father. Mr. Rutherfield took a cigar from his mouth and smiled at his daughter . . . a benevolent smile. With his plump ruddiness, his genial gaze, it might have been thought that he was the most kindly of men.

'Well, my dear, did you see—er—Captain Lindsey?' he murmured. 'That is what you went out for, isn't it? Most improper . . . without a chaperon.'

Fiona smiled back at him, a hard, icy smile.

'I don't need chaperoning any longer, thank you. I can take care of myself. And I did *not* see Captain Lindsey.'

Mr. Rutherfield's eyelids creased now into a smile, which made him look like an amiable pussy-cat.

'Too bad,' he said. 'These hospitals have strict rules, of course. Never mind. You can send him the cuttings from the local paper about your wedding, my dear. Perhaps even a photograph.'

Fiona went scarlet, then speechlessly rushed past her father and up the stairs. She had never hated anyone so much. She thought:

'He must be the hardest, cruellest man on earth. He would do anything . . . anything to get his own way. He is a dictator . . . a little Hitler . . . a Mussolini . . . I *hate* him.'

Upstairs in her room, Louise timidly

questioned her. 'Fiona dearest, where *have you* been?'

Fiona looked at her face in the mirror. She hardly recognised that flushed, stubborn young face with the glittering eyes, the feverish colour, the passionate, wilful mouth.

She said:

'Never mind. Tell Conchita to run my bath. Let's get dressed.'

'You know Daddy is planning for you to marry Philippe at once?'

'I know.'

Fiona turned and placed both hands on her young sister's shoulders and looked hard into the big blue eyes.

'And do you want that? Do you want to see the man you love take his final vows to me? Will that please your prim and proper little soul, *ma petite soeur*?'

Louise blushed and clutched at the gold cross which she wore. She could not understand Fiona in this daring fiery mood. She whimpered:

'You've no right to ask me such a question . . .'

'And Daddy has no right to ask me to marry a man whom I look on as a brother, when I belong body and soul to another . . .'

'Body and soul?' repeated Louise, stuttering. 'Oh, *Fiona!*'

'Yes, body and soul,' repeated Fiona, and flung her arms above her head with an ecstatic movement. 'Oh, don't look so shocked, darling. You're not a nun and neither am I. We are both human . . . women who are meant to love and be loved. I love Bill and I want to feel his arms around me, just as you must want Philippe's around you. And if I don't marry Philippe . . . he will turn to you.'

Louise, as pale now as she had been red, gasped:

'You mustn't say such things. You can't break your vows. Oh, you scare me when you talk so wildly, Fiona . . .'

'Run to your *prie-dieu*, sweet, and pray for me. But no prayers on earth will separate me from Bill, now. I love him and he loves me, as no two people have ever loved before. Romeo and Juliet . . . Abelard and Heloise . . . Antony and Cleopatra . . . all the great lovers of history . . . I think of them today and understand at last why they wished to die rather than leave each other.'

Louise gulped. She did not reply. Deep down in her virginal heart, she knew that this lovely, crazy sister of hers spoke the truth. She knew that often she—Louise—had lain awake at night, and dared to picture herself in Philippe's arms . . . but had cast the thought from her as being shameful and hopeless. How could Fiona dare speak like this of Captain Lindsey? *What did she mean to do?*

Conchita, the pretty dark-eyed Spanish girl who was personal maid to the Misses

Rutherfield, called from the bathroom:

'Señorita . . . your bath is ready. Venga!'

Fiona slid out of her clothes and into a white wrapper. Taking a comb she ran it through her tawny hair, then twisted the red-brown curls into a knot on the top of her head. She stepped into the sunken green marble bath, with the steaming water that Conchita had perfumed with Chanel bath-salts. As she stood there a moment, Louise looked half fearfully at her sister's exquisite body, so perfect from milk-white shoulders, down to the tapering leg, to the small feet. 'With those tawny curls pinned high on the small head,' thought Louise, 'she is like the Goddess Psyche . . . in her bath . . . and the god of Love, himself, would adore her.' Would all that glamorous loveliness ever belong to Philippe d'Auvergne? In this instant, at the mere idea, there shot through Louise's veins an anguish of jealousy. She covered her face with her hands, and knew that it would kill her if, indeed, she must stand by and see that marriage take place.

CHAPTER NINETEEN

In the library of the Villa des Fleurs, later that night, when the heat of the golden day had become the chill of a clear moonlit night,

Fiona faced Philippe, her *fiancé*, alone. Alone for the first time since his arrival from Toulouse, which had been just before dinner. The meeting then had been conventional and in front of the Rutherfield family; he had given her a swift kiss on either cheek and remarked on her charming appearance. (She wore a mist-blue dinner dress with greeny-blue flowers at her belt.) Then settled down to a long meal and general discussion. There was no mention of personal affairs . . . even of the immediate wedding for which Philippe was supposed to have come. They talked of the war . . . of conditions in Casablanca . . . anything but themselves. But Fiona was conscious of high tension in the air. She caught Philippe looking at her strangely from his bright dark eyes; once or twice frowning as though in grave speculation. And she knew that her father had been to the airport to meet him and that Philippe had been told about— Bill.

Louise—with the resilience of extreme youth—was the only happy one at that dinner. She chatted vivaciously to Philippe, keeping her admiring blue eyes upon him. He answered with his customary grace and amiability. But he kept his dark brooding gaze upon the tawny-haired elder sister in her mist-blue dress and whose long lashes veiled her eyes from him.

Now they were alone; Mr. Rutherfield and

Louise and that vague Miss Macdonald had mysteriously vanished. The betrothed couple stood by the wood-fire which gave out a pleasant pungent odour. The room, with its books, priceless Flemish tapestries of gold, Florentine brocade, was full of warmth and cleverly shaded lights. No sound to be heard except the crackling of the logs in the grate, behind a beautiful wrought-iron screen, and outside the faint mysterious cries from the native quarters of the city.

Fiona, with quickened heartbeats, at last raised her eyes to her *fiancé* and gave him an almost imploring glance. He returned it coldly. He spoke in a colder voice than she had ever heard from Philippe, who had been her girlhood's companion, as well as her lover. He said in his own language:

'You needn't tell me. I know all.'

She replied in French.

'My father has told you then?'

'Everything.'

Her teeth sank into her lower red lip. Nervously she wiped the palms of her slender hands with a chiffon handkerchief.

'Ah! I wonder. How much?'

'Everything,' he repeated, and the face he turned to her now was pale and glistening a little as though with perspiration. His hair looked dank and black and his lips were compressed, as though he laboured under a terrific strain of emotion.

200

'You have betrayed our love,' he added, in a thick voice.

She blushed brightly and shook her head.

'I beg you, Philippe, *mon cher*, not to put it that way. It is dramatic . . . unnecessary. I have not betrayed our love. I have . . . never loved you in that way. You knew it.'

It was his turn to blush . . . he was a proud young man and he suffered from mortally wounded vanity, as well as from wounded love.

'I always hoped—' he broke off, significantly.

'Philippe, be rational. I was promised to you in marriage by my father . . . It was a mutual arrangement between our two families . . . and I was a mere schoolgirl at the time. I have always loved you as a brother . . . never as a future husband.'

He clenched his teeth, took a handkerchief from his pocket and wiped his damp, haughty face.

'It is intolerable. I have always looked upon you as my promised wife. You can never have cared at all for me.'

'Oh, I have indeed, but not as a woman loves her lover, Philippe,' she said gently. 'I only wish it could have been otherwise.'

'You will learn to love me once we are married,' he said stiffly, icily, but his dark eyes looked at her with barely concealed passion. She never seemed more desirable to him than tonight, when he had actually been told, first

201

by her father, now by herself, that she did not wish to marry him.

Fiona caught her breath.

'I *cannot* marry you.'

'That is outrageous and nonsensical!' he exclaimed. 'It has been arranged . . . settled . . . my family arrive tomorrow. The wedding is to be almost at once.'

'It isn't possible now. I love someone else,' she said, through dry lips.

'An English captain in the Merchant Service . . . a nobody whom you met in Edinburgh . . . an upstart, who has dared to take liberties—' Philippe broke off, almost choking, and coughed into his handkerchief as though ashamed. Fiona looked at him in misery. She was fond of him, she hated to hurt him. But she must fight for her freedom . . . for Bill . . . now, or never.

'Listen, Philippe,' she said. 'Try to understand the truth and forgive me. Let me tell you . . . everything.'

'I refuse to listen,' he almost shouted the words. She had never seen the gentle, gracious young man so violently disturbed. She realised suddenly what a terrible thing was the passion of love. It could make—or mar—save or destroy a human being. Jealousy . . . possessiveness were turning the gentle Philippe into a savage, who would know no mercy and give no sympathy. Yet, she had counted on his co-operation.

She had said to herself so many times: '*He will understand and be kind . . . he will release me.*'

Frightened and disappointed, she began to pour out her story of her accidental meeting with Bill Lindsey; the gradual growth of their love; their unwillingness to do the wrong thing, yet their inability to part from each other. She implored Philippe to have pity on her.

'I was never meant for you . . . I should never have been betrothed at such a young age. Let me go . . . give me my release from our bond, I beg of you, my dear, dear Philippe.'

He looked at her almost in horror.

'It is impossible. My father . . . my uncle and aunt are on their way here this very night. I could not tell them that our engagement is to be broken.'

Fiona went very white. Her great eyes stared at him.

'You must release me . . . oh, you *must.*'

As he turned from her, his thin body trembling with a kind of nameless rage and disappointment:

'No, I absolutely refuse.'

'My father has got round you . . .' she said with passionate hatred. 'I know it. But has he told you how vilely *he* has behaved and blackmailed me into continuing with our engagement?'

'I will not listen to you, Fiona. Your father

has done right. You must be saved from yourself. You are infatuated with this atrocious person, who is a rough sailor . . . one of our own employees . . . you have disgraced us all. But I will forgive you. There are excuses, I have left you alone too long. You are beautiful and impulsive. I tell you, I understand and will forgive. But you must give your word of honour never to see this man again.'

Fiona gave him a look of despair.

'*Mon dieu*, can I not make you believe that I love him? He is nothing like what you say. Daddy has misled you. Bill is—'

'Be quiet, Fiona,' broke in Philippe hoarsely. 'I will pardon you, I say, but the matter is closed. You become my wife as soon as the legal part of it can be arranged.'

'Oh!' she said in a choked voice. 'Now you have joined Father. You are against me. How *can* you . . . how can you wish to force my hand, knowing that I love another man?'

'Because I believe you are suffering from a childish infatuation and that you will belong entirely to me, once we are married,' he said stubbornly.

She was speechless. Her heart was beginning to sink lower and lower. She had never anticipated this obstinacy on her *fiancé's* part. How could she run away with Bill if her betrothal to Philippe remained as it was . . . a legal bond between them? She must make Philippe relent . . . she must . . .

204

'I beg you to help me—' she began huskily.

He interrupted:

The matter is closed. Please never refer to it again. *Please*, Fiona . . .'

With this, he turned, and with his handkerchief pressed to his lips walked out of the library.

He walked out of the villa and on to the terrace. He felt suffocated. He was torn between his blinding desire for Fiona and his despair over her frank admittance of her love for another man. When he had last seen her, he had imagined that such a man existed. But he had always believed that he would win her in the end. Now, when she had actually demanded her freedom, he had swung to an obstinate determination to keep her . . . never to let her belong to that other man. And yet when he thought about it, out here in the cool night, his passions dying down, he was sadly confused in his thoughts. What use to possess an unwilling bride? What kind of happiness could he hope for? Yet he could not face his father, his relatives, tomorrow and suffer before them the shame of a rejected suitor.

He stood staring down at the glittering lights of Casablanca. A light touch on his sleeve made him turn round. He saw Louise— a scarf about her fair curls—large eyes full of sweetness and concern.

'Come in, *mon cher Philippe* . . . don't stand out here alone,' she smiled.

He melted at her touch, with the quickness of his race to feel sentiment and pleasure in a charming feminine sympathy. He put his arm about Louise's slight shoulders and gave a deep, long sigh.

'*Petite sœur* . . . little sister . . . I am a very unhappy man tonight.'

She trembled at his touch, then suddenly, to his surprise, broke away from him.

'I am not your little sister yet . . . I am *not*,' she said a little wildly, 'and I cannot bear you to be unhappy.'

Then she turned and fled back into the villa. Philippe d'Auvergne stood staring after her. Experienced with women as he was, he could not be blind to the meaning of her words and her behaviour. It was a shock to him. But not an unpleasant shock. Little Louise . . . pretty, fair-haired Louise with her delicacies, and her devotions and her quaint primness . . . *was in love with him.* That must be it. That was why she did not wish him to call her 'sister'. Poor, dear *petite* Louise . . .

Philippe stood still in the moonlight for a long time ruminating on the ironies of life and love and the strange influence these two girls had upon his life.

He wanted Fiona . . . and it was Louise who loved him. Strange unaccountable fact.

When he returned to the library, Fiona and Louise had retired. Mr. Rutherfield was sitting over a cigar and whisky-and-soda. He looked at the young Frenchman intently.

'Well . . . have you got your young woman under control?' he asked with a lightness which he did not exactly feel.

Philippe bowed stiffly.

'I have told Fiona that I will never give her up.'

'Good,' said Harry Rutherfield. 'Then tomorrow we will go to *le Maire* and arrange for the marriage to take place, shall we say the day after that?'

'As you wish, sir,' said Philippe d'Auvergne.

But there was no smile on his face and no pleasure in his heart. He suffered . . . and he wondered if poor Louise was suffering too . . . from this heavy burden of unrequited love.

Upstairs Fiona refused to have any discussion with her young sister. Louise, too, was unsympathetic, and even sullen tonight. They exchanged only a few words. Fiona said:

'Philippe refuses to set me free.'

Louise said:

'You are hurting him, and I hate you for it.'

Fiona tilted her beautiful head proudly, and with wounded gaze on her sister replied:

'I, too, am hurt. And the man I love will be hurt. You don't think of that. But I shall never marry Philippe. *Never* . . . something must and will prevent it.'

Brave hopeful words. But Fiona felt far from brave or hopeful after she had said them. She did not sleep at all that night; she was

207

tossing and turning, tortured with anxiety. If she could not get Bill soon, she would die of this love, she thought.

The morning brought fresh torture. Fiona had crept downstairs before anybody was up, telephoned to a local grage and ordered a car to be outside the gates of the villa at twenty minutes to twelve. She must keep that tryst with Bill at noon . . . she must see him, whatever happened.

At breakfast time, the heads of Philippe's family arrived at the d'Auvergne villa in Casablanca. Gaston d'Auvergne, Henri Concours and his wife. Mr. Rutherfield gave orders to Miss Macdonald to prepare lunch for them all. To Fiona he said briefly:

'You will take your mother's place at the head of the table and entertain the party. Tomorrow your marriage takes place.'

She said nothing, but felt a desperate desire to rush out of the villa now, and never return to it. But she maintained some degree of composure. She helped Louise arrange the flowers. They both wore light dresses, for it was a warm brilliant morning. Philippe, who had stayed here last night, had gone to his own home to welcome his relations. Just before leaving, he had sought out his *fiancée*, kissed her hand with formal courtesy, looked deeply into her eyes and murmured:

'I beg you to do what is right . . . I rely on you.'

She had not replied, but the hand he kissed was ice-cold.

She had no definite plan as to what she meant to do. She could not see a straight road ahead for any of them. But she knew that she must keep that appointment at the hospital with Bill.

She knew, too, that Louise suspected that she was scheming something . . . but she avoided her young sister's reproachful gaze, and escaped from the villa at the appointed time.

At noon she was waiting in the closed car outside the gates of the hospital on the Bousbir Road.

And now fresh anxieties assailed her. Would her darling be strong enough to dress and come out? Would he be discovered, and prevented from coming? What would she do if he failed to turn up? An agony of longing for his strong presence, his hands, his lips, possessed her. She sat there, staring out of the open window of the car, her face almost as pale as the ivory silk suit which she was wearing.

'Bill . . . Bill . . . my darling, come to me . . .' she said aloud, her eyes straining, watching, waiting for his familiar blue-clad figure to appear.

CHAPTER TWENTY

At last that longed-for figure appeared. Left arm in a sling. Right hand leaning heavily on a stick. Bill walked slowly, as though he had no strength in his body, and as he drew near the merciless sunshine revealed the new pallor which the torpedoing, and the days in bed, had brought to his darkly tanned face.

Fiona caught her breath hard with excitement. She opened the door of the car and called to him:

'Bill . . . oh, Bill!'

He looked at her with a brief, almost shy smile and brought his hand up in salute.

'Hello!'

'Jump in . . . oh, quickly, before you're seen,' she said breathlessly.

He stepped into the car and sat down heavily and with a sigh beside her. Fiona said to the driver:

'To the Sphynx . . .' Then, as the car moved and turned around in the direction of Casablanca, she added: 'That is the only place I know. I believe it is always packed with officers drinking at this hour, but nobody who knows me is likely to be there.'

'I am in your hands, darling,' he said.

She leaned toward him. He caught a breath of the scent she used, looked into her magnificent shining eyes, and almost wonderingly touched a strand of the silken hair that curled against her lovely neck. He added:

'Gosh . . . it's good to see you again, sweet. You are so damned beautiful . . . it just knocks me down every time I see you.'

The boyish praise thrilled her. She took his right hand and carried it to her glowing cheek.

'I've longed for this moment . . . been half crazy to see you. Yolande helped us . . . my little French friend.'

'My friend now, too, from this moment onward. She and that nice ward sister, Jeanne Somebody or other, were in on it. The M.O. saw my arm and changed the dressing and told m I couldn't get up for a few days. As soon as he and the Matron moved into another ward, I dressed . . . in a borrowed uniform. Mine was ruined by sea-water. I haven't a rag to my back. Everything went down. This belongs to another chap in the English Navy, who is in the same ward.'

'You look fine, Bill . . . but are you strong enough to be out like this?'

He did not tell her that he felt as weak as a rat, and that the walk down that drive had set his heart thumping and the sweat pouring down his cheeks. He took the slender hand that gripped his so hard, and kissed the palm repeatedly, passionately.

'I couldn't live without seeing you, Fiona,

211

sweet. Tell me what's happening at home. Is *he*
. . . back?'

'Don't ask me any questions for a moment,'
she said in a low voice. 'Just hold me . . . close
to you . . . close . . .'

He put his uninjured arm about her. She
melted into that embrace. As the car moved
swiftly down the white road to Casablanca,
their lips met and clung in a kiss that robbed
them both of strength, of the will to reason or
analyse. The world lost, they surrendered to
each other's kiss with a completeness of
passion and ecstasy which neither of them had
dreamed possible. To Fiona, it was heaven
after the days and nights of tortured thinking.
And Bill Lindsey asked himself during that
kiss why he had ever doubted that this girl
loved him. She was love incarnate; all the
warmth and beauty and sweetness of her,
strained against his pounding heart.

'Darling, my darling,' he said. 'My sweet
darling.'

'I love you,' she said in a suffocated voice. 'I
shall never love anyone else . . . never.'

Like one fainting with the force of emotion,
she leaned her lovely head against his shoulder
and shut her eyes. The man bent and touched
the long heavy lashes with his lips.

'Heart's desire,' he whispered. 'I adore you.'

'Why can't we go away together now . . .
never return to the rest of the world . . . but
just lose ourselves in this love . . . and stay

alone together . . .' she said in a voice of despair.

'Darling, I have no right to suggest any such thing,' said Bill Lindsey, 'I told you that in Edinburgh. But I also repeat what I added then . . . I'm so darned crazy about you that if you love me enough I will run away with you. Right now.'

She pressed hot eyes against his shoulder. If it were only as easy as that! She whispered:

'We're up against a hopeless difficulty at the moment. I want to leave all and run away with you . . . and I can't?

'Why not?'

'Philippe is back.'

Bill stiffened at the mention of that name.

'And have you told him . . . about us?'

'Yes.'

'Well, if he's anything of a man he'll release you. The marriage tie is sacred, but an engagement is made either to be carried out or broken. That is what it is for surely . . . a period of test, of experiment . . . and if either of the pair find it a mistake, it should be broken without argument.'

Fiona gave a dreary little laugh.

'Oh, my Bill, how easy that sounds. How *English*. But I'm half French and he, Philippe, is a Frenchman. Our betrothal was a legal affair, and binding without the mutual consent of the two parties concerned.'

'Good heavens!' exclaimed Bill, staring at

her. 'Do you mean that the man is going to force you to go on with it?'

'Yes,' she said in a broken voice. 'Last night he told me that he would never set me free. His relatives are all here. The wedding is supposed to be performed tomorrow.'

Bill Lindsey drew away from her. In shocked silence he considered what she had just told him. His mind was chaotic and his body weak. He could not contend with such a crisis in his emotional life. It was too much for him. He was a simple, easy-going young man. Such complexes, such complications defeated him. But he did know that he loved this girl to the pitch of madness, and that it would be death to him to let her marry another man.

They had come to the winding streets and lattice-roofed alleys of Casablanca. Now the air was noisy with the sound of native vendors . . . the high-pitched voices of women and half-naked children running through the bazaars. Motor-cars, donkeys, camels, jostled against one another in the dirty streets. There was a pungent, unpleasant odour of raw hides drying in the hot sunlight. Everywhere, brilliant colours . . . scarlet and blue-dyed slippers, woven rugs and scarves, hanging out for sale, mountains of vegetables and fruit . . . brass trays and ornaments, multi-coloured beads. Spiced cakes, the aroma of strong coffee . . . leather carafes of wine.

Everything passed before the eyes of the

man and girl in the car, like a kaleidoscope . . . making a crazy pattern. In reality they saw and heard nothing but each other. So they came to the broad, modern boulevards and to the famous Sphynx Bar where already French officers and one or two smart women were drinking *apéritifs.*

'Are you well enough to get out of the car or will you stay in it?' Fiona asked Bill anxiously.

'I'll get out,' he said in a laconic voice.

She gave him an arm and felt him shaking. She was filled with an impotent sense of love and despair. She worshipped him, and was making him suffer. It was terrible. But she was helpless.

They sat together at a small corner table and drank black coffee. Bill wiped the dew from his forehead. Fiona said:

'I know you should be in bed. This will give you a temperature, and I shall be to blame.'

'Darling,' he said, 'what does a temperature matter?'

'And you'll get into a row for leaving hospital without permission.'

He smiled tenderly into her great miserable eyes. 'Captain Lindsey can take a tick-off, my sweet. That's all the M.O. can do to me.'

'Oh, Bill,' she said in a choked voice, 'what can I do?'

'I honestly don't know, Fiona. It's beaten me. You say you can't get out of this engagement in this country and if the fellow is cad enough to hold you to it . . . well, where are we?'

'But I'll never marry him. I'll *never* consent,' she said in a passionate undertone.

'Even so, where are we?'

'At least it means I shan't be his wife, and he'll get tired of such a betrothal and finally let me go.'

'Meanwhile there will be a packet of trouble for you and I shall feel I've ruined your life,' he said gloomily.

'You must never feel that. You have *made* it. I didn't know what it was to live until you loved me.'

'You're a darling, Fiona . . . but I wish to heaven you'd been free.'

'I'd give my soul to be free.'

He put a hand over hers.

'You're an excitable, strange little thing. Sometimes I don't understand you. Why did you let me go in Edinburgh . . . without a fight? You're fighting now. You seem to be in earnest and yet.'

'Of course I am and I always was,' she interrupted. 'You need have no doubt about my love for you, whatever the issue.'

And she would say no more on that subject. For she could not tell him how her father had threatened to ruin him. Even now she was terrified for him . . . she was only too well aware that there would be hell to pay back there in the Villa des Fleurs if she refused to

216

go through with her marriage tomorrow.

Neither of them noticed a swarthy Spaniard in an ill-fitting grey suit and gaudy taste in ties, and with a sombrero on his knees, sitting at a table in the shadows behind them. Smoking a thin black cheroot, he watched the pair closely. Miguel Cortez had been well paid by Mr. Rutherfield to do his stuff where the British mercantile officer was concerned. He had seen Miss Rutherfield and the officer come into the Sphynx. He knew what he must do . . . what had been planned when the Captain first landed so unceremoniously in Casablanca.

Miguel Cortez was cunning as a fox and without scruple. For money he would have sold his own mother into slavery. What he had to do now was nothing. It did not concern him personally. Other people's sufferings were of no account in his life. He was as cold, as cruel as a snake. But he adored the gold that the great Harry Rutherfield could put into his little leather pouch.

After another five or ten minutes he finished his Pernod and slouched out of the Sphynx Bar by a back door. Almost immediately he re-entered the Bar from the front. There he saw to it that, by making movements with his sombrero, he attracted the attention of the young couple who had been hand in hand, staring miserably into each other's eyes. They both looked toward the Spaniard. Fiona had been saying:

217

'Bill, have faith in me. Somehow I'll break away. Only don't desert me. I couldn't bear that now.'

'I'll never desert you, my darling. But it worries me . . . knowing you have a *fiancé* . . . the whole show in fact . . . I like to play fair . . . I always have . . . I'd like to go to M. d'Auvergne myself and—'

'You couldn't,' she broke in. 'You'd get no further with him than I have done. Oh, darling, I know how honest you are. But you mustn't feel guilty. I never loved Philippe. I've never kissed any man as I've kissed you. I am all yours.'

Deeply moved, Bill crushed the small hand he held and was about to answer her, when Miguel Cortez moved . . . like the snake he was, he sprang toward them and struck.

It was to the girl he addressed himself, with a great show of politeness and apology.

'Señorita Rutherfield . . . You do not know me, but I know you. I know, also, your father. I have lived hero in Casablanca all my life. I knew, also, your revered aunt, and your honoured mother.'

He put a hand over his heart and bowed.

Fiona thought: 'What a quaint little man . . .' She said:

'What do you want, señor'?'

He looked to the right and left, then whispered:

'I am romantic, señorita . . . I know life . . . I

218

know, as everybody does in the city, that you are affianced to M. d'Auvergne.'

Fiona blushed and frowned.

'Well, señor . . . what of it?'

Bill, wishing for the hundredth time that he had not lost his pipe at the bottom of the sea, lit a cigarette. His head was spinning. Gosh, he felt bad. That shoulder of his burned like fire. He ought to get back to the hospital.

Cortez said in Fiona's ear:

'I have just been out. Your father is at the Roi de la Bière' (he mentioned the name of the most popular café in the town) 'with M. d'Auvergne. He mentioned in my hearing that when they had finished their drinks they would come on here. You would not wish to be seen here, señorita. As a friend, I give you this warning.'

Fiona sprang to her feet. Her father and Philippe coming here! That would be awful. They must not find her here with Bill. There might be a scene. Philippe might even threaten Bill and he, hot-spirited, would retaliate, and he was not nearly well enough to tackle such a situation. She did not pause to inquire more closely into the Spaniard's story or his reasons for this friendly action. She took what he said for granted.

'Bill, we must go at once,' she said.

You are too late, señorita,' said Cortez, with a flash of white teeth. 'Mr. Rutherfield is already driving toward the Sphynx. You must

219

go, señorita . . . through the back entrance. I will see the Captain back to the hospital.'

Bill stood up unsteadily.

'What's all this about, darling?'

She answered agitatedly:

'Father . . . Philippe are both coming here. There mustn't be a scene. You couldn't stand it. You are ill. This man will see you back to hospital. I'll disappear. I'll write to you . . . or send a message through Yvonne. Oh, darling, I daren't let you in for a scene. I *must* go . . . good-bye . . . God bless you.'

She was gone before he could answer her. He sat down again and leaned his aching bead on one hand. He felt ill. Had he been well . . . strong . . . nothing would have pleased him better than to have stood up to the great Rutherfield . . . and to the French fellow who was cad enough to refuse Fiona her freedom.

Miguel Cortez looked at the young English officer slyly. His plan had worked one hundred per cent. He was enchanted with his own cleverness. He said:

'Come, señor . . . I will take you to your hospital.'

In a daze, Bill staggered out of the café with the little Spaniard. The glare of sunshine hurt his eyes. He was conscious now only of one desire . . . to be back in his cool bed . . . to sleep. The meeting with Fiona . . . that passionate embrace in the car . . . all seemed like a splendid but hazy dream.

Cortez hailed a native-driven, ramshackle old taxi. He put Bill into it. Bill muttered:

'This . . . isn't my car.'

'Your car has gone, señor,' said Miguel smoothly. 'This one will do as well.'

Bill leaned back and shut his aching eyes.

'Tell him to get me back to the hospital double-damned quick.'

Miguel smiled. He whispered in the driver's ear. The driver, a Senegalese, grinned and nodded. They left the boulevards and turned into a narrow alley. Bill Lindsey, during that drive, passed into a state of semi-consciousness and Miguel Cortez had no difficulty whatsoever in achieving his object.

The car reached the outskirts of the city and stopped before a narrow white house with blue-shuttered windows, standing in a desolate, uncared-for garden. Agile as a jungle animal, Cortez jumped out and assisted the young officer, who swayed against him, his face deathly. Bill looked with glassy eyes at the man and mumbled:

'This is . . . not . . . hospital . . .'

Cortez made no reply, but tapped twice on the door. A face looked through a grille, then the door was unlocked. A girl stood there; a Spanish girl wearing a black silk dress and a black lace net over a hair of such gleaming gold that it was obviously dyed. She was young and had an exquisite figure, but her face was of marred beauty, large black eyes looked from

221

under blue-painted lids with a cynical weariness and indifference. Hand on her hip, she stared at Miguel (well known to her) and at the tall fair Englishman in his blue uniform. In their language she said to Miguel:

'*Hombre!* What is it you bring to me?'

'Get him in and in a room quickly, Mercédès. And do not let him out for several days. You will be well paid. When he recovers tell him he came to you of his own free will and that you are—'

The girl interrupted:

'I know what to tell him. That I am Mercédès, who is the toast of the lowest cafés in Casablanca and out of bounds to the British and American officers, eh?' she gave a harsh little laugh.

Bill passed a hand across his eyes. All was going dark. As he lurched against Mercédès, she exclaimed:

'*Santa Maria!* But this is a man . . . a Viking of a man . . .'

She used the words Yvonne had used, twenty-four hours ago. But Bill Lindsey did not hear them. He had passed into oblivion.

CHAPTER TWENTY-ONE

The luncheon party at the Villa des Fleurs was over. The Rutherfield family and their guests sat on the verandah in the sunshine, looking down towards the blue, silken sea, drinking coffee. The men smoked cigars.

It had been a festive meal. Louise had been given special leave to remain off duty from the hospital wing. It was an accepted fact that the elder sister, of course, would be giving up her nursing altogether for the moment. Tomorrow was to be her wedding day.

The two heads of the Anglia Shipping Line—Harry Rutherfield and Gaston d'Auvergne—were in excellent spirits. They laughed and chatted in the French language. The Concours were equally merry. Philippe's uncle was a short, stout little man with a pointed beard and curly grey hair. Madame Concours was equally stout: a kindly little woman with a faint moustache, and round black eyes, typical of her race. She wore a black and white spotted silk dress with a high collar and a large flat locket, set in brilliants, containing the miniature of her only son Pierre, who had died in childhood. Philippe, among other things, was now the Concours' heir. They adored him. They had been pleased about his betrothal to the elder of the

Rutherfield sisters. They thought her beautiful and intelligent, and knew that she had been well brought up.

They had come from Paris to Casablanca laden with presents for the young couple, and had a trunk full of exquisite clothes for Fiona—the best that could be procured in war time from the leading dress-salons in the capital.

During that luncheon party, the 'bride-to-be' had sat like an image, hardly speaking or moving, eating nothing at all. She sat in her mother's place at the head of the table, as her father had wished, perfectly dressed in a white linen suit, with pearls about her neck and in her small ears. Henri Concours sat on one side of her, her *fiancé* on the other. When they spoke to her she answered mechanically. Once or twice Philippe bent close and whispered:

'For heaven's sake pull yourself together...'

She made no reply, but her large brilliant eyes stared beyond him. Her thoughts were not here. *She* was not here. She was still in the Sphynx Bar, with Bill. She was overcome with anxiety about him. For she knew now that neither her father nor her *fiancé* had been down in the town this morning, Louise had told her that both of them had been here, in her father's study.

Why, then, had that wretched little Spaniard frightened her into leaving Bill? What could it mean? And Bill had looked so ill. She could not rest in peace until she knew that he was safely back in hospital.

Out on the verandah she drank some coffee and tried to talk to Philippe's aunt. Madame Concours, in her high-pitched voice, chattered incessantly. What time was the wedding to be? Was *M. le Maire* coming here to the villa to perform the ceremony? Where were Fiona and *cher Philippe* going for their honeymoon?

These and a dozen questions. And Fiona, her throat dry, her face drawn and grey with worry, answered '*Je ne sais pas.* I do not know, Tante Thérèse . . .

She wished they would leave her alone. She wished Philippe would not keep staring at her in that sullen, formidable fashion and that little Louise would not look as though a dagger had entered her tender heart every time the word 'wedding' was mentioned.

The whole thing was a farce. She would never go through with this marriage tomorrow . . . *never.*

The lunch party seemed to last an interminable time. It was Madame Concours, herself, who finally broke it up. She had eaten far too much and was suffering from indigestion. She smothered a hiccup behind a lace-edged hand-kerchief and fanned her perspiring plump little face, suggested that she and Henri should return to the d'Auvergne villa and leave '*cher petite Fifi*' to rest. The sweet child looked fatigued, she said.

225

Henri Concours beamed upon Fiona.

'*Eh bien* . . . of course she must rest. The bride must have cheeks like roses and eyes like stars tomorrow, eh?'

Fiona suffered him to kiss her resoundingly on both cheeks, and was then clasped to Tante Thérèse's ample bosom.

She felt sick . . . sick to the very soul and almost fainting. She had eaten no food and her head was spinning. Indeed, she felt so genuinely ill this afternoon that she believed she would soon be able to tell everybody that the wedding was to be postponed on account of a severe breakdown . . . and it would be true.

At length she got away from prying eyes . . . and staggered up to her own bedroom and locked herself in.

'Oh, Bill!' She murmured his name with a heartrending sob and sank on to her bed, burying her white young face in the pillow. And once again she lived those passionate moments in his arms this morning, remembering the almost desperate passion of his long, wild kisses. Oh, she loved him so much. She could not tolerate life apart from him; certainly she could not become Philippe's wife to-morrow. *It would kill her.*

Was Bill safely back in hospital?

If only she knew! But she could not even ring through to her friend Yolande. The girl had told her that it was forbidden for the junior nurses to receive calls.

The rest of that day seemed to drag interminably. Louise came up at tea-time and tried to get her sister to go downstairs.

'Philippe is asking for you, darling. *M. le Maire is* coming for sherry at six. There are plans to be made. You must come.'

'Tell them I am ill . . . I am going to bed. I shall not come downstairs again.'

Louise argued in vain and finally went away. She told Philippe what Fiona had said. The young man, who had been desperately worried, himself, all day, blushed angrily and clenched his hands. He did not believe that his *fiancée* was ill. She was merely dissembling . . . deliberately avoiding him. And what of tomorrow? All plans for the wedding had been made.

Just before six, he himself went up to Fiona's door.

'I beg you to control yourself and come down,' he called to her. 'You must meet *M. le Maire* . . . and tonight we are all dining at my home. You *must* be there, Fiona. Be rational.'

Her voice came back faintly:

'I am ill, I must be excused.'

'I don't believe you,' he said, and wiped his hot forehead and neck.

No answer. Philippe stared, wretched, at the door. 'Fiona . . . *nom de dieu* . . . what of tomorrow?' at length he said hoarsely.

'The wedding cannot take place, Philippe. I

227

tell you I am ill.'

'I will give you until tonight to reconsider your decision,' he said, biting his lips. 'You cannot do this to me. It is an outrage.'

No answer. He turned away and went downstairs, and out into the garden. He felt choked with rage and thwarted desire. And the main force of his anger was directed against the unknown Englishman, Lindsey, whom Fiona loved. He wished violently that these were the days of the old duels in France, so that he could have summoned Captain Lindsey, crossed swords with him, and *killed him.*

Louise saw him wandering aimlessly through the grounds of the villa, and her big blue eyes filled with tears. If only she could comfort him . . . her poor, dear Philippe. What a day! What a lunch party! And what would be the end of it all?

Later that night Rutherfield, himself, returned in his car from his offices in the town and was informed by a desperate Philippe that Fiona wished to postpone the wedding on account of illness.

Rutherfield's eyes narrowed to pin-pricks. He put a hand on the young man's shoulder.

'Keep calm, Philippe. I will manage this. It is purely an attack of nerves. Many brides are the same. You need not be worried.'

'It is more than nerves. She detests me,' said Philippe bitterly.

Harry Rutherfield gave his genial, deceptive smile.

'Now, now, my boy. You are exaggerating. Fiona will be all right. You will see.'

He patted his back and went up to his daughter's room.

'Open the door and let me in. I wish to speak to you, Fifi my dear,' he said, and added softly: 'You *will* open it, or I will break it down, which will scandalise Miss Macdonald and the servants and rouse attention from the hospital quarter.'

A moment's pause. Then Fiona unlocked her door. Her father stepped in. He saw her standing before him, her tawny hair wild and disordered, her face ghastly. He had never seen the girl look like that before and it shocked him somewhat. But he had no pity, no remorse on account of this misery for which he, himself, was responsible. He said gently:

'Come, come, my dear. This is no way to behave. *M. le Maire* will be here in a moment, and poor Philippe is distracted. It is too late for any postponement of your marriage now.'

Like a creature at bay she faced him.

'You know how I feel. I still love Bill Lindsey. I cannot and will not marry Philippe,' she said.

'And what of our bargain? You are backing out of a promise, Fiona. It is unworthy of you.'

She gave a wild laugh.

'It was an unworthy bargain for you to strike

229

with me. It was a form of blackmail.'

He sighed and shook his head.

'How can you be so pig-headed . . . so stupid about this third-rate mercantile officer?'

'He is the finest man in the world and I love him.'

'But you will marry Philippe,' persisted her father.

'No . . . no . . . I won't . . . I won't . . . You can't make me go through with it,' she said in a hysterical voice. Before Mr. Rutherfield could reply to this, Louise put her head in the doorway.

'Daddy . . . an urgent telephone call. I said you were busy and they said it was important. Will you speak?'

He frowned; then glanced at the ivory telephone beside Fiona's bed.

'Oh, very well . . . have it put through up here.'

Louise retired. Rutherfield picked up the receiver and Fiona, sick at heart, walked to the window and stood staring out. The golden day had ended in black clouds and a sullen-looking sea. The air was sultry unseasonably hot. Fiona, who knew this coast, suspected that a thunderstorm was brewing. Her head was aching violently and she did, indeed, feel ill. The air was charged with electricity, thunderstorms always affected her, upset her equilibrium.

She barely heard what her father was saying.

She was thinking only of Bill and how to escape tomorrow. Then she heard her father's voice. He had hung up the receiver and walked to her side.

'Fifi . . . Fifi . . . listen to me, my child.'

'Well—what is it?'

He was smiling . . . that sinister smile which she had grown to dread.

'I have news for you,' he said softly. 'News of your friend Captain Lindsey . . . the finest man in the world, I think you called him.'

Fiona came to life. The colour darted to her face and throat and she clasped her hands together nervously. 'What news?' she asked.

Mr. Rutherfield eyed her almost pityingly.

'It will be a shock to you, my dear. You had a high opinion of Lindsey, I know.'

She stared.

'What is it? What has happened to him? Go on—tell me.'

'This call was from the Chief of Police.'

'The police?' she repeated. 'What have they got to do with Bill?'

'They were asked to co-operate with the Naval and Military Hospital in a search for Captain Lindsey, my dear. He disappeared from the hospital at noon today. It has been ascertained that he borrowed a naval uniform and slipped out of the ward and, in spite of the M.O's orders to the contrary, left the building.'

Fiona's heart thudded wildly.

'Well—what of it? That is not a serious

crime.'

'Serious enough, but he did not return to the hospital,' said Mr. Rutherfield, watching his daughter closely.

Fiona's thoughts were chaotic. *Bill had not returned to hospital?* Where was he, then? Where had he gone after she had left? What had that Spaniard been up to? Oh, heavens, why had she left him? Only because she had believed that her father and Philippe were approaching and she had wanted to spare Bill from a scene.

She said:

'Well . . . where can he be? He must have been taken ill, of course.'

'Oh, they have found him now,' said Mr. Rutherfield. She swallowed hard.

'Where . . . where?'

'You will not care for the truth, my dear, but it is well you should know what kind of fellow Lindsey really is.' Trembling violently, she stared at her father.

'What do you mean?'

'The police rounded him up, a short while ago, in the *Maison Blanche* . . . a nefarious villa on the outskirts of the city, kept by a woman of ill-repute, whose daughter is a dancer in one of the lowest Arab cafés . . . a place out of bounds to officers. He had gone to the café with this girl. She told the police that he had picked her up soon after one o'clock. He was discovered, half an hour ago, in this villa dead drunk.'

232

Fiona gave a gasp.

'That isn't true. He was ill . . . He must have been taken there by that Spaniard . . . I know . . . I saw him . . .'

'You know nothing and saw nothing,' said her father in a warning voice. 'And Captain Lindsey is under arrest. When he is well enough he will be chucked out—relieved of his command. And now, my dear, hadn't you better pull yourself together and go down to Philippe?'

She tried to speak, to protest. No words came. The news she had just been given of Bill had come as a horrible shock, and on top of all that she had been through today, it was too much for her. She gave a little sighing moan and suddenly crumpled up on the floor at her father's feet.

At that moment a bright flash of lightning illuminated the room, followed by a deafening peal of thunder. The storm which had been brewing all afternoon broke in full violence over the Villa des Fleurs.

CHAPTER TWENTY-TWO

Harry Rutherfield looked down at his daughter's prostrate figure. Personal gain, obstinacy, all that was ruthless in him suddenly gave way to paternal instinct. He bent over

Fiona and his eyes were ashamed.

'Fifi,' he said, 'Fifi, my darling child . . .'

No answer from her. Her long lashes curved against the soft pale cheeks. The rouged lips were half open as though in silent protest against this latest grief and pain.

Rutherfield strode to the bell and rang it. Conchita came running in, saw the Señorita huddled on the floor and uttered a piercing scream. It was drowned by another violent peal of thunder, and the Spanish girl, who hated storms, flung an arm up to shield her eyes. Rutherfield shook her.

'Pull yourself together,' he said roughly. 'Get your mistress into bed. I am sending for *el medico* . . .' (He used the Spanish term for doctor.)

Conchita knelt beside Fiona, muttering and weeping.

'*Dios mios* . . . What is it . . . my lady . . . my pretty lady . . .'

Fiona opened her eyes and looked dully up at Conchita's frightened face.

'Bill,' she moaned, then slid into complete insensibility once more.

Louise, who had been downstairs talking to Philippe and *M. le Maire*, who had already arrived and was drinking sherry with the bridegroom-to-be, was hastily summoned by her father. She turned pale and rushed upstairs to her sister. Rutherfield telephoned to the English doctor from the *Clinic Anglaise*, an elderly, capable man who had been one of the physicians in charge of the late-lamented Tante Marie.

Dr. Gibson's verdict upon Fiona put the final nail in the coffin of Harry Rutherfield's hopes that his daughter's wedding to young d'Auvergne would take place tomorrow.

'She has had some kind of shock . . . she is in a bad state,' he told Mr. Rutherfield gravely. 'Her pulse is very slow and there is every sign of a nervous breakdown. Miss Fiona must be kept in bed, and incidentally, marriage for her just now is out of the question.'

Rutherfield compressed his lips.

'How long will this condition last?'

Dr. Gibson shrugged his shoulders.

'One cannot tell. In a case like this it is impossible to prophesy, but she is young and has a fine constitution and may mend rapidly. She is, on the other hand, highly strung. She appears to be in a state of mental anxiety. Perhaps you know why?'

'Yes, I know,' said Fiona's father briefly.

'I advise,' added Dr. Gibson with a discreet cough, 'that you suggest to her *fiancé* that he does not visit her for a few days at least. She is best quite alone, except for her sister or immediate family.'

He then handed Rutherfield a prescription, mentioned that he had given Fiona a hypodermic to quieten her, and departed.

As the two men walked out of the villa,

Dr. Gibson looked at the angry sky. Torrents of rain were falling. The temperature was dropping rapidly. At frequent intervals lurid flashes of fork lightning zig-zagged across the horizon. The whiteness of the houses and *terrasses* of Casablanca looked whiter than ever against the intense gloom.

'Bad weather,' murmured Dr. Gibson, and, bidding Mr. Rutherfield good night, hurried through the rain into his car. A Senegalese chauffeur held the door open for him. Harry Rutherfield did not wait to watch the doctor's car vanish down the drive. His own face was as stormy and dark with gloom as the weather. He hastened into the drawing-room where, at Miss Macdonald's command, a fire had been lighted. *M. le Maire* had gone. Philippe stood leaning against the mantelpiece. He looked anxiously up at Fiona's father as the large figure in the light grey suit entered.

'Well? What does the doctor say?'

'That your wedding cannot possibly take place for a few days,' said Rutherfield briefly in English, then added in French: 'I regret, my boy. It is formidable. But Fiona has had a complete breakdown.'

Philippe turned very white. His lips worked. His thin, sensitive face contracted as though he were about to cry. Then he sank into a chair and locked his hands together.

'*Mon dieu* . . . it is the end,' he said in a tone of despair.

Mr. Rutherfield frowned. There were moments when he wished his future son-in-law were less effeminate, that he had a stronger character. He growled:

'Stuff and nonsense, it is not the end. It is merely a postponement.'

'I tell you all is ended,' said Philippe, breathing fast. 'Fiona is crazy about this other man. Her illness is a subterfuge and—'

'Oh no, it is not,' broke in Rutherfield. 'She is genuinely ill or I would not have accepted that old fool Gibson's diagnosis. But as for Captain Lindsey, it is the end for *him* . . .'

Philippe raised a distorted face.

'What do you mean?'

Rutherfield, lighting a cigar, brusquely recounted to Philippe the story that he had told his daughter, omitting, of course, the mention of the fact that the Spaniard, Cortez, had acted under orders—orders to get hold of and ruin young William Lindsey by any method he chose to manoeuvre.

Philippe's face changed colour. He clicked his tongue. It was shocking, he said. Of course Fiona was mad—must never be permitted to give way to this infatuation. The Englishman must be a low type. He deserved arrest and dismissal, etc, etc. A flow of French, to which Rutherfield listened, well satisfied that Philippe was once more beginning to believe that he held a chance with Fiona, and that Lindsey would soon be out of the way. All of which Rutherfield encouraged, and following upon which Philippe drove to his father's villa to break the sad news of his *fiancée*'s sudden illness. After that he must acquaint *M. le Maire* and alter the arrangements for tomorrow.

Upstairs, in Fiona's room, Miss Macdonald took charge. She adored illness and nursing, and she had nursed both these young girls before in their youth. She cleared the room of flowers, lit a fire and drew the curtains to hide the now less frequent flashes of lightning. She and Conchita had undressed Fiona, who lay in bed, quiet, drowsy from the effects of the hypodermic. Louise, as usual on the verge of tears, sat beside her sister and thought how dreadful it all was. But what, exactly, had caused Fiona's breakdown she did not know. Her father had not told her. Fiona, before she succumbed to the dope given her, kept moaning Bill Lindsey's name and tried to tell Louise a jumbled story about a treacherous Spaniard and a plot, but it was all unintelligible to Louise, who came to the conclusion that poor Fiona was raving.

And now . . . no wedding tomorrow. Tante Thérèse and Oncle Henri would return to Paris, disappointed. All those beautiful delicate trousseau garments that Louise had helped to unpack must be put away. It seemed unbelievable. Louise, as she sat there, thinking everything over, supposed that she ought to feel down in the depths about it all. But she was only human, and her young ingenuous heart rejoiced secretly. To her, personally, this illness was no calamity, but a blessing in disguise. For it meant that Fiona would not become Madame Philippe d'Auvergne tomorrow, and that she, Louise, need not steel herself to hide the intense pain of standing by and watching that marriage consecrated; nor would she be left alone with Daddy and Mac. She still had her beautiful sister with her . . . crazy, foolish, whatever she was, Fiona was still the dearest thing on earth to Louise.

Poor dear Philippe would need comforting too. She would go downstairs presently and condole with him. Delicious thought!

Fiona stirred and moaned:

'*Bill* . . .'

Louise bit her lip, glanced agitatedly at the old Scottish governess who was tip-toeing about the room, tidying, and then, as Mac went out to fetch something that she needed, Louise hastily bent over her sister.

'Fifi . . . dearest . . . don't keep mentioning that name. You must try not to . . .' she said.

Fiona's lashes lifted. Her eyes looked glazed.

'Louise . . . we must save him . . . justice . . . not his fault . . . oh, he wasn't drunk, Louise . . .' she muttered.

'Who wasn't drunk, darling?' Louise stroked one of her sister's long slender hands.

'Bill . . . save him . . . go to him, Louise.'

'Darling, how *can* I?'

'You must . . .' Fiona tried to sit up. Louise saw that she was flushed as with fever, and the sweat was pouring down her cheeks, darkening the glorious bright hair. 'Must . . .' she repeated thickly, wildly. 'For me . . . for me, I beg you, Louise!'

'Oh, Fill dearest. I'd do anything for you, but what . . .'?'

'Go to . . . hospital . . . on Bousbir Road . . . see Bill. Tell him . . . I'll give evidence.'

'What evidence?'

But Fiona had fallen back on the pillow. Her eyes closed again. Louise shrugged her shoulders and, clasping her little gold cross to her delicate young bosom, murmured a prayer. Poor darling Fiona . . . she must indeed be raving. What was it all about . . . this nonsense about giving evidence and going to see Bill in the hospital.

Fiona spoke no more that night. Dr. Gibson had done his job and promised her father that the girl should be kept quiet for the next twelve hours at least. The hypodermic he had given her was strong. She slept heavily until morning. Soon after dawn the faithful and devoted Miss Macdonald crept in to look at Fiona, and found her lying there with eyes wide open, cheeks pale red, eyes still glazed and so weak with fever that she could hardly raise her head. At once Mac sent for Conchita. They sponged the beautiful exhausted body until Fiona was cooler. Then brought her a hot drink. She accepted the ministrations apathetically. Mac, with a kindly smile, patted her hand and said:

'Just concentrate on getting well, dear. You'll soon be all right. It's just a little breakdown. But your wedding need not be postponed too long. Don't be too miserable.'

Her words were only calculated to make Fiona more miserable. She lay mute, staring in front of her with large, hopeless eyes. It had been a night of semi-consciousness, half waking, half sleeping, and of terrible dreams. Bill centred in all those dreams. Once she had seen him lying in the arms of a dancing-girl, and she had laughed when she, Fiona, had tried to take him away. He had told her that all was over between them . . . the dancing-girl was his new love. Fiona had wakened from that dream, sobbing wretchedly. She knew that it was only a dream, the result of the morphia she had been given. But she could not get it out of her mind. Bill had been found in a house of ill-repute, with a Spanish dancer. Oh, just supposing he had gone there of his own free will? Men were like that. Perhaps he had grown weary of frustration, of loving her, Fiona . . . knowing her to be so far out of his reach. Perhaps, in a fit of despair, he had turned from her to this evil, painted woman of Casablanca. Fiona, carefully brought up though she had been, knew that such creatures existed; had read French novels; was not altogether ignorant of the sordid side of life. But she had imagined Bill Lindsey to be a man above such an action. She still believed it. But the dream had been vivid and terrible, and it haunted her.

She must get in touch with him. She must, at least, make some effort to ensure that if he had been taken to that place against his will, her evidence could be used in his favour. She wanted to tell him that she was prepared to announce to his superiors that she had seen him yesterday morning at the Sphynx Bar and that he had been ill. They must find that little snake Cortez.

Fiona waited for the kindly Mac to depart, then rang for Conchita, and told her to send the señorita Louise to her.

Louise, sleepy, sweet and very young-looking in her dressing-gown, hurried to her sister's side.

Fiona gripped her hand hard.

'You must help me . . . you must. It will kill me to lie here and feel I can do nothing. If you don't help me, I'll get up and go out myself, even if I die of fever,' she said in a choked, urgent voice.

'Oh, dear!' Louise uttered her usual weak protest. 'What is it now, Fifi?'

Fiona recounted the story of yesterday. Louise's big blue eyes looked as round and big as saucers as she took in every word Fiona said. She gasped at the end of it:

'He was found in that dreadful place . . . with a dancing-girl! . . . Fifi! . . . How could you still care for such a brute? You must be quite unbalanced.'

'I don't believe he went there of his own accord. He loves me. He told me so . . . he held me in his arms and told me so only yesterday,' said Fiona, in a triumphant voice.

Louise shook her fair curly head.

'It is all . . . awful . . . I don't know what to believe.'

'Believe me. And I believe in *him.*'

'But how can it all end except in catastrophe? Daddy has set his heart on this marriage and Philippe told me last night that he is not too unhappy, because he is sure you may be well enough to marry him next week.'

Fiona set her teeth.

'He is wrong. Daddy is wrong. But we won't go into that now. Louise, you have always been my darling little sister, and you must help me now. Either you drive to the hospital and get Yolande to smuggle you into Bill's room . . . or I go myself.'

'You have a temperature. You're weak as a baby. Mac has just told Conchita so.'

'I shall go all the same.' said Fiona.

Louise believed her. She knew that her sister was entirely capable of carrying out that threat. And if she did, she would certainly get pneumonia.

Reluctantly Louise promised to go to the hospital, if she could get away today, without being seen.

'Of course you can get away. Aren't you supposed to be on duty?'

'No—I was allowed off for your wedding.'

'Get into uniform, anyhow, and look as though you are going into the Red Cross wing. Then get a car and drive to the hospital. Look for Yolande. In your uniform, no one will think it amiss for you to be there.'

'What use will it be? What can I say to Captain Lindsey?' Fiona clutched her sister's hand.

'You needn't say anything. I'll write. Bring me a block and pencil. *Please*, darling . . . if you love me . . . do this for me.'

Louise sighed. but she promised to do as she was requested. But somehow she felt that in doing so she personally, rather than Fiona, was being disloyal to Philippe.

CHAPTER TWENTY-THREE

In a private room in the big hospital on the Bousbir Road Captain William Lindsey lay in a most unenviable frame of mind, and an equally wretched condition of body.

The doctor in charge of his case had just left him. The dressings on his injured arm had been changed, and despite what the M.O. had acidly termed 'his disgraceful debauch', the wound was doing nicely. The blinding headache and slight feverish attack from which the Captain suffered today was the result of too much drink rather than his wound. So the doctor announced. But Bill thought otherwise. He *knew*. He was well aware that his physical malaise this morning was the consequence of some kind of drug. He was sure of it.

He had only the haziest recollection of all that had happened to him from the moment that Fiona had left him in the Sphynx Bar. It was like a nightmare, and a constant irritation because he could not remember things clearly enough to define them and lay a really plausible story in front of the authorities. He only knew that he had been tricked by that rotten little Spanish tyke, who had interfered with him and Fiona and told them some trumped-up story about Mr. Rutherfield and young d'Auvergne being about to discover them in the Bar. Fiona had been frightened away for his sake. He remembered fainting during that drive; then waking to find himself in a strange house lying on a divan in a horrid ill-ventilated room furnished in cheap Moorish style. All sunshine and fresh air shut out. The windows, he remembered, were shuttered. There were dead flowers in a vase, and flies everywhere. He remembered looking around him and wondering where the devil he was, and why he had been brought here; and of hearing strange sounds . . . sometimes native music . . . sometimes a tinkling piano and a French song being sung in a shrill, feminine voice . . . doors banging, intermittent shouts of laughter . . . or sounds of a woman weeping. A strange assortment of noises.

Then a door had been unlocked and a girl had glided in and sat down beside him. He had a hazy recollection of having seen her at the door when he arrived at this place. He recognised the golden hair behind the black net, painted eyelids and short silk dress. She bent over him and invited him to drink. With a throat dry and head buzzing, he accepted the wine she offered. (Later he knew himself to be all kinds of a fool. That wine had been drugged.) He had gulped it thirstily . . . then fallen asleep again. At intervals he awoke, and she was always there, this girl, with more wine for him. (Little wonder, when they found him, they smelled the liquor and imagined him dead drunk!) He remembered, too, the girl trying to make love to him.

'You have beautiful fair hair and are strong and brown . . . Mercédès will give you her heart . . .' she murmured in Spanish. But he pushed her roughly away, told her to go to hell and tried to reach the door. He must get away. The whole place was nauseating. He staggered as far as the door, heard Mercédès pleading with him, and fell . . .

When again recovered, it was to find a couple of French military policemen shaking him. The *Maison Blanche* had been raided. Captain Lindsey, his uniform crumpled and stained with wine, and still only semi-conscious, was taken from the weeping, cursing Mercédès and driven back to hospital. There to be left to 'sleep off the fumes'. This morning a stern and unsympathetic doctor told him disgustedly that he had disobeyed all orders, had broken hospital bounds without permission and had been found intoxicated in uniform in a villa of ill fame, forbidden to French and British officers of the Army and Navy.

The amazed and horror-stricken Bill had started to protest . . . and had been told that he could reserve his story for the Seamen's Board, when he came up before it, which would be as soon as the condition of his arm permitted. The doctor added:

'I dare say you'll be relieved of your command, Lindsey, and you deserve it. You have disgraced your uniform.'

He left Bill to digest those words in silence and alone for the rest of the morning. And a most unpleasant morning of reflection it was too. For he could see that, whether he had been the victim of a 'frame-up' or not, the result was the same. He could never prove that he had not gone willingly to that villa; and he could not even begin to put up the story of why he had gone, without implicating Harry Rutherfield's daughter.

The whole thing was a nightmare. Sick at heart, and hardly able to lift his head for pain, Bill strove for a solution to the problem. Of all the damnable things to have happened to a chap, he thought bitterly . . . this was the limit . . . especially to one who had always prized honour and decency above all things . . . Now he was accused of dragging his uniform in the mud. Things looked black. And unless he could give a satisfactory explanation of his presence in that Spanish woman's villa, he would find himself no longer captain of a ship, but a ruined man, starting at the bottom of the ladder again.

That would be the end for him and Fiona. Under such conditions, how could any man ask Fiona Rutherfield to link her life with his?

Bill groaned and tossed from side to side in an agony of mental misery. But wretched though he felt, bodily and spiritually, he still thought with intense love and tenderness of Fiona. The whole trouble had started through him going out yesterday to meet her—but he could not blame her for that. He could only blame himself. She had been so sweet . . . so adorable. And she, poor child, was so un-happy herself. Wasn't today to have been her wedding day? What was *she* doing this morning? It only added to Bill's misery to picture Fiona back there at the Villa des Fleurs, fighting her own difficult battle.

It was soon after lunch hour, when the wards in the big hospital were quiet and most of the patients preparing for their siesta, that the little French nurse, Yolande Deuchars, put her head in at Bill's door.

'A visitor for you, *Monsieur le capitaine*,' she whispered. 'But only for an instant. I will keep guard in case Sister Leonard appears.'

Bill nodded apathetically. He was feeling so rotten he didn't really want a visitor. As for that old cat Sister Leonard, she had been helping to make life a burden for him all morning. Whenever she came in here, it was to utter a jibe about his despicable behaviour.

Then he saw a slender figure in the blue coat and skirt of an English V.A.D.; a sweet serious face framed in fair hair, and two large, rather scared blue eyes. He stared up at her questioningly. She coloured, and pulling a letter from her pocket, handed it to him.

'My sister, Fiona . . . asked me . . . to bring you this,' she stammered.

Bill's brown gaunt face burnt red.

'Of course . . . you are Louise. I remember. We met in Edinburgh.'

'Yes,' she said stiffly.

He gave her a half-humorous, half-cynical smile. 'Obviously you still mistrust me and disapprove.' She cast down her long fair lashes.

'It is not for me to judge, Captain Lindsey. But my . . . my sister is ill and threatened to get up and come here herself, which would have been madness, so I came.'

'Fiona . . . ill?'

There was a sharp note of anxiety in his voice that took the edge off Louise's disapproval. She looked up at him more kindly.

'It is nothing much . . . a little fever . . . a breakdown. She was upset . . . when she heard about you. It is a terrible scandal.'

The word struck him as being stilted, strangely old-fashioned. He lay back on his pillows, holding Fiona's unopened letter in his hand. He was looking under thick, knitted brows at the young V.A.D., as though trying to understand her. Only the tender chin, the long swan-like throat, the graceful build were the same . . . proclaimed their close relationship. Louise added:

'Please be quick . . . I dare not be found here. I don't want to get Yolande into trouble. There has been trouble enough.'

'You're dead right there,' said Bill briefly, and fumbled with the flap of the envelope with his one hand.

Louise added:

'I'll do it . . .' and slit the flap for him, then sat silent while he read the letter. She eyed him curiously. He was changed since she had seen him in Edinburgh. He did not look so vital and boyish. The months had aged him. She remembered that he had been through a shattering experience; his ship had been torpedoed. He had suffered. There were new lines carved on either side his lips. But he was wonderfully handsome, she had to admit. How bright and thick his hair was; his eyes had the clear deep blue of the sea. Oh, she could see what attracted Fiona . . . but she steeled her heart against him. He was a bad man. He kept low company . . . whilst pretending to love Fiona . . . that was contemptible. Philippe was upright and honourable. He would never have behaved so unpardonably.

Bill, heart hammering, was reading every line written in Fiona's big, flowing hand.

My darling, beloved Bill,

Father has told me all that has happened. I know where you were found. I want you to know that I don't believe you guilty. You must have been tricked into that dreadful house. If there is an enquiry, I will give evidence. You must be saved. As soon as I am well again, I intend to run away to you. I can't bear to be separated from you any longer. I love you better than life itself. I would rather die than leave you again.

Bill, my darling, never leave me or stop loving me. I'll stand by you in this, whatever the result. And when I'm gone, I'm sure Philippe won't try to keep me as his betrothed. He will want to get rid of me. So much the better. I belong to you

251

now. Remember that and be sure of my love and my faith in you.

Oh, darling, I love you so much.

Your most unhappy, Fiona.

Bill Lindsey read this rather childlike, piteous letter twice. Every word hurt and yet enraptured him. Hurt because he had entered her young life only to ruin it. Enraptured because he was so proud to be loved by her in this frank and heartwhole manner. Her pathetic faith in him gave him back his courage, his belief in himself.

He raised his eyes to Louise and said:

'Do you know what she has written?'

'I know that Fiona is mad and wishes to break away from home and make her life with you,' said the girl coldly.

'You think that madness?'

'Yes,' she said.

'You don't think me good enough for your sister?' Louise blushed.

'That is not the point. She was officially betrothed to M. d'Auvergne. It is a sin to break that betrothal.'

'Isn't that very out-of-date, my dear child?'

'Perhaps. We have been brought up in an old-fashioned way. And it is my father's wish. It will distress him terribly if Fiona does this thing.'

'Do you, none of you, consider *her* happiness?'

252

'I think she would be equally happy with Philippe,' said Louise stubbornly, although it hurt her to say so.

'You are going against Fiona's own wishes. She is convinced that her happiness lies with me.'

'She may be mistaken.'

'She may be,' said Bill in a low voice, and suddenly screwed Fiona's letter up in his hand. 'You may be entirely right, my dear. And now I'm in the devil of a mess and have less right than ever to ask for her love and loyalty. Oh, I wish I knew what to do!'

It was a bitter cry from the man's soul. Louise, young though she was, recognised the note of extreme suffering in that cry. She looked at him with real pity now.

'I'm terribly sorry . . . for you both,' she murmured.

He shut his eyes.

'Go back and tell her not to wreck her life for me,' he said in a stifled voice. 'Tell her I love her and always will, but that I can't allow her to leave her home, her security, all she has had, for a man who is about to be disgraced and ruined.'

'Why did you do it?' sighed Louise.

'Do what?'

'G-go to that d-dancer,' stammered the girl.

Bill gave a harsh laugh.

'So even you, her sister, think I was swine enough to go straight from *her* arms to a cheap

253

dancing-girl . . . good grief, what an idea! You're wrong, my child. Dead wrong. And *she* is right to trust me *that* far. I'm not guilty. *And I swear I'm going to find that Spanish chap who framed me, and prove it.* But until I'm reinstated in the eyes of my superiors, I shall not let Fiona come near me again.'

Now, for the first time, Louise knew that William Lindsey truly loved her sister. She looked at him with new eyes . . . with admiration and respect.

'I think that is wonderful of you,' she said.

'Cut out the pretty speeches and go back to her,' he said, more roughly than he intended, for he was sore at heart. 'Give her my message . . . and then leave me in peace. But . . . thank you for coming.'

Louise bit her lip. She felt miserable and undecided. Somehow she felt that for Fiona's sake she should be doing more to comfort this man.

'Go along . . . don't worry about me,' Bill said with a short rasping laugh. 'Just take care of *her.* And let me know when she is well again. I don't like to think of her as ill.'

'I promise to let you know. And I wish . . .'

'Wish I'd never got mixed up in your nice well-ordered lives, eh?' he finished for her.

Louise, half crying, shook her head. No, that was not at all that she had been going to say. She wished, suddenly, that Fiona could have her Bill. In spite of Philippe's existence.

She was beginning to realise—at last—what it must be like for a woman to be the object of Bill Lindsey's love. He was a strong, courageous, splendid man.

She turned and walked quickly out of the room. Bill unclenched his fingers and smoothed out the crumpled note and read it again. Then with a look of pain in his eyes he put the note to his lips.

'Fiona . . . my sweet love . . . my poor little girl,' he groaned.

Back in the Villa des Fleurs, a somewhat chastened Louise delivered Captain Lindsey's message. Fiona, who had been sleeping under the influence of another sedative, was now wide awake and much stronger. The fever had subsided. She sat up in bed, looking wan and big-eyed, a white feather cape around her bare shoulders, her tawny hair falling like smooth satin against her neck. Her great greenish eyes stared at Louise. She listened intently to her. She made her repeat several times all that Bill had said. Then with compressed lips, Fiona said.

'So he thinks he can make me leave him . . . now that he is in real trouble?'

'He did the right thing, darling . . . he does not want you to leave your security and

'Don't tell me again. I know how his brain works. Fie loves me. He does not wish me to ruin myself for his sake. That's all. Isn't it? *Isn't* it, Louise?'

'Yes,' faltered the younger girl. 'And I . . . I admit he is splendid . . .'

'That is the word,' said Fiona, drawing a deep breath. 'He is *splendid*. And I'm not going to be ruined because of him. I am going to be saved from a life of wretchedness with the wrong man, and lead a marvellous and wonderful one with the right man . . . whether he is in command of a ship or the humblest seaman of the crew. Oh, Louise, you don't know how much I love that man!'

Louise was, indeed, only just beginning to get the full value of this passionate devotion between Bill Lindsey and her sister, and it startled and amazed her. She recognised the strength and glory of it in comparison, for instance, with her own timid embryonic love for Philippe. She ceased to protest against Fiona's love-affair. She began to think that it might be best for Fiona to go her own way . . . best for Philippe . . . for all of them.

'What are you planning to do, Fifi?' she asked, staring curiously at her sister's face, which was transfigured with the force of her emotion.

Fiona said:

'I'm going to send another letter to Bill . . . I'll post it to Yolande and she will give it to him. I am going to tell him that I will never give him up and that as soon as I am fit enough I will leave home and go to a hotel and wait for him to join me. I will *make* Philippe call off our marriage . . . force his hand, despite Father . . . despite the world. Then Bill and I will get married, and we will face life, and whatever is in store for us, together.'

CHAPTER TWENTY-FOUR

Louise looked at her sister with mingled awe and admiration. (At the bottom of her heart, she was still loyal to Philippe and still thought that Fiona was doing wrong. But admire her she must, for her strength of character and the way in which she loved Bill Lindsey.)

Louise gave a little sigh.

'Oh, I give it up, darling. You must go your own way now. But it will kill Daddy and Philippe.'

Fiona's sweet red lips twisted into a somewhat cynical smile.

'I doubt if it'll kill either of them, darling. But first of all I've got to get well . . . and so has Bill. Oh, tell me how he looked . . . what he said . . . tell me all over again.'

So, all over again, Louise repeated exactly what had passed between herself and Bill at the hospital. Fiona hung on every word.

'He was very pale—really ill, do you think?'

'Y-yes, I must say he looked a bit ill.'

'Oh, my poor Bill!' Fiona clasped her hands about her knees and her face screwed up like a child about to weep.

'Oh, he'll be all right, I expect,' said Louise quickly. 'Don't distress yourself, Fifi darling. *You* aren't at all well, and you must be quiet.'

Fiona gave another deep sigh.

'It doesn't matter about me. I've just had a stupid breakdown. My nerves have gone to pieces. But *he* has a horrid wound in his arm and he ought never to have got up. It's my fault. I let him come out and meet me. I blame myself entirely—' She broke off, a catch in her throat.

Louise stared.

'You did meet him out, then?'

'Yes, and I *know* he was not drunk when they found him. He was ill. The doctors must be fools not to see how ill he was. He could hardly stand when we were in the Sphynx Bar.'

'The Sphynx Bar!' repeated Louise, her blue eyes huge, and uttered the name as though it were 'the devil'. Fifi her sister, in the famous Bar . . . without a chaperon! It was really shocking.

'I must find that Spaniard who told us those lies about Daddy and Philippe being on their way. I know he is responsible for all this trouble. He is the one to give evidence. He took Bill to that dancer's house. I know Bill would never have gone there on his own.'

'You seem to trust Captain Lindsey completely. I wonder—' began the younger girl, but Fiona interrupted:

258

'There is no need to wonder. I know Bill.'

'Oh, well,' said Louise weakly. 'I give in.'

Fiona caught her sister's hand and pressed it.

'Poor darling Louise. I know you think me a lunatic. But you'll see . . . it'll all come right. And don't feel too sorry for Daddy and Philippe if I run away. I am sure they will recover. It is only you I hate leaving.'

'When do you intend to go?' asked Louise anxiously.

'I'm not sure. But I'll let you know. You'll keep my secret, won't you, Louise?'

'Oh yes,' said Louise, with a sigh. 'I'll keep it.'

From that hour onward there burned in Fiona a new spirit; one clear idea, and one only. To get well enough to leave the Villa des Fleurs, cut away completely from her *fiancé*, her family and her old life, and dedicate that life to Bill Lindsey.

She sent Bill another letter, through Yvonne.

Oh no, my darling, you can't get rid of me so easily (she wrote, with a glint of humour), *I'm much too much in love with you now, and I am not going to let you make a sacrifice and give me up just because you are in difficulties. After all, that is when a woman should stand by the man she loves. I know you are innocent, Bill. I don't believe a word they say about you being*

259

intoxicated in that dancer's house, and I know you were taken there by that Spaniard. I am going to find him, and make him give evidence in your favour. I will face the whole world with you.

I can see that I must take drastic action now or I will never get away from Philippe. If I sufficiently disgrace him, no doubt his own people will wish him to break with me. So I shall leave home and say that I have gone to you. I will go to a hotel. I have some money that my father gave me for clothes and things. I shall not hesitate to use it until we can be married, and then you, my husband, will keep me. Yes, my darling, I am throwing myself into your arms now. Will you take me, or tell me you don't love me any more? Oh, my soul, I adore you. I want nothing but you on this earth. I shall love you until I die . . . and long after that.

Your Fiona.

She knew that this warm outpouring from her heart would reach him. Little Yolande, kindly friend, would see to that. Which, of course, she did. And within twenty-four hours, Fiona, whom the doctor had allowed up for the first time, received her answer—her first love-letter from William Lindsey. She recognised Yvonne's writing on the envelope and her heart gave a great lurch of excitement as Louise handed her the post. There was a note, also, from Philippe, accompanied by a

260

huge bunch of scarlet carnations. This note she did not look at. She knew Bill had written, and that was what she had been waiting for, hardly able to eat or sleep. She tore open the flap and devoured the enclosed letter. Bill had a clear firm writing, easy to read.

Oh, my darling, what a wonderful letter you sent me (he wrote). *I can't tell you what it did to me. I just felt a great weight has rolled off me and that my heart is light again. After I had sent that message by your sister, I experienced the most intense depression of my life. I love you, Fiona. I love you with every particle of my being. To give you up would take away my reason for existence. But I felt I ought not to let you go on with this thing now that there is a black mark against my name. After all, as an officer of the Anglia Line, I had little enough to offer Harry Rutherfield's daughter. But now when I may be proved guilty of this offence which I did not, in fact, commit, I may have still less to offer. I know I ought to give you up. But your marvellous letter has defeated me. You believe in me and you seem to love me as I do you. All right, my darling, we'll fight this thing together. You've honoured me with your faith and your willingness to share my life. I'll give that life to you. Everything I do in future will be for you and you alone. I am at your feet. And now my one wish is to get fit and face up to whatever is in store . . . with you.*

261

I dare say if you do this thing, they'll let you go, and the moment you're free you must marry me. I'll take care of you to the best of my ability. Let me know where to find you. Yolande is a brick. She's ready to help us keep in touch.

I can't begin to tell you what I feel for you. I can only say 'Thank you' and God bless you, my beautiful, lovely darling.

Yours for ever,
Bill.

When Fiona finished reading that letter, the tears were in her eyes, and her face was transfigured with happiness. She closed her eyes a moment, and so intense were her emotions that she could almost *feel* his lips against her mouth . . . his arms holding her against her heart. She whispered:

'You and I together . . . against the world . . . Bill, Bill, my beloved . . .'

She immediately answered that letter with another passionate assurance of her love and faith, and gave it to her sister to post.

'You look radiant, Fifi,' Louise said sadly. 'Does this man mean so much as all that? Oh, I can't help feeling sorry for Philippe.'

Fiona thrust the bunch of carnations into Louise's arms.

'Take them away . . . to your own room. *I'm* not sorry for Philippe. He has been so egotistical. I told him I loved Bill and wanted my freedom, and he refused it. Why, he isn't

262

human.' Then, as she saw the hurt expression on Louise's face, Fiona added: 'Sorry, dearest . . . I always forget how devoted *you* are to him. Philippe is all right. But he is a marionette. His father . . . my father . . . pull the strings and he jerks. It doesn't appeal to me. I like a man . . . a real man . . . like my Bill.'

Louise struggled suddenly between laughter and tears.

'Oh, dear . . . "like my Bill" . . . it sounds to me like a song. A Cockney song. You and your Bill. Honestly, Fifi, you don't know how you've changed. You're a completely different person. You seem so much older and more determined in every way.'

Fiona held Bill's letter against her cheek.

'That is what love—real love does to you, Louise.'

Louise, adjusting her nurse's veil, shook her head and sighed, thinking of her poor dear Philippe. She had been alone with him last night. He had come round to inquire about Fiona, whom he had not seen in person since her breakdown. Mac, being busy with her patient, had left them together. He had seemed *distrait* and depressed. They had sat by the wood fire in the elegant little yellow and white *salon*, which used to be Tante Marie's favourite room in the villa . . . and Louise had talked to Philippe while he smoked one of Daddy's cigars.

She had been so happy because he had

spoken more confidentially to her than he had ever done before, and had not as usual called her his '*petite soeur*'. He had treated her more as a friend. (She preferred friendship from Philippe rather than a brotherly attitude.) He admitted to her that he knew that Fiona did not love him, and that he had begun to wonder whether he would ever make her care as he did, and whether their marriage would not, after all, be a mistake.

He had asked her to keep these confidences entirely to herself. It had done him good, he said, to pour out his heart to Louise, because he was feeling very miserable, but he did not wish Fiona to know what he felt and thought. So nothing would induce Louise to tell Fiona about that conversation. But she, herself, could not forget one word of it. And each time she thought it all over, she wondered how long it would be before Philippe reached the conclusion that he was no longer in love with Fiona.

Whatever the young man felt about his affianced wife, however, Mr. Rutherfield was still determined that Fiona should carry out that marriage contract. And if Fiona had changed, so, too, had their father, reflected Louise. She could see that he had lost a lot of his joviality. Today he was a harassed, serious man, and very unsympathetic about Fiona's troubles. Louise excused him on the grounds that he was bitterly disappointed in Fiona and that he only wanted what he thought to be right and best for her. But she *had* noticed how lacking he was in tenderness toward Fifi just now.

After Louise had arranged Philippe's carnations in her own room, she took Fiona's letter out to the post-box which was within sight of the big wrought-iron gates of the Villa des Fleurs. Then she must hurry to the hospital wing. It was time she was on duty.

It so happened that Mr. Rutherfield's car turned into the drive just as Louise reached it. Harry Rutherfield saw his youngest daughter's slim uniformed figure and stopped the car.

'Where are you off to, my dear?' he smiled at her. He had nothing but tenderness in his heart for this docile delicate member of his family.

Louise coloured and said:

'I . . . I'm going to the post, Daddy.'

He glanced sharply at the letter in her hand.

'Who has my darling been writing to?' he asked with a gay smile.

'I . . . it's a letter Fifi has written,' she stammered.

'Oh, a letter Fifi has written. Well, well, show me, darling . . .'

Swallowing hard, Louise showed her father the letter. He scanned the address: *Nurse Yolande Deuchars, The Naval and Military Hospital, Bousbir Road.*

That was enough for Rutherfield. He knew

perfectly well that the letter had one enclosed for Captain Lindsey. He sat back in the car, still smiling gaily.

'Nice girl, Yolande. Run along, my pet, and post it . . .' Greatly relieved, Louise hurried off.

But ten minutes later, when she was busy in the wards, her father also was busy . . . retrieving that letter. He was extremely anxious to know what was transpiring between Fiona and William Lindsey. It was a simple matter to get hold of the letter. He drove to the post office, informed the postmaster that an important letter had just been dropped into the box on the hill by mistake, and the post-master, anxious to do anything to please the great shipowner, sent a representative with a key immediately to open the box.

In his study, Harry Rutherfield, chewing a cigar, perused the passionate words written by his eldest daughter to the young English officer.

The contents of that letter infuriated him, and at the same time he was amazed by the concentrated feeling in those words. Fiona had certainly 'got it badly'. There was little left in her of the unawakened simple child whom he had liked to pet and also to dominate in the past. This was a woman, writing to the man she loved. It was also the letter of a very determined woman (Fiona was not his daughter for nothing) announcing her

266

intention of leaving her home and family for William Lindsey.

The last paragraph caught Rutherfield's attention:

I am much better this afternoon and will be out tomorrow. I have wonderful recuperative powers, Bill dearest, and will soon regain my vitality. My first action will be to hunt for that disgusting little Spaniard. He is the man who must account for what happened to you. Then I am going to start packing, and find a suitable hotel. You, I hope, will soon be strong enough to leave hospital, even for a few hours, to join me. But this time, take care, my adored darling, and get full permission. Do nothing on my account to hurt your career any more. Oh, I love you so madly, darling, I am completely and for always
Your
Fiona.

Harry Rutherfield's face was a puce shade when he finished this letter which had not been meant for his eyes. He shook with fury. So Fiona meant to defy him, good and properly . . . and to run away with that fellow. How the devil was he going to stop it? He could ruin Lindsey . . . but he could not, in the year 1939, lock his twenty-one-year-old daughter up and keep her a prisoner. If she intended to ruin herself, she could join Lindsey and nothing could prevent it. Of course,

267

Philippe need not release her. No priest in Casablanca would marry Fiona to another man. But supposing, notwithstanding all this, she was mad enough to go to Lindsey and stay with him?

Supposing, too, she got hold of that rat Cortez and he went over to her side and gave evidence on Lindsey's behalf?

Rutherfield acted in his usual swift, ruthless way.

He sent word to Miguel Cortez to meet him in the town. The Spaniard did so, and later that night the two men had a quick, confidential talk.

'It is imperative that you give Casablanca a wide berth for a few weeks,' Rutherfield told Cortez brusquely. 'Here is some more money. Take it, and take yourself to Tangier . . . or any other part of Morocco that suits you. But stay out of this town until my daughter is married to d'Auvergne.'

Cortez bowed obsequiously and his eyes glittered as he took the wad of notes from the shipowner. He would go to Tangier tomorrow morning, he said. But, certainly, señor. He had relatives in Tangier. He would stay there until the señor said he might return. Return he must eventually, as he had a mother in Casablanca and she was old, poor soul, and bedridden. He was a good son . . . the angels knew that . . . whatever wrong he had done, he was a good son and must return to look after his mother, etc., etc., until Rutherfield shut him up and left him.

Cortez took himself and his money to a café, ordered a drink, and chuckled to himself. This business of Mr. Rutherfield's daughter and the English captain was going to be a lucrative one for him. He was enjoying himself. The senor was already a little 'windy'. So much the better. He would go on paying. As for Miguel's mother . . . that was a pretty story, but the good lady had long since died and been buried in the Spanish cemetery here. And Miguel did not, perhaps, care to remember that she had died of an illness brought on by extreme poverty, because Miguel had stolen all her savings and spent them on a woman of the town.

Rutherfield returned to his villa and decided to say nothing to Fiona, but to watch her. He also cautioned Miss Macdonald.

'It is best for you to know that our poor Fiona has developed a mad infatuation for a worthless drunkard who wears a uniform which he has already disgraced,' he told her. 'Whatever happens, she must be kept from meeting this fellow. If she tries to go out alone, let me know instantly.'

'Oh yes, at once, Mr. Rutherfield,' said the old Scottish governess, shocked. 'Och, what a terrible thing. The wee girrl's derranged, surely.'

Mr. Rutherfield twisted his lips.

'Maybe it *is* a question of derangement. But you and I know what is best for her. Her marriage to M. d'Auvergne must take place as soon as she is better. I leave it in your hands.'

Miss Macdonald retired, determined that the foolish Fiona should be very carefully watched indeed. She was entirely on Mr. Rutherfield's side.

CHAPTER TWENTY-FIVE

It was a week later when Fiona, wearing a dark scarf hiding the glory of her hair, and sun-glasses hiding her eyes, slipped out of the Villa des Fleurs and made her way down to the centre of the town.

Fiona knew perfectly well that her father had told Mac to watch her. But Fiona had eluded the Scottish governess. She was supposed at this hour to be resting. Louise was on duty in the hospital ward. Mac had said that she would come to Fiona with a cup of tea and wake her about four.

Almost as soon as Miss Macdonald had left, the girl had got up, dressed and packed a small bag. She was feeling well and strong again. Every day she had felt more and more exasperated, impatient to get out of the villa . . . and away from the whole family. Philippe, she knew, was hanging about miserably, waiting to be allowed to see her. Her father she looked upon as a cruel, ruthless individual, prowling around, ready to spring on her and endeavour to keep her imprisoned here. Louise was her only friend, and Louise could do little, really, to help.

The last letter from Bill, sent by Yolande, had told Fiona that he, too, was better. The arm was healing quickly now and he was up, and expected to be allowed out at the end of the week. He had already been interviewed by a senior officer of the Anglia Shipping Line, who had reprimanded him severely and told him that his case was going up before the Seamen's Board in London, and that as soon as he was well, he would be sent back there to attend the inquiry.

To that, Fiona had but one reply.

I too, will go to England. I'll follow you, my dearest, and stand by you, whatever the result of the inquiry.

Now she felt that she must take decisive action; once having made the break, she would write at once to Philippe and demand her freedom.

Fiona did not even turn her lovely head to look back at the home of which she had once been so fond, and which once she had rightfully thought the most glamorous place in the world. Today it was for the most part a

271

hospital; and the rest a prison. She regretted nothing but leaving her young sister and Conchita, who had always been her devoted maid.

Nobody saw her go. No one followed. Mr. Rutherfield was in Gibraltar for twenty-four hours. Fiona had known that and had thought it a propitious time to run away.

The afternoon was full of golden calm. Casablanca lay white and shining in the sunlight. In the distance Fiona could see the violet blue silk of the sea. But her eyes turned toward the Bousbir Road, and her heart was heavy with longing for her lover. When would Bill be able to get to her? When?

She picked up an old Spanish *fiacre* half-way to the town, drawn by an aged horse, covered in a fly-net. It ambled lazily along. Fiona said: 'Take me to the Hotel Splendide.' But she did not mean to stay there. The luxury, super-modern hotel had been built just before the war. It was the sort of place to which Harry Rutherfield would take his family. Fiona had dined and danced there many times in the past. But today was different. She had to be careful of her money. What she had would not last long. And it might be some time before Bill would be able to take care of her. Already she had made up her mind that if it was a question of following Bill to London, she was ready to pawn her diamond clips (which had been her mother's and which had been given

272

to her on her nineteenth birthday) in order to pay her fare.

The *fiacre* moved slowly down one of the big boulevards, and stopped before the huge white building which was the Hotel Splendide. Fiona took her suitcase and stepped out. She paid the driver and dismissed him. Then, without another look at the luxury hotel, she walked on down the boulevard. She must find a much smaller and cheaper dwelling.

Several men, Europeans, stared curiously at the slim mysterious figure of the girl in the dark suit. Nothing much was visible of her pale face, which had grown thinner since her breakdown in health, accentuating the outline of the high cheekbones, giving her a Slavonic appearance. The sunglasses were a disfigurement. But even so, men noticed the lissom grace of her figure and the delicate beauty of her ankles. Once a native of the city sidled up to her and murmured something in her ear. In horror, Fiona shrank back and walked quickly on. She must learn not to be afraid, now that she had burned her boats and left the shelter and security of her home, she told herself. Please heaven she would soon be with Bill. Meanwhile she must find a suitable home.

She decided to ask one of the nice-looking French policemen, standing on his chalked circle in the centre of a cross-roads.

The policeman, answering in French,

recommended m'amoiselle the Pension Braemar, not far away. It was small and highly respectable, he said, run by a Scottish lady. The officer's own sister-in-law, an English girl, had stayed there.

That sounded exactly right to Fiona. The very name 'Braemar' summoned up memories of Scotland; of the grey dignity and austerity of Edinburgh; and those days when Bill had been her patient in Aunt Jean's house in Moray Place. Darling Bill! Her eyes brimmed at the thought of him. She had given up the world for him. Now he *was* her world.

She found 'Braemar' one of the older houses in Casablanca in the Rue d'Orlay, standing a little back from the pavement, and approached by a paved pathway on either side of which were orange trees. The stones were chipped. The paint was shabby. The curtains in the tall narrow french window were faded linen. But through an open door Fiona caught sight of a spotless red-tiled hall and flowers; an appearance of order and cleanliness. And she knew at once that 'Braemar' would shelter her, and that here she would come to no harm. She knew it even more when she interviewed the proprietress, Miss Ritchie, a tall, bony lady wearing spectacles and a green overall. Her hair had once been fiery red and had faded— her bright blue eyes and freckles still proclaimed her Lowland descent. Her burr was unmistakably 'Edinburgh'; different from the accent of Miss Macdonald, who came from the Highlands. As soon as Miss Ritchie spoke, Fiona felt that she was back in Scotland's capital. Her face lit up and she said:

'Oh, you're from Edinburgh . . . I *know* you are.'

'Ay, I am that,' said Flora Ritchie, and her own eyes brightened. 'D'ye ken my country, then?'

'I know Edinburgh,' said Fiona, 'the castle and the crags above it, and Holyrood and the Royal Mile. Oh, I *loved* it, in spite of the east winds.'

'Och, I'd give a fortune to feel the sting of the east wind down Princes Street. Ye can keep the sun and what's to be found in this God-forsaken country,' said Flora Ritchie. 'French Morocco . . . why, heavens, child, the glamour lies under the dirrt. But it's clean and fine in Scotland. Come in. Come in. I've a room for anyone that can tell me aboot Edinburgh the noo. I've no' had time or money to go back there, but when I die the word "Edinburgh" will be found written across Flora Ritchie's heart . . .'

Fiona stepped into the cool house, and into Miss Ritchie's own private room, which was as English as it could be, full of homely things. And there Fiona had tea with the woman, and knew that she had found sanctuary. She gave her own name. Miss Ritchie knew nothing of Harry Rutherfield or his family. She had kept this modest *pension* for the last twenty years, having come out here originally as a governess to a French family, rather like Miss Macdonald. Since then she had catered for the type of English or French tourist who could not afford more than two or three pounds a week, and who gave places like the Splendide a wide berth. When Fiona said that she had come here to visit her *fiancé*, who had been torpedoed and was in hospital, Miss Ritchie saw no reason to disbelieve the girl, and so glad was she to have somebody to talk to about her beloved Scotland that she let Fiona have one of the best bedrooms for the least money. 'Best' though it was, the little room in 'Braemar' was shabbier than any Fiona had occupied so far in her young life. Bare wooden floor, with a few cheap rugs; a bedroom suite of unvarnished deal and an old brass bedstead with springs that needed overhauling. Paint that had blistered everywhere from the sun. Rush blinds that needed renovation. But it was all scrupulously clean, and as Fiona unpacked her suitcase she looked around and thought:

'This could be paradise . . . with *him* . . .'

At the mere thought, she blushed vividly, flung herself on the bed and hid her burning face on the cool pillow. She was not his wife yet . . . but one day soon, she would be. Oh, what a terrible, wonderful thing was this love. It burned her up. She cared for nothing, nobody now, but Bill. Already her family, her beautiful home, Philippe d'Auvergne, seemed phantoms of the past. Nothing was real but this shabby room in the *pension* and her high hopes of being with Bill soon.

Almost immediately she put on her hat and went out again. She left the Pension Braemar behind her and walked to the Boulevard de la Gare. She had an object now. To find the Spaniard who had guided Bill to his ruin and make him admit it.

First she went to the post office and sent a telegram to Bill, giving him her address and new telephone number. She also sent a note by special messenger up to the Villa des Fleurs, to Louise, giving the girl her address.

I trust you on your honour not to give it to Philippe or Daddy (she wrote). *You must never let me down. But if you want me, darling, I am here . . .*

Louise loved her father and she loved Philippe. But honour was dear to her devotional little soul and her sister knew that wild horses would not drag from her the fact that Fiona was to be found at the Pension Braemar.

For the next hour, Fiona commenced what she half knew to be a fruitless errand. She went to the Sphynx Bar and sat there awhile, drinking orangeade, watching for the Spaniard, whom she thought might come in at

277

this hour. Her heart shook every time she fancied she saw a man who resembled her father, or one of the d'Auvergnes. She dared not be found here. She went on to the Café de la Bière . . . to four or five other cafés; her great feverish eyes searching, always searching for the Spaniard. He must be found. He alone could defend Bill when the time came.

She did not, of course, see Miguel Cortez, nor did she know his name, so could not ask for him. At one or two cafés men spoke to her, admiringly. She fled in fear and disgust. At one place she dared finally to question the bartender. Did he know a little Spaniard, who wore a light grey suit and sombrero and had a thin black line of moustache?

The bartender, a Frenchman, who had spent some time in New York and spoke a mixture of French and Yankee slang, grinned at her.

'Say, baby, lay off Spaniards. No' much good, and no dollars, I guess. You find nice rich *Americano* and—'

'I want this man for business reasons . . . not for what you imagine,' Fiona broke in, crimsoning angrily.

He grinned harder, leaning his elbows on the counter and staring at the pale, exquisite girl's face.

'What's your name, honey?'

Fiona could have hit him. But she continued to question. She was working for Bill . . . only for Bill. She went so far as to mention that there had been an incident when an English Merchant officer had been found in a dancer's house . . . had the bar-tender heard about it? He had. It was a public scandal, he told her, and roared with laughter.

'She's clever . . . Mercédès . . . she been going down-hill; losing her looks. But say, baby, she's popular again since that raid on her villa.'

Fiona stared at the man. He disgusted her, but she was fascinated by his information. So he *knew* about Bill being arrested. It was a public scandal, he said. And the dancer's name was Mercédès.

'Where is . . . the villa?' she asked breathlessly.

' 'Way outside bazaar. You don' wanna go there, baby. You have dinner with nice *Americano* instead.'

'Listen,' said Fiona, her heart hammering. 'Where can I find . . . this dancer?'

'Mercédès? She dance every night at Café Ton-Ton in Rue Blanchette. But you don' wanna go there, baby—'

Fiona cut the man short. She threw a five-franc note on the counter and turned and walked out of the bar. The bartender shouted after her. 'Baby, come back. *Venez ici . . .*'

But Fiona had gone. She was walking rapidly back to the Pension Braemar. Her thoughts were in a whirl. So the dancer in

279

whose house Bill had been found was called Mercédès and she danced every night at the Café Ton-Ton in the Rue Blanchette. She, Fiona, could go there. A taxi would take her. She *would* go there . . . later tonight. She would see Mercédès, herself, and make her tell the truth about Bill. Mercédès would know quite well that Bill had drunk nothing . . . that he had been ill when the police found him in her villa.

'I'll appeal to her,' thought Fiona feverishly. 'I'll make her own up . . . I'll get a confession from her even if I have to give her my diamond clips as a bribe.'

Her mind was made up. And there was no one to warn her to keep away from one of the most nefarious cafés in Casablanca. She knew no fear tonight. She was inspired by her tremendous love for Bill; her wish to save him . . . to save his reputation which meant so much to him.

So excited was she by her own plans that she could hardly eat the fish supper which Miss Ritchie served in the genteel dining-room, where six genteel lodgers gathered for the evening meal at seven o'clock. There were four men, clerks, working in French and English firms, and two women, one a typist and one an elderly dress-maker. Pale, tired, devitalised creatures. Fiona shone among them like a jewel. They looked at her well-cut clothes, wonderful face, her tawny mane of

280

hair and her slender grace, and marvelled that this young beauty should have come among them in the Pension Braemar.

Fiona hardly ate and hardly spoke. The men stared at her, fascinated by her loveliness. The two women thought her stand-offish and were offended. But Fiona was living in a world of her own. Her thoughts rotated about Bill. It was as though her great passion for him was burning her up, exhausting her of all other thoughts or emotions.

Supper over, there followed several dull, difficult hours for Fiona. She went to her room and lay on her bed, concentrating on her plans, trying in vain to rest. She knew that it would be useless for her to try to contact the dancer, Mercédès, until later. She was crazily impatient, and finally, at ten o'clock, she slipped out of the Pension and found a cruising taxi and told the man to take her to the Café Ton-Ton.

'In the Rue Blanchette?' he asked.

'Yes.'

The driver stared. He knew the place. What man didn't! But this girl looked quiet and decent. Funny place for *her* to choose, he thought. But it wasn't his business.

Fiona got into the car. The man drove quickly down the wide boulevard and into a quieter, narrower street, toward the harbour. The Rue Blanchette overlooked the sea.

It was a mysterious purple night. Great clear

stars hung like jewels in the sky over Casablanca. The air was warm and full of the faint sighs and sounds of music and laughter from the cafés and bazaars.

It was not until the taxi pulled up before a shoddy-looking building, with a torn awning bearing the words 'Ton-Ton', that Fiona began to feel afraid.

She hung back, half inclined to tell the driver to take her straight back to the Pension; to Miss Ritchie's genteel respectable dwelling where she was so safe.

Then she thought:

'It is for him. I may be able to get the evidence that will save *him.*'

She paid the driver, and with a pulse fluttering in her throat she knocked on the door of the café. She stood there in the purple dusk, under the stars, with the dark shadows of the harbour and the sea lapping against the stone walls behind her. There was not a soul in sight. The shuttered houses and cafés were all closed. The place seemed dead, deserted. It had an atmosphere of secret evil. Who was to know what lay behind those doors . . . or whose eyes peered through the shutters, watching, waiting . . . spying . . . ? For this was one of the most sinister and dangerous quarters in Casablanca. The notorious Rue Blanchette.

CHAPTER TWENTY-SIX

Fiona stared at the door before her. She saw a knocker and above it a kind of grille. She put out a hand that trembled a little and touched the knocker. The sound seemed amplified by the silence of the shadowed street. Her heartbeats quickened and she caught her breath as she saw two eyes peering at her now behind the grille. She heard a woman's voice . . . possibly an old woman's . . . for it was hoarse and quavering.

'*Qui est là?* Who is there?' She spoke first in French, then English, with a strong accent.

Fiona answered in French:

'I . . . I wish to see Mercédès.'

'Mercédès is busy.'

'I can wait,' said Fiona desperately.

'Who are you?'

'Never mind. I . . . I wish to see her.'

A low evil chuckle from the old woman the other side of the door.

'Many wish to see her. *Ha! Ha! Ha! Entrez . . . Entrez, mademoiselle.*'

The door opened. Fiona stepped in. She stood blinking for a moment. The lights inside were strong, after the darkness. She was in the café and it was garishly illuminated and everything seemed to Fiona very red . . . red lampshades . . . red plush sofas all round the

283

walls . . . tables laid for supper . . . mirrored walls. There were several men of various nationalities drinking and smoking. In one corner a group of girls in tawdry evening dresses. The atmosphere was thick with smoke and the place had a strong odour of French cigarettes, of garlic and coffee.

Fiona looked nervously around her. One of the men, a pallid creature wearing a deplorably cut, lightish blue suit, looked up at her. He then turned to his companion, an older man with a beard, and he too looked at Fiona, then shrugged his shoulders. They exchanged a jest and laughed. Fiona felt her cheeks grow hot. She knew that she should not have come here. She was doubtless laying herself open to insult. She had put on a quiet grey dress and tied a scarf over her glorious hair, and she had hoped to make herself inconspicuous.

The old woman who had let her in glanced at her inquisitively, then motioned her to a table.

'Sit down . . . I will tell Mercédès. But she will not have much time for you. She dances at eleven o'clock. It is nearly that.'

'Tell her it is very important,' said Fiona in a low voice. The old creature shuffled off, chuckling.

'It is always important . . . always,' she croaked.

Fiona, ill at ease and without lifting her gaze

to the men, whom she felt were staring at her, sat down.

To the left of her was a piano. Two men—dressed in dirty white linen suits—they looked as though they might be South Americans—were holding a conference by this piano. One held a guitar and twanged a note of it now and again. The other ran a dirty hand up and down the piano keys. This, Fiona presumed, constituted the orchestra.

At the far end of the café sat a man and girl in day-clothes, huddled together, her head on his shoulder, his right arm embracing her, whilst with the other hand he carried a drink to his lips. Now and then he put the drink down, turned and kissed the girl, who responded languorously.

Fiona regarded this scene with horror. After her strict upbringing by her father and Tante Marie and the extreme innocence of her life, she was unprepared for any such scene as the one she now surveyed in the Café Ton-Ton. She felt hot with shame and longed to get out. She was petrified that at any moment some man would come across and speak to her.

Then the old woman came back.

'*Venez* . . . come, mademoiselle. Mercédès will see you. She is finishing her dressing. You must be quick.'

Fiona thankfully followed the woman through some curtains into a small back room. Here, too, the lights were bright, concentrated on a dressing table at which was seated the Spanish girl, fixing a flower in her golden hair. Fiona—now that she was face to face with the dancer—felt so nervous that she was tongue-tied. She stared at Mercédès only half remembering the errand on which she had come. She thought at first glance that Mercédès was beautiful with that glistening hair, huge black eyes and the long voluptuous body. She wore a black lace evening dress. Her shoulders were bare, ivory-coloured. There was a tortoiseshell Spanish comb in her hair and a little black mantilla floating from it. There were tawdry red silk roses pinned to her corsage. At second glance Fiona saw that she was altogether tawdry and that the natural beauty of her face was destroyed by its viciousness.

Mercédès turned slowly in her chair and stared in her turn at Fiona . . . looked with genuine surprise and curiosity at the well-dressed, aristocratic girl. *Madre di Dios*, she thought, but what brought *her* here?

Then Fiona found speech.

'I have come . . . to ask . . . to ask your help . . .' she stammered.

Mercédès opened wide her eyes. Her lashes fascinated Fiona. They were so long, each one seemed varnished so that they stuck out in a stiff fringe.

'You want my help?' Mercédès said in French, which she spoke with a strong Spanish

286

accent. 'And how can Mercédés help mademoiselle?'

Fiona licked her dry lips.

'It . . . it is about . . . my . . . my future husband.'

'I beg you to explain. What have I to do with mademoiselle's future husband?'

'He was found . . . in your villa, señorita,' said Fiona desperately.

A moment's pause. Then Mercédès' eyes narrowed and a secret, unpleasant little smile curved her scarlet mouth.

'I see. Well, a good many men are found in my villa, mademoiselle,' she said with deliberate insolence. 'How does that concern you?'

'This . . . this officer . . . we are going to be married. I am concerned for his future,' said Fiona breathlessly, gaining courage. 'He has been wrongfully accused of being found in your villa, intoxicated. Señorita, you know that he was ill and that it was a Spaniard . . . a countryman of yours . . . who brought him to you. I want you to defend him . . . to bear witness to the truth. Otherwise he will be ruined.'

Mercédès did not speak for a moment. Her brain was nevertheless working. She knew, now, exactly who this girl was. Miguel had told her the whole story. She knew also that it was Captain Lindsey to whom mademoiselle referred. But Mercédès had been well paid by

287

Miguel, and more *pesetas* had been promised. She was not at all prepared to support Fiona's story and uphold the English captain. It would pay her better to stand by Miguel.

Fiona leaned forward.

'Señorita Mercédès, I beg you to help us,' she said earnestly. 'If you knew how much this means . . .'

She paused. Mercédès had kicked her chair back and sprung to her feet. Under the thick coat of paint her face was red and angry. She looked what she was now . . . a virago. She said between her teeth:

'Get out of here . . .'

Fiona also rose, in a bitterness of disappointment. 'Please . . .' she said. 'You *know* that Captain Lindsey was not drunk—'

'Shut up!' said the Spanish girl. 'And get out of here. I know nothing. Many men come to me . . . and many are drunk. Your . . . future husband is no different from the rest. Get out. I am busy and have no time for you . . . you little fool!'

Fiona went white.

'You won't help to defend an innocent man?'

Mercédès put a hand on her hip, threw back her head and laughed.

'There are no innocent men. Get out, I say, or I will tell old Carmen to throw you out, and she is strong, *Dios*, but she is strong . . . despite her age.'

288

Fiona gave one look at the dancer's malicious face, then with all her hopes dead, turned and ran blindly out of the dressing-room into the café. The two musicians were playing a rumba. The one with the guitar was singing in a nasal, sentimental voice. One or two couples, clutching each other feverishly, were dancing.

Fiona had but one clear idea now. To get out of this place. But as she crossed the floor, the young man in the light blue suit who had first noticed her moved quickly and barred her exit.

'Why the hurry, *ma belle*?' he said in French. He was a Frenchman, living in Casablanca.

Fiona looked at him in dismay.

'I . . . I must go . . . at once . . . please, m'sieu.'

He smiled, put out a languid hand and curled his fingers around her wrist.

'*Mais non* . . . stay awhile. Dance with me. You have a most alluring mouth, mademoiselle.'

Frightened, she drew back, staring around as though for help.

'Let me go . . . please.'

He laughed again, said something which she did not understand, and put an arm about her, trying to make her dance. Hot with fright and nerves, Fiona struggled to release herself. He seemed amused and only drew her closer.

She knew, then, that she had been mad to

come to this place. She had had some difficulty in getting in. She might find it equally difficult to get out. Nobody was taking the smallest notice of her struggles with the young Frenchman. The others were far too interested in one another.

Through chattering teeth, Fiona said:

'Let go of me . . . *let go of me . . .*'

'*Mais non, chérie,*' he said soothingly, and tightened his hold of her.

She thought, despairingly:

'Bill . . . Bill . . . what shall I do? I came here for you . . . I've failed . . . I've just made a fool of myself . . . and now I don't know what to do . . .'

At that moment the lights were lowered. The band—augmented now by a drummer with cymbals, broke into the opening bars of a *Flamenco*. The couples on the floor melted away. Mercédès came in. A spotlight was flashed upon her, as she slithered across the floor, clicking her castanets.

The Frenchman, who was holding Fiona in a vice-like grip, drew her to a side-table and forced her into a seat.

'Together we will watch, *chérie* . . . Then you shall dance with me,' he murmured.

She could not move in his grasp. She was helpless. Cold, sick, she sat there, staring blindly at the Spanish dancer's swift-moving graceful figure.

What was she going to do? she kept asking

290

herself. How could she get out of this terrible place? Who would help her? Nobody. Not a soul cared whether she wanted to stay or to go.

Although the café was plunged in darkness now, save for a light by the piano and the spotlight which followed the undulating figure of Mercédès, Fiona could see more people coming into the room. Fresh visitors, of course, to see the notorious dancer. All men. Vaguely Fiona could see their figures. But not a decent woman. There were no decent women here. Only the paid 'hostesses' of the café . . .

Fiona experienced a sense of utter disgust and fear as she sat vainly trying to release her wrist from the tentacle-like fingers of her companion. Now and then he tried to kiss her. She shrank back. She heard him laugh, and he told her that she was *ravissante*.

When would Mercédès stop dancing? When would those lights go on? Desperately Fiona tried to drag her hand away. Her wrist was sore, bruised from the silent struggle. But the man won every time.

Then she fell his arm around her. He whispered:

'Stop trying to get away, *chérie*. You are going to stay here . . . with me. It isn't often that Jean Doré becomes so interested in a girl. But you are unlike any girl I have ever seen. Stop struggling and kiss me . . . my angel . . .'

She felt his breath on her cheek.

It was too much for Fiona . . . the contact with the hateful man and his words. She sprang to her feet and screamed.

'I want to get out . . . I want to leave this place. *Help* me . . . someone . . .'

Her voice, shrill and hysterical, rose above the sound of the *Flamenco*. The clicking of castanets ceased. The music stopped. A man's voice said: '*Nom de dieu*, what is this?' The lights flashed on.

Mercédès stood in the centre of the floor, panting, furious. Fiona stared wildly around her. The café seemed full of people now . . . full of men. Something in her snapped. She began to scream and scream.

A young man in a dark suit, and with a pale sculptured face, suddenly rushed across the dance-floor and reached the side of the screaming girl. Her scarf had dropped, revealing her long tawny hair. He stared down at her convulsed, terrified face.

'Fiona . . .' he said incredulously. '*Fiona . . . c'est toi . . . bon dieu . . .*'

She looked at him through a mist, and recognised the man to whom for so long she had been affianced. She burst into tears and exclaimed in English:

'Philippe . . . thank *God* . . . take me out of here!'

The Frenchman who still held Fiona's wrist gave Philippe d'Auvergne an ugly look.

'What the devil . . .' he began.

Philippe cut him short.

'Let go of this lady's hand . . . let go, I say, unless you want me to fetch the police.'

Jean Doré released Fiona and fell back. The word 'police' was enough for one who was 'wanted' in several of the big cities in France. And there was an air of command about the aristocratic young gentleman which was not often to be found in the Café Ton-Ton. For all he knew, ruminated Jean Doré, this was a member of the hated police.

Philippe took the half-fainting Fiona by the arm and walked with her out of the café. Mercédès and her audience stared, as though amazed, and in dead silence.

A few curt words to old Carmen, and the door was immediately opened and closed on the couple speedily and with curses. They were not the kind Mercédés wanted in Café Ton-Ton.

Out in the cool night air, Fiona revived. She clung to Philippe's arm, sobbing spasmodically. He stared down at her, his face haggard in the starlight.

'In heaven's name, what were *you* doing *there*?'

'Oh, Philippe . . . if you hadn't come . . . it would have been terrible. I was terrified.'

'I should think so,' he laughed curtly. 'It is a dangerous quarter, this. And that café is the haunt of the worst set in Casablanca. I, myself, have never been there before. But I wished to see this girl Mercédès.'

Fiona stopped crying. She looked up at Philippe from suffused eyes.

'You wanted to see her, too? That is why I was there. To make her tell the truth about Bill.'

'You must be crazy.'

'I am . . . if to love is crazy,' she said, with a short, unhappy laugh. 'Bill has been wrongfully accused. I hoped Mercédès would consent to tell the truth about him. But she refused. Why did you wish to see her?'

'Not out of desire to save your Englishman's skin.' said Philippe bitterly. 'Only from curiosity. Your father told me the whole affair. I wondered what manner of girl Mercédès was to induce Captain Lindsey to be unfaithful to *you.*'

Fiona went scarlet.

'That isn't true,' she said furiously. 'He was never unfaithful. He was ill and taken to her house against his will.'

D'Auvergne looked down at Fiona in an unbelieving way. How was it possible, he wondered, that this girl . . . such a child, she had always seemed to him . . . could love William Lindsey so madly that she believed every word that he said . . . and would go to lengths like these to help defend him? It struck Philippe suddenly, in this hour, that he was no longer jealous of Lindsey. It was as though his passion for Fiona had died within him, leaving

294

him cold . . . almost disinterested . . . no longer caring whether Fiona wished to marry him or not. She had hurt him too profoundly. Never, never would he recover from this shock tonight of finding her in the Café Ton-Ton. He had been unable to credit his own hearing when he had first heard her voice in the darkness, screaming . . . then his sight, when he had actually seen her.

He felt a sudden queer desire to be with Louise. He was dead tired . . . emotionally played out. Louise loved him. Louise was pure and cool and deeply religious. He would like to kneel at her feet and put his head on her lap and pray and weep like a boy.

He said:

'My car is here. I will drive you home.'

'I am not going home, Philippe.'

'You are more than mad. Your father is searching Casablanca for you.'

'I shall never go home. I am going to marry Bill . . . as soon as I am free.'

He looked down at her proud, passionate young face. Strange, how little she moved him any more. Indeed, he felt nothing for her . . . not even resentment. He pitied her. He thought it was dreadful that she should allow her mad passion for the Englishman to wreck her life in such a way.

'Philippe, please drive me to the Boulevard de la Gare, then let me go. I . . . am in a nice *pension*. But I shall not tell you where. You will only give me away to my father.' He shrugged his shoulders and opened the door of the car.

'I will do as you say. But you are not responsible for your actions.'

Oh yes, I am. What I did tonight was mad, I admit. But I am still determined to find that Spaniard who helped to ruin Bill. I shall not sit calmly by and see Bill lose his position through my father.'

Philippe did not answer. He was half in mind to race the big Lancia straight up to the Villa des Fleurs and deposit this crazy girl there. But on second thoughts he did as she requested, and drove her to the town. He knew perfectly well that if he got her as far as the villa, she would only run away again. It would be futile. So he drove her to the Boulevard de la Gare. As they moved along, Fiona said:

'Philippe, I know I've hurt you . . . that I should have married you. But you must forgive me. I never loved you. I do love Bill. *I must* go to him now.'

'So far as I am concerned, you can do so. I have finished with you,' said Philippe d'Auvergne coldly. 'I will inform my parents and your father tomorrow that our contract is to be broken . . . immediately.'

CHAPTER TWENTY-SEVEN

At the Pension Braemar, Miss Ritchie, in a dressing-gown, and with her hair in a net, opened the door to Fiona.

'Och, what an hour to come back!' she said, a trifle testily.

Fiona offered profuse apologies. As she went upstairs. Miss Ritchie added:

'It's no' the thing for a r-respectable young gir-rl to be out so late in Casablanca.'

Fiona, her cheeks hot, nodded.

'I . . . I wasn't alone,' she said, swallowing hard.

'Ooh, well, it's no' my business,' said the good Scottish lady kindly. 'And there's been a gentleman telephoning several times tonight.'

Fiona, hand on the banisters, looked at Miss Ritchie with wide eyes.

'Oh . . . was it Captain Lindsey?'

'Ay. Disappointed he seemed you were out. He said he'd call here in the morning.'

'Call here!' repeated Fiona, her heart leaping with delight.

'Ay . . . he said so.'

Fiona went up to her room. She sat down on her bed and covered her flaming face with her hands. What a night! What a *nightmare*, indeed! That dreadful café . . . that hateful Spanish creature, Mercédès . . . and the *dreadful* Frenchman.

It was a miracle that Philippe had been of the same mind as herself and chosen to visit Mercédès tonight. Otherwise, she might still be struggling to get away from the place. She thought over Philippe's last words to her:

'I shall not tell Mr. Rutherfield that I found you in the Rue Blanchette. He would be too distressed. Certainly I shall say nothing to poor little Louise. And you can count on your immediate release from our contract.'

He had spoken coldly, even scornfully, as though he felt it to be beneath his dignity now to own her as a *fiancée*. She realised how she had failed him. But it was not her fault. The betrothal manoeuvred by her father should never have been allowed to take place. She could never justly blame herself for falling in love with Bill Lindsey.

It was a triumph to know that she had secured her freedom. What else mattered? Nothing. Now she could belong to Bill. And Bill was better . . . he was to be allowed out and was coming here to see her tomorrow morning.

Fiona undressed and got into the high white bed, which had a mosquito-net over it. She was too excited to sleep. Her brain was in a whirl. She was just beginning to realise what a colossal step she had taken in leaving her home and breaking the old ties . . . for Bill. And she would not have been human had she not felt a tremor of trepidation; a half-scared, lonely little feeling. It was to be Bill and herself . . . alone . . . against the world . . . against her clever, influential father's vengeance.

Sleep evaded her until dawn. Then only for a few hours did she find oblivion from her feverish thoughts. At half past seven she was up and dressed. She put on the pale blue coat and skirt and cream silk shirt which she had brought with her, made up her face (she was too pale and tired-looking for her liking) and did her hair with great care. Bill was coming . . . at last.

She went down to breakfast. The sun was shining brilliantly. The day promised to be a splendid one. Excitement choked Fiona so that she could barely eat her *croissants* or drink the strong coffee supplied to the paying guests at 'Braemar' . . . She kept looking out of the window. When would Bill come? When?

She was relieved when the other guests one by one departed to their various jobs. She walked into the shabby genteel sitting-room, which had Egyptian embroideries on the walls, and a set of ivory elephants on the mantelpiece, which were Miss Ritchie's pride. There were two pots of rose geraniums on the table. The windows were shuttered to keep out the strong sunlight, although there was nothing much left to fade. The colour had long since gone out of the worn rugs and cushions.

It was a cheerless room. But to Fiona . . . it was paradise itself . . . for when Bill came, she could be alone with him in here.

For two hours after breakfast she waited, alternately in a state of excitement and depression. Finally a car stopped before the *pension.* Through the slats in the shutters, Fiona's eager gaze saw a figure in blue uniform step out, a big fair man with one arm in a sling. A suffocating sensation of joy within Fiona's heart blotted out all other feelings. She ran to the door and stood waiting there. Bill came through the front door, and paused and took off his peaked cap, looking around him. Then he saw the slim girl in the pale blue suit . . . saw her transfigured face and great luminous eyes.

'Fiona!' he exclaimed.

'Bill,' she said huskily.

He moved into the room and shut the door behind him. She ran to him and he caught her close with his strong right arm. The world ceased to exist for them both as their lips met in a long, desperate kiss.

One kiss was followed by another and yet another . . . it was as though they could not stop kissing—they clung together yet more closely . . . Fiona's arms twined about Bill's neck. Her face was pale now with the intensity of her happiness.

At last he let her go and drew breath. His strong brown face was like hers, transfigured.

Keeping an arm about her, he drew her to the sofa and they sat down together, looking into each other's eyes.

He said:

'*You sweet*! Oh, my *adorable* darling . . .'

'Oh, Bill . . . Bill . . . everything is worth while now.'

'I don't deserve that you should love me so much, my darling,' he said humbly.

'You do, you do indeed.'

'You know that I worship you.'

'We love each other. We could never possibly have said goodbye. We *must* be together.'

'Yes, I realise that,' he said seriously, keeping his gaze on her. He still found it hard to understand why this glorious girl should care for him so deeply. She was exquisite this morning in her blue dress. He drank in the sight of her great greenish eyes under the faintly blue-shadowed lids . . . her silken, red-brown hair, caught her delicate fragrance. Picking up her hands, he looked in silent reverence at the long slender fingers with the smooth coral-tinted nails, then kissed each in turn. She said:

'Tell me everything about yourself . . . quickly . . . what is happening?'

Bill told her briefly. He was allowed out now, but the arm was still discharging a little, and until the wound had closed he could not leave the hospital and go to London. In its

301

way, that was as well, he said, because it meant he need not leave Casablanca—and her. It also gave him time before he faced his Board to try to find that little devil of a Spaniard and wring the truth out of him.

Fiona bit her lip.

'Yes, we must both look for that man. It is our only hope.'

'I shall also see the woman, Mercédès, as soon as I can discover where I was taken that night,' said Bill Lindsey grimly.

Fiona flushed and her lashes drooped. She held tightly on to his hand.

'I . . . can tell you that. But it is useless. She won't talk.' Bill stared at her.

'How in the world do you know?'

'I saw her, Bill . . . last night.'

'*You* saw that woman?'

She told him what had happened. He listened, staring at her incredulously with his bright blue eyes. His face went white under the bronze and the muscles of his cheeks tautened. He exclaimed:

'Good heavens! . . . You went alone to such a place?' She nodded. He drew her close, with an involuntary movement.

'Good heavens!' he repeated. 'You did that . . . for me?'

'Yes, Bill.'

'I am stupefied, darling! It was truly grand of you, but you should never have done it. It makes my blood run cold to think what risks

302

you took.'

'Philippe saved me.'

Bill listened to the rest of her story and his brows contracted.

'That's not so good.'

'It *is* good. It has finally decided him that I am mad and that he doesn't wish any longer to marry me,' said Fiona with a laugh. 'I am to be released at once from my contract.'

Bill's face brightened.

'Well, darling, that's better.'

'Isn't it marvellous? Bill, Bill, we can be together now and no one can separate us.'

'Oh, my sweet,' he said huskily, and bent down to kiss her again . . . to cover her lovely face with kisses. 'It sounds almost too good to be true. I can get a licence . . . and make you my wife . . . Oh, darling . . . it's a great thought. But are you *sure* you want to throw everything up like this . . . and come to me?'

'I am sure. Haven't I proved what I feel for you, darling?'

He said:

'You have, indeed. And I'm not hesitating a moment longer. You may find yourself the wife of an able seaman instead of a chap with a master's ticket . . . but I'll do what I can to make something of my life for you with you . . . my adorable Fiona.'

She sighed happily and shut her eyes and lifted her lips to his.

So engrossed were the lovers in each other,

neither heard sound of familiar voices raised in altercation outside the door of the Pension Braemar.

There, in the sunlight, stood a scared-looking Louise, with her father. Mr. Rutherfield was smiling.

'No need to be worried, my dear, just leave Fiona to me,' he was saying.

'But you shouldn't have followed me, Daddy,' the girl answered reproachfully; 'it wasn't fair. Fifi trusted me with her address. She will think I've betrayed her. I had no idea you would follow . . .'

'My dear child, I knew if I let you go out by yourself this morning that you would lead me to her.'

Louise's fair face was pink and distressed.

'It wasn't fair, Daddy . . .'

'Nonsense, Louise. I must be allowed to decide what is best for my own daughters. Fiona is behaving like a lunatic. I shall insist on taking her home. You need not wait. You can take the car and go straight back and wait for us.'

Louise hesitated, then with a shrug of her shoulders turned and stepped into the car. It had been a shock to her when, just as she walked up the path to Fiona's *pension*, she had seen her father approach. Much as she loved and respected him, she was a little upset by such cunning.

Mr. Rutherfield rang the bell. Miss Ritchie,

at that moment passing through the hall, opened the front door.

Mr. Rutherfield raised his hat courteously.

'I believe my daughter, Miss Rutherfield, is staying with you,' he said, with a genial smile. 'Might I see her—if she— is here?'

'Och, ay, come in,' said Miss Ritchie. 'The bairn is in yonder room with her boyfriend.'

Harry Rutherfield raised his brows.

With her boyfriend, eh? So William Lindsey was here? Well, there was nothing like killing two birds with one stone. He would deal first with Fiona—and then with young Lindsey.

Well pleased, he walked to the door indicated by Miss Ritchie, and opened it.

CHAPTER TWENTY-EIGHT

Fiona and Bill were sitting side by side on the sofa, both hands locked, eyes gazing into eyes. They turned their heads simultaneously as the door opened and saw to their profound astonishment a big man with a deceptively genial face and smile. A man in a smart suit obviously made by the best English tailor; a flower in his buttonhole, and carrying pigskin gloves, panama hat, and a malacca stick.

For an instant Bill Lindsey, rising slowly from the sofa, stared at the intruder without recognition. But he soon knew who it was. For

305

the girl leaped to her feet and gave a startled cry of:

'Daddy!'

'Gosh!' said Bill Lindsey, under his breath, and his blue eyes narrowed. He knew now that he faced Fiona's father . . . and the head of the Anglia Shipping Line.

Mr. Rutherfield put down the hat, gloves and stick.

'Well, my dear, so here you are,' he said pleasantly. 'And this young man, I presume is . . . Captain Lindsey?'

'Yes,' said Fiona, in an almost aggressive voice, and gave her father a challenging look from her brilliant eyes, 'he is.'

Bill moved stiffly to attention.

'Lindsey, at your service, sir.'

'Ah . . . h'm,' said Harry Rutherfield, and put his hands behind his back and went on smiling at the young pair. That smile heartened Bill. But it did nothing at all to give Fiona encouragement. She knew her father too well. Pale, agitated, she waited for him to speak. He did not pay much attention to her. He was examining William Lindsey curiously. Almost regretfully. Fine looking chap, he thought. Healthy-looking, with brown of the sun on his lean face, and in his gold-touched hair, and the blue of the sea in his eyes. A real sailor. Rutherfield, who could sum men up, knew at once that this one was to be trusted, fundamentally decent. A pity that he must be

306

instrumental in the ruin of such a man. Lindsey was the type the Anglia Line liked in their employ. A *great* pity Lindsey had ever aspired to Fiona Rutherfield. Women were ever the cause of disaster to men, reflected Rutherfield sadly, as though it were the most simple thing in the world for him to transfer his own guilt to his daughter because she had been charming enough to attract Captain Lindsey.

He said:

'Well, well, I must say these are not the circumstances under which I relish meeting you, Lindsey. I'd preferred it could have been that I complimented you on your behaviour as an officer in command of that fine ship *The Albatross* . . . a great loss to the Company, by the way . . . brat instead, I had to question very severely your behaviour with my daughter . . . *and* your infamous conduct with a notorious—'

'Stop, please!' It was Fiona, who cut in breathlessly, her cheeks aflame now with indignation. 'You know perfectly well that Bill was not responsible for what happened the other night.'

'Not responsible because he was blind drunk,' said Rutherfield, in a snapping voice, and his smile faded.

Then Bill moved forward. He was a little white about the mouth.

'If I might speak in my own defence, sir . . . I assure you that *I* was *not* drunk,' he said. 'I am not a heavy drinker at any time, and on that particular evening I had only had one *apéritif* with Fiona. But I was a sick man. I oughtn't to have left the hospital. To that much, I admit. I had no right to be out. But I was in a fainting condition when that Spanish chap got hold of me, and instead of driving me back to hospital, as I expected, he drove me to some damn' fool villa and left me in that woman's clutches. No doubt she poured drink and dope down my throat. I wouldn't know. I can remember nothing. But I repeat—I was not responsible, and I shall stick to that story when I go up before the Board.'

Rutherfield listened to this in silence, without looking at the young man. Perhaps some degree of shame troubled him. He knew only too well what Miguel Cortez had done. But he soon banished the feeling and spoke sternly to the young officer.

'The Board will decide what is to be done with you, Lindsey. In peace-time I would have no hesitation in dismissing you from our service. However, you are now under Government control.'

'It's just as well. The Government will give him a fair hearing, but you are prejudiced and you've done this to him deliberately!' exclaimed Fiona in a passionately resentful voice.

Bill caught her hand.

'Hush, darling. Let me deal with this.'

Mr. Rutherfield shook his head and sighed.

'You see, amongst other things, Lindsey, how you have demoralised my daughter. She was a sweet, obedient child before you came into her life, and was about to marry a fine man, chosen by those who know what is best for her future. You have come between her and her *fiancé*. You have corrupted her so that she has become scarcely recognisable to her own family.'

Fiona listened to this masterpiece of hypocrisy with rising fury. But Bill said in a cold, level voice:

'You must pardon me, Mr. Rutherfield, if I do not admit to having corrupted Fiona nor having come deliberately between her and her *fiancé*. When we first met in Edinburgh, I had no notion that she was even engaged. Later, when I knew, I was already deeply in love with her. I went away, believing it to be my duty, but fate threw us into contact again and I then realised that she had never really cared for M. d'Auvergne. It has been an "arranged" affair, which is, in my opinion, out of date, and totally unfair to any girl.'

'Enough of this,' said Rutherfield, his face very red, 'I know what is best for my daughter. Enough of this whole ridiculous business. Fiona will pack her bag and come straight home with me. You, Lindsey, return to your hospital and do not dare to communicate with Fiona again.'

An instant's silence. Bill hesitated. He could not wholly forget his invidious position, and the fact that Fiona was throwing up a great deal by linking her life with his. But she took his hand, pressed it hard, and said in a passionate undertone:

'Don't listen to him, Bill. He can't separate us. He cant . . .'

Bill drew breath. He turned to the 'big man'.

'I'm sorry, sir. Fiona has consented to marry me as soon as it can be arranged,' he said.

Mr. Rutherfield's face was almost purple now. He shouted at the young man.

'You blithering young ass . . . you can't do such a thing! She's under contract to Philippe d'Auvergne and—'

'Philippe, himself, is dissolving the contract,' broke in Fiona. 'I saw him last night and he wants nothing more to do with me. He is telling his father so this morning.'

The colour faded from Mr. Rutherfield's face. He could barely speak, so choked was he with rage. Then he said in a whisper:

'You mad girl! You've ruined yourself . . . and perhaps your whole family.'

Bill pricked up his ears.

'Pardon me, sir,' he said smoothly, 'but was Fiona marrying this French chap for her own life's happiness, or in order to do a service to her relations?'

'I think you've got something there, darling,'

said Fiona, with a brief laugh and a dark glance at her father. 'There must be a strong reason why my father should be so insistent on this link-up of our family with the d'Auvergnes. Maybe he doesn't altogether trust Gaston d'Auvergne and thinks it wise to cement the partnership by an ally in the offspring.'

'Maybe, darling,' said Bill seriously, talking to her as though no one else were present.

Mr. Rutherfield put a handkerchief to his lips. He was shaking. His daughter had hit the truth rather too astutely for his liking. He felt, for the first time in his life, defeated. It was not a feeling he relished. He, who had always prided himself upon getting what he wanted . . . doing what he wanted. He looked at the young couple, who were smiling into each other's eyes with such utter devotion and tenderness. He could see that here was no usual love between a man and a woman, but a tremendous, vital passion that could not easily be annihilated. He could threaten, punish . . . ruin the boy . . . disinherit his daughter . . . but neither of them would care. They lived in a world of their own. A world of overwhelming love.

For one obliterating moment, Harry Rutherfield regretted what he had done to William Lindsey. He remembered his own youth . . . before he had become so involved with high finance and let a shell of greed for gold, for power, grow around all his nobler instincts. He remembered his first great love .. . for the mother of Fiona and Louise . . . and his deep grief when she had died. Nothing had been the same since then. And he had in the ensuing years increased his power, his fortune, and deteriorated in his own soul. He knew it, and saw himself naked and ashamed. But only for an instant. Then the darkness closed around him again. He crashed a fist down on a small cedarwood table so violently that it rocked on its legs.

'You fools!' he thundered. 'If you think you can defy me, you're wrong. I shall never stand by and see you marry my daughter, Lindsey, nor shall I allow Philippe to break his contract. She shall marry him yet . . . I shall go to Gaston d'Auvergne now, this moment, and make sure of that.'

A tiny tremor of apprehension shot through Fiona. If Philippe were to listen to her father . . . to break his promise to set her free . . . that would complicate matters considerably. But she held her head high and, putting an arm through Bill's, stood leaning her lovely slender body against his.

'Do whatever you like,' she said. 'I shall never leave Bill now . . . never. And if you're so anxious to unite our two families, why not marry Louise to Philippe? She would be only too delighted.'

Mr. Rutherfield flung her a look of malice

and resentment, picked up his things with a trembling hand, and walked from the room. As he reached the door, he turned and flung a parting shot at the young officer:

'Remember, Lindsey . . . I have weight with the Naval Department . . . and what I say about the employees on my ships goes. If you're chucked out now, you'll never get back. I'll see you don't. They'll keep you on the seas for the duration, but if I testify to your rotten record, they'll never give you another ship, and when the war ends you'll never get taken on by another decent shipping line. I'll see to that.'

Bill stiffened in every limb. Such hatred, such vindictiveness, revolted his simple, honest soul. He began to understand a little why Fiona had grown to despise her own father. He said:

'Thanks, sir. I'll remember what you say.'

'Go to the devil, then, but you'll not take my daughter with you. She'll never be in a position to marry you, I'll see to that!' shouted Rutherfield. He walked out and slammed the door.

Fiona ran to Bill. He caught her close. She sobbed:

'Oh, my darling, my *darling* . . . my own father is trying to ruin you. It *kills* me . . . I can't bear it.'

He tried to comfort her, uttering every endearing word he knew. He covered her bright beautiful head with kisses.

'My adorable darling, don't cry. Don't shed a tear for me. I'll be okay. I'm innocent and I shall prove it. We'll make that creature, Mercédès, or the Spaniard talk. We'll defeat the old boy somehow. Gosh, he's a hard nut, Fiona. It's shaken me a bit to realise that he's so anxious to ruin me.'

'He's not sane,' wept Fiona. 'I know I hit the nail on the head when I suggested it's s-something to d-do with his business affairs that makes him so crazy to have this marriage with Philippe come off. Oh, Bill, I hope he doesn't stop Philippe from releasing me.'

'I hope not, my darling. If he does . . .'

'I shall still remain with you,' she finished for him.

He looked at her with great tenderness and, pulling a handkerchief from his pocket, dabbed the tears from her cheeks and glistening lashes.

'My dearest dear . . . you couldn't do that.'

'I'll stay near you, anyhow . . . I'll never go back to my father's house.'

'We must trust to luck that you'll be able to marry me, darling. But you've heard for yourself . . . the old boy means to do me in good and proper. You can see what you'll be marrying.'

'I love you,' was her answer, and she pressed her warm wet cheek against his.

'Oh, my darling,' he said, 'thank you for such love. Thank you, darling. I'll fight the world for you. I swear it.'

Their lips met and clung in a long, fierce kiss. For a few moments they were lost to the world again in each other's arms. Then Bill made an effort to come back to earth.

'I must be a bit practical, sweet. You've chucked everything for me. I must look after you. Do you mean to stay on here for the moment?'

'Yes. Miss Ritchie is kind and the *pension* is clean—and reasonable.'

'What about £ s. d. ?'

She coloured a little and laughed.

'I'm all right . . . for the moment.'

His blue eyes examined her earnestly.

'Swear you'll ask me for what you need?'

'If and when I need it, darling Bill.'

'I'm to be your husband, darling, so you mustn't mind calling on me.'

'I won't,' she said softly.

He glanced at his wrist-watch.

'Gosh! How the time passes when you're with the one you love. I must get back to hospital for lunch.'

'You must?'

'Yes, darling. I get electrical treatment at two o'clock.'

She touched his sling.

'Oh, darling, is it getting better?'

'Much better. No need to worry.'

Hungrily she looked up at his brown face.

'If only we could be together . . . and I could

315

look after you.'

'I hope that'll soon be possible,' he said.

'When will you come again?'

'This afternoon between tea and dinner . . . and any other time I get off. But I've got a job to do, my sweet, and it's a job that must be done.'

'What?'

'To find that Spanish fellow who double-crossed William Lindsey and punch his face in, darling, then make him talk.'

Fiona sighed deeply.

'Oh, darling, I hope you do. I'll look for him too.'

'No more nocturnal visits to low cafés on my behalf,' said Bill, shaking her gently. 'You're much too beautiful and precious to go wandering around Casablanca at nights. You stay in . . . and be a good girl.'

She hugged him and lifted her glowing face for his kiss.

'I'll be good. Oh, I love you so, Bill.'

'I'll fight the world for you,' he said for the second time, and gave her a last, long kiss.

CHAPTER TWENTY-NINE

One week later Fiona returned to the Pension Braemar, hot, tired and discouraged, having spent a couple of hours wandering around the boulevards, hoping to catch a glimpse of the little Spaniard who had led Bill to his ruin. Her search had been in vain. And every day this week it had been the same. She had spent most of the long, lonely hours when Bill was not able to visit her making the same weary, fruitless search. Bill, also, had done his share, mostly at night. And, as he told Fiona, he had visited three-quarters of the cafés and dancing halls in the town. But never a sign of the Spaniard. He seemed to have mysteriously disappeared. And why he had acted as he did and given Fiona that fictitious warning that evening, neither Fiona nor Bill could wholly fathom. Unless he had been hired specially to do the dirty trick . . . and they both knew that was a possibility.

The result was the same. Bill's reputation among the senior officers in Casablanca with whom he had to come in contact was pretty poor, and the younger men at the hospital treated him with good-natured contempt. They did not judge or condemn him, but they told him openly that he had been a 'dope' to get himself into such a mess. It was a heinous offence for an officer in uniform to break bounds and be found drunk in the house of a woman like Mercédès. Letting the Service down and all that. But they all thought Lindsey a good sport and a damn' nice fellow and were sorry about it.

Bill was more than sorry. As the days went

by and his arm continued to heal, and he knew that the time was fast approaching when he must face his Board and realised that he had no witness as yet for his defence, he grew more and more depressed. It was grand knowing that Fiona was so utterly in love with him and the hours spent with her were as heaven to him. But he had always loved his job on the sea and valued his good name, and it could not but worry him when he considered what he had lost. It worried him equally to know what Fiona was losing through associating herself so closely with him. But she was always so supremely happy in his company that he had not the heart to show his depression to her. He was always gay and optimistic when with her. Fiona hid her own qualms from him rather than allow him to feel a guilt complex about her. So they fondly deceived each other, and when they were apart the reaction was all the worse. They lived only for the moments they could share. And the wonderful hours there were . . . in Miss Ritchie's humble *pension*, or in some quiet little café . . . or in a hired car in the country, right away from the town.

So passed that first week. But this afternoon as Fiona returned to the *pension* she was more than usually down-hearted. She, too, knew that Bill's sojourn in hospital could not last much longer and that soon he would be sent home. What her own fate would be she dared not think. She had planned to write to Lady

Inverlaw and throw herself on her mercy . . . ask her if she could have her up in Edinburgh for awhile, until she could marry Bill. Aunt Jean was human . . . and she had never approved of the *mariage de convenance* . . . Fiona knew that.

Meanwhile, Fiona had not set eyes on any of her family. Louise, whom she had hoped to see, wrote to tell her that she was virtually a prisoner in the Villa des Fleurs. Her father had forbidden her to go near the Pension Braemar and Miss Macdonald watched her every action. Louise, too, was miserable and depressed and begged Fiona to come home. In her last letter she had written:

Daddy is in a terrible mood and quite frightens me. Nothing is the sane and Philippe has not been here since you left. I am so unhappy, I think I shall ask permission to leave this world and enter a convent . . .

Fiona had wept over that. She did not like to feel her little sister was so unhappy. Pretty Louise must never become a nun. Where was Philippe? If only the foolish boy would turn in his misery to the one who loved him. What was happening about the marriage contract? That was the burning question which remained unanswered for Fiona and Bill.

Fiona had heard no more from her father, or her one-time *fiancé*. The question of finance would soon arise. (Horrid shadow that must always blot out a little of the sunshine of glamorous love.) She had only a limited amount in her possession, and although the terms of the Pension Braemar were cheap enough, Fiona wanted to keep something for the future. She could not ask Bill . . . for he had only his small savings, and he wanted those to safeguard her, he said, once they were married . . . especially if he was shortly to forego his captain's pay and start again as an ordinary seaman.

Fiona considered that tomorrow, if things had not altered, she would take her diamond clips to Marquis Ltd., the Parisian jewellers in the Boulevard de la Gare, and sell them. Then if Aunt Jean would have her in Edinburgh, she could afford to go to Paris, and thence to Scotland . . . to wait for Bill.

But what they both hoped for, of course, was the release from Philippe d'Auvergne, so that they could be married before they left Casablanca.

Fiona entered the *pension* and went up to her bedroom. Oh, she was so tired. Her feet ached from the unaccustomed walking. And her appearance depressed her. Her suit needed sponging and pressing. She wanted Conchita's services badly. She had brought nothing here but a suitcase. She had written to Louise for more clothes, but Louise had replied that her father would not allow a single thing belonging to Fiona to leave the villa. She wished now that she had brought more away at the time. But she was not going to let her father break her spirit by such clean actions as keeping back her clothes. It was nothing . . . when she thought of the enormity of her love for Bill and his for her.

She took off her shoes and lay down on her bed, and closed her eyes. She would be seeing Bill tonight . . . his coming always turned purgatory into paradise . . . and she longed for hint with all her heart.

'You're getting thin and you're quite slim enough, my sweet,' he had said yesterday. 'You must take care of your darling self.'

He was always the same . . . so tender, so solicitous . . . such a wonderful lover.

She was so exhausted that she dozed for an hour. Then she found that it was supper-time. Manga, the little half-caste maid, who had Moorish blood in her, was banging the big beaten-copper gong downstairs. Swiftly Fiona got up, washed and changed into her one and only dress, and made herself as lovely as she could . . . for Bill. He would be here in an hour.

But two hours later a white-faced, harassed Fiona was pacing up and down in the sitting-room, still waiting for Bill. He had not come, and he had not telephoned. She could not think what had happened and jumped to the conclusion either that he was ill or had met with an accident.

Miss Ritchie tried to induce her to go to bed.

'Och, bairnie, you look worn out. It's past nine. Get some rest.'

'It's early yet,' said Fiona impatiently.

'It's no ear-rly for me,' said Flora Ritchie. 'And it's no likely the young man will come now.'

Gloomily Fiona stared out of the window. It was almost dark . . . the black-out would soon have to be done. She felt sick with disappointment.

She still hoped that Bill would appear, or that the telephone bell would ring. But he did not come.

At eleven o'clock she was forced to go upstairs to her room. The guests at Braemar had all retired and Miss Ritchie wanted to lock up.

Fiona, full of forebodings, undressed, got into bed and cried like a child.

In the morning, surely, there would be a letter . . . an explanation. She was up early, pale, eyes rimmed with red, waiting for the post. But when it came there was only a short note from Louise.

Mac is going out this afternoon and if Daddy doesn't see me I mean to slip out and drive down to you, darling. We must have a talk.

That would have cheered Fiona up yesterday. Today it did nothing to uplift her spirits.

At noon she telephoned the Naval and Military Hospital. She did not give her name, but said that she was a 'relation' inquiring after Captain Lindsey's health.

The answer she received was a considerable shock.

'Captain Lindsey left the hospital after dinner last night and has not returned,' she was told. When she questioned her informant further, it brought no satisfaction. Nobody knew where he had gone or what had happened and the police were searching for him now.

The police . . . that word struck terror into Fiona's soul. Chilled to the bone, white and big-eyed, she left the telephone-kiosk. Her heart was hammering. Bill must surely have been on his way to see her . . . and had come to some harm. Surely, surely, he would not for the second time be found in a low house, forbidden to officers . . . for if so, he would most certainly be dismissed his ship, if not kept under arrest.

Fiona looked wildly around her. She knew, for a certainty, that something terrible must have happened to Bill. Perhaps he had met that Spaniard and had a fight with him and been knifed. Yes, *perhaps Bill had been murdered.*

At the mere idea of this, Fiona went a little crazy. She turned, rushed upstairs, found her hat and bag and tore out of the *pension*. She hailed a passing taxi and said hoarsely:

'Drive to the Villa des Fleurs.'

As they turned through the wrought-iron gates, with many conflicting emotions she looked at the lovely, familiar gardens of her old home . . . the beautiful white villa, flying the flag of the *Croix de Rouge*. She paid the taxi and rushed into the front hall, crying:

'Louise . . . *Louise* . . .'

Louise appeared at the top of the staircase.

'Fiona . . . Oh, *darling* . . . you've come home?' she cried joyfully.

Fiona ignored this.

'Come downstairs quickly . . . I must talk to you. Where is Daddy?'

'At the office. Mac is shopping. I was going to creep down to see you after lunch. Oh, Fifi darling . . . why have you come here?' said Louise excitedly.

'Something terrible has happened,' said Fiona.

Louise stared at her sister. She saw now how ghastly Fiona looked.

'Oh, Fifi . . . what now?'

Fiona told her. Louise, also pale, drew back and instinctively touched her cross.

'There is something evil in all this. Our Lady protect us . . . something is evil here.'

'I agree . . . and it is trying to kill the man I

love,' said Fiona hysterically. 'I tell you, he has been done away with.'

'More likely he has had another spell of drunkenness,' said Louise in a low voice.

'It isn't true. I know him. Oh, Louise, believe me. That isn't true.'

'Well, what can we do about it?' asked Louise helplessly.

'We must get help. Philippe must help us. He and his father have power in Casablanca . . . as much power as Daddy. Louise dearest, I implore you, even if you never do another thing for me, help me now.'

'But how?'

'Go to Philippe . . . or send for him . . . better still, tell him to come here at once, to see you.'

'Fiona, I can't. Besides, he wouldn't come,' said Louise, her fair face puckered with distress.

'Yes, he will. I have a feeling he will if you send for him.'

'But why should he do anything for Captain Lindsey?'

'I know Philippe. You know him. He is at heart a sentimentalist. And he is no longer in love with me. He will be. a friend. I will throw myself at his feet. We must both appeal to him,' said Fiona wildly.

Louise argued a moment longer. But Fiona was adamant, and so strongly did she press her cause that finally the younger girl did as she was directed. First she telephoned to the d'Auvergne villa. But they were told that M. Philippe was not there. He had gone to his father's office.

Louise then telephoned to the office. There she managed to make contact with Philippe. In a trembling voice she said:

'Philippe . . . something terrible has happened. Will you come straight to the Villa des Fleurs?'

'Why, Louise *ma petite*, what has happened?' came his surprised voice.

'Oh, come now . . . please . . . at once, and say nothing to my father,' said Louise breathlessly.

'But of course, if you want me, Louise,' said Philippe, for he had always been devoted to the girl whom he had once imagined would be his sister-in-law.

Louise put up the receiver . . . and looked at Fiona. 'He is coming,' she said.

Fiona collapsed into a chair and put her face in her hands.

Ten minutes later Philippe d'Auvergne, very stiff and pale and proud, stood between the two sisters, listening first to Fiona's frenzied appeal to him; then to Louise. His first words were discouraging.

'I do not see why I should be called upon to act in this matter,' he said.

Fiona, tears streaming down her cheeks, turned from him.

'I know that, Philippe. I have no right to ask you for help. But I'm desperate. I can think of no other way. I *know* that Bill is innocent. I shall *die* if he is not found and all this matter put right.'

Philippe shrugged his shoulders, but it was Louise then who dared to catch his hand in hers.

'Philippe, *mon cher, cher* Philippe . . . you have known us both since we were children. We have always been friends, before all this terrible affair started. You were so kind, so good to us. Be kind now, Philippe. Poor Fiona cannot help her love for the Englishman. It is too much for her. Forgive her, Philippe, and help her . . . for my sake.'

He looked a trifle wonderingly at the younger girl. Her usually pale young face was flushed with the ardour of her emotions, her great blue eyes were swimming. He could see the rise and fall of her young breast, the quivering of her slender fingers in his. He knew that Louise loved him. His facile emotions were stirred to pity . . . then more than pity. Desire for Louise as a woman, desire to receive from her the passionate love and admiration that the older sister had denied to him, fired his imagination. He flushed and caught her hand to his lips.

'Sweet,' he murmured. 'So sweet and gentle . . . so thoughtful of others . . . and so good. For you a man would do much.'

Louise stared up at him speechlessly. A happiness that was almost unbearable flooded her very soul. Then:

'Philippe,' she said, in a smothered voice.

He kissed her hand again.

'You are a little saint,' he said. 'I will forgive Fiona. I will help her . . . for *you*.'

Louise said:

'I thank you . . . from my heart . . .'

Fiona, still weeping, added:

'Dear, dear Philippe . . . all my life I will be grateful.'

'Come,' he said. 'Both of you come with me. We will go in my car to the Chief of Police. He is my great friend. We will find Captain Lindsey and restore him to Fiona . . . and discover the truth of this mysterious disappearance and of the allegations against his character.'

CHAPTER THIRTY

Fiona gave a cry of joy and gripped Philippe's hand between both of hers.

'I thank you . . . with all my heart, I thank you,' she said in a voice that was choked with sobs.

He gazed at her wet, pale impassioned young face with curiosity. *Mon dieu!* How she loved this Englishman. There could be no doubt as to that fact. She loved him and would sacrifice anything for his sake. That seemed strange and almost pathetic to Philippe d'Auvergne, who had once desired Fiona above all other women for his wife. He had lost his love for her, too. But not his admiration. All his life he must admire her for her beauty, her strength of character, her sincerity. For at least she had never been anything but honest with him, and in Philippe's cynical opinion real honesty is rare in the 'gentle' sex.

He spoke to her with feeling:

'My poor little Fiona, have courage and trust me. I will do all I can to help you. But if we discover that your Captain Lindsey is— shall we say—no good . . . do not blame me, *ma petite.*'

Her lips curved into a ghost of a smile.

'We shall never find that, Philippe,' she said proudly.

He pressed her hand and then let it fall. Turning to Louise, he gave her a warm, intimate look that brought the rich blood to her fair transparent face.

'Let us go,' he said.

'Oh, dear . . .' sighed Louise tremulously. 'What will Daddy say?'

'He will be none too pleased with me,' was Philippe's grim answer. And he had a disagreeable recollection of the last half-hour recently spent with Harry Rutherfield in his office. Rutherfield, in a towering rage, after leaving the Pension Braemar yesterday had sent for Philippe and told him that he must get Fiona away from that place and from Lindsey and marry her at once. Philippe had replied coldly that he no longer wished to marry Fiona and that he had already given instructions to his father's solicitors to tear up the betrothal contract. A 'scene' had followed, but Philippe had been adamant. He had finished with Fiona. So far as he was concerned she could go to Lindsey and never return.

Then Gaston d'Auvergne had intervened. The French head of the Anglia Shipping Line had not indulged in any 'scenes' nor lost his temper. He had—as always—been exquisitely polite, smooth and diplomatic. It was as well, he had said, to leave the young couple to unravel their own tangles. If his son had lost interest in Mademoiselle Fiona (and little wonder, after her treatment of him), far better to call the whole thing off and without rancour . . . the families could remain good friends. Harry Rutherfield was left to rage and fume in vain. He knew well enough that Gaston d'Auvergne did not mind whether his son married Fiona Rutherfield or not. He had no ulterior motive, as Rutherfield had, in arranging the alliance between the families.

Both men were greedy for power, for money. But they differed in that d'Auvergne had never doubted his partner's integrity, and

330

Rutherfield never quite knew where he was with the smooth-tongued politic Frenchman.

The hour that followed Philippe's arrival at the Villa des Fleurs was full of excitement and anxiety for Fiona. Philippe drove, first, to the headquarters of his friend the Chief of Police, M. Voldaire, who interviewed him—and Fiona—in his office near the Central Station.

M. Voldaire, a small man with shrewd bright eyes and a well-waxed moustache, sat back in his chair, twiddled a fountain-pen in his hand and listened—first to Philippe's introduction, then to the story that Fiona Rutherfield poured out. He watched her as she spoke. He knew human nature. He knew at once that this lovely girl, half English, half French, had warm passionate blood in her veins and a wildly romantic disposition. At the same time he was sure that she spoke the truth, and that although she was speaking in wild defence of the man she loved she did not exaggerate. He took a note of all that she said about the Spaniard and the dancer, Mercédès.

At length he spoke.

'M'amselle,' he said, 'this is not an easy affair. We are already working in conjunction with the Naval and Military Police in a search for Captain Lindsey. He has not been seen since yesterday evening, at a quarter to eight. when he left the hospital to visit you, so you tell me, at the Pension Braemar.'

'That is true,' said Fiona.

'Recently Captain Lindsey was found in a state of intoxication in the house of Mercédès, who is . . .' he coughed and glanced apologetically at Louise, who demurely looked downward . . . 'ahem . . . I need not enlarge upon what manner of woman she is.'

'But he was taken there, against his will . . . too ill to resist,' interrupted Fiona. 'I have already explained that.' M. Voldaire nodded.

'I will take that into account. But he cannot again have been so . . . er . . ill last night that once more, unaware of what was happening to him, he was . . . er . . . decoyed into some notorious woman's house, m'amselle.'

'Then he has been murdered,' said Fiona in a passionate voice. 'It is the Spaniard . . . in my father's pay.'

'Fiona!' broke in Louise, resentfully.

'My dear . . . be careful what you say . . .' added Philippe, frowning.

Fiona flung back her head.

'It is time you all knew that my father has a strong motive in trying to force me to give up Bill and marry Philippe. I never meant to tell, but in Bill's interests I *must*. If he is to be found . . . the truth must be told. My own father, up in Scotland before the war, blackmailed me. He told me that he would offer Bill command of *The Albatross* on the understanding that I let him go out of my life and married Philippe. Had I refused, he would have ruined Bill—dismissed him from the

332

Anglia Line. Is that right or just? Is it normal? No . . . there was a sinister reason behind the whole of his efforts to separate me from Bill and to hurry on my wedding with Philippe d'Auvergne. And if that reason is discovered then we may also discover the truth about Bill . . . and the recent catastrophes which have befallen him.'

'I don't believe Daddy has anything to do with this,' began Louise, her face puckered like a child's.

Philippe came up to the back of her chair and laid a hand on her shoulder.

'*Soyez tranquille, ma petite* . . . keep calm . . . let us consider what Fiona is saying . . .'

And the young man was uneasy. For he, too, had been wondering since yesterday why Harry Rutherfield should have been so *abnormally* upset by his decision to rescind the contract.

M. Voldaire was thinking rapidly. He, too, was a little uneasy. Mr. Rutherfield was a 'power' in this town. Even the Chief of Police was unwilling to offend Mr. Rutherfield. On the other hand, he had equally little wish to disgruntle the d'Auvergnes . . . Gaston was a friend of thirty years' standing. Philippe he had known since he was a small boy.

M. Voldaire walked to a file and drew out a sheaf of small photographs.

'Would M'amselle examine these,' he said, smiling in a fatherly fashion, 'and tell us if amongst these faces she recognises that of the

Spaniard who spoke to her in the Sphynx Bar.'

Fiona took the large sheets of pictured faces . . . criminal faces, most of them . . . Europeans, natives . . . a motley crew who had at some time been convicted and imprisoned in Casablanca and whose dossiers were held here for reference.

With a rapidly beating heart Fiona looked intently at the various faces. It seemed for a moment that she was to be disappointed. Then with a cry she pointed at one familiar countenance.

'Yes . . . here is the man,' she said excitedly.

M. Voldaire and Philippe bent over her shoulder. The Chief of Police smoothed his long moustaches and cocked a bushy eyebrow.

'Ah ha,' he said. 'Miguel Cortez . . . *Numéro quarante-quinze.* Let me look him up. If I remember rightly, that gentleman was sent to prison in the winter of last year for assaulting and robbing an American tourist . . . *attendez, m'amselle.*'

He hastened to a cupboard and pulled out a large ledger. Fiona watched him, her soul in her eyes. If only they could find the Spaniard, maybe they would find darling Bill . . . through him.

Voldaire returned.

'I am right. Miguel Cortez, a Spaniard, born in Ceuta . . . well-known for his criminal activities throughout Spanish and French Morocco. Several times imprisoned. Lately known to be living in Casablanca. We are aware of his lodgings and hide-outs. I will give orders, *m'amselle*, for my men to make an immediate search for him.'

With swimming eyes, Fiona turned to Philippe.

'You see,' she said, 'already what I have said is proved correct. The man who took Bill off that night has a criminal record. You will see . . . Bill is innocent. We must find him . . . oh, we must!'

Philippe murmured a few comforting words. Louise sat silent. She did not like the implication that had been put upon her father. But whenever she met Philippe's gaze her heart bounded and her spirits soared. There was something new and warm and sweet in his expression. She *adored* her Philippe and he no longer loved Fiona. He was free to love elsewhere. It was an exciting, perilous thought for little Louise.

Within an hour of Voldaire's 'sleuths' going out, they returned with a report upon Miguel Cortez. The house in which he usually lodged had been found locked and shuttered, but they broke in and found a woman there . . . evidently afraid of the police, and trying to evade them. They forced her into the admission that she used to live with Cortez, who had recently acquired some money . . . much money . . . and had boasted that it had been given to him by an important gentleman

335

who resided in Casablanca. Cortez had gone to Tangier, but returned yesterday. The woman told what she knew out of spite because Cortez had refused to take her to Tangier with him. He had gone in search of new love, she was sure, although he had told her that it was part of his bargain with the gentleman that he should leave Casablanca for a spell. Upon questioning her more closely the inspector discovered that when Cortez returned he quarrelled with this woman and changed his lodgings. She had followed him and knew where he was to be found.

The police went to Miguel's new quarters, a house which was also well known to them at headquarters . . . being a low type of gambling-den near the Rue Blanchette.

Here, the police found Cortez, himself, and cross-questioned him. They had no evidence at the moment on which to arrest him, but in view of what Miss Rutherfield had told them they tried to extract from him the information that they needed about William Lindsey. The Spaniard blustered but seemed scared. He had a purple bruise over his right eye, and had obviously been involved in a recent fight. He was sullen and refused to speak. But the inspector was of the opinion that he knew something.

Fiona listened to all this, sprang to her feet.

'He knows where Bill is . . . he has seen him . . . perhaps fought him . . . perhaps that

336

mark on his forehead is from Bill's fist!' she said hysterically. 'You must arrest him, M. Voldaire.'

The chief eyed her kindly, but shook his head.

'*Mais non, m'amselle* . . . that would be foolish, even were we within our rights.'

'Then what can we do?' asked the girl agonisedly. 'Where is Bill? He may be dead . . . dying . . . oh, I can't bear it.'

'Take my advice and go home,' said Voldaire, 'to await events. I fancy, m'amselle, that we will soon have news for you. We have told Cortez that we have finished with him, but from now on . . . we are going to watch. Sure enough, he will give himself away . . . in time.'

Fiona and Louise were now in each other's arms. The sisters were weeping. Fiona with the anguish of her thoughts . . . Louise out of sheer nerves and sympathy.

Philippe led them out of the Bureau himself, deep in thought. He had another plan . . . a plan which he intended to carry out, without the assistance of M. Voldaire or his sleuths.

Fiona refused to return home. She preferred to stay at the Pension Braemar. Louise went back alone to the Villa des Fleurs . . . there to explain, as best she could, her long absence and escape from Miss Macdonald's watchful eye. But Louise, although her blue eyes were red-rimmed with weeping, had a curiously contented little smile on her mouth. A secret smile. And a lovely secret all her own to compensate her for any of the anxieties that beset her concerning her family. For when Philippe had driven her home, and they were alone, he had stopped the car outside the gates. Lifting her hand to his lips, he had said:

'May I come and sit with you tonight, *chère* Louise?'

She had answered quickly, naïvely:

'Oh, Philippe . . . you know how much I would like that.'

He then said with a deep look from his dark eyes:

'I know, dear little one . . . and I am filled with a new enchantment. I find that I could never again wish that you might become *ma petite soeur . . .*'

That made her whole heart tremble and leap. With another swift kiss on her hand, he had driven on and his last words had been: 'Until tonight . . .'

Nothing very much . . . yet so much did it mean to Louise that she could not be too unhappy about Fiona and her misfortunes. For she knew that Philippe, just as Fiona had always hoped, had turned to *her* on the rebound. Tonight, perhaps, he would tell her what lay in his heart and she could at last speak to him of the adoration in which she had always held him. She flung herself on her *prie-dieu*, and lifting her eyes to the little blue

338

and gold Madonna standing in a niche in the wall of her boudoir, prayed long and ardently for Philippe . . . for his love . . . and for the safe return to Fiona of William Lindsey.

CHAPTER THIRTY-ONE

It was about half past four that same afternoon that Philippe d'Auvergne, with a grim determined look on his thin pale face, called at the Villa des Fleurs and asked to see Mr. Rutherfield.

Many times he had called here at this beautiful romantic villa, he reflected. But never before on such an errand. Truly, life was an astonishment . . . one never knew what next would come along as a complication. However, this time, he felt that he held the key which would unlock all doors and solve all the immediate problems.

Harry Rutherfield received the young Frenchman with his usual geniality and warmth. Cigar in hand, he sat at the desk in his library, where he had been writing letters.

'Glad to see you, Philippe, my boy. I hope and believe that you have decided to revoke your decision about Fiona.'

'No, sir,' said Philippe in an icy voice, and with such hauteur that the older man stared at him. 'I shall never revoke that, because I am of the opinion that the best thing that can happen to Fiona is that she should marry Captain Lindsey without further delay.'

Rutherfield stared harder, the cigar suspended in his hand. Then Philippe added quickly:

'Mr. Rutherfield, I have known you since I was a boy. You are my father's partner. The father of two girls whom I respect and admire. But I have no hesitation in saying here and now that you have behaved like a blackguard, sir, and that you deserve no mercy from either Captain Lindsey or your family.'

Harry Rutherfield's face took on the purplish hue which indicated loss of temper with him. He sprang to his feet.

'You . . . you young puppy . . . how *dare* you?' he began to splutter.

Philippe interposed:

'Mr. Rutherfield, the game is up. Or . . . if it is still being played, I hold the trump cards in my hands . . . on behalf of Fiona.'

'What the devil do you mean, Philippe?'

'I mean that I have Captain William Lindsey in my car, outside this house, sir. Also that at this moment my old friend M. Voldaire is holding Señor Miguel Cortez in safe custody.'

Rutherfield's colour faded. He gave a gasp and sank back into his chair. The cigar fell from his nerveless fingers. Mechanically he picked it up. He looked at the young man with bolting eyes. He seemed to shrink, visibly, in

340

that moment. He made as though to speak, but no words came, only his lips opened and quivered.

Philippe spoke again, and spoke for a long time, and what he had to say this time left Harry Rutherfield in no doubt as to the fact that the 'game' was indeed up. It appeared that Philippe had gone to see Cortez and, knowing that threats would wring nothing from the crafty Spaniard, had bargained with him, and placed a large wad of notes in front of his gaze. Cortez could never resist money. He had that same morning interviewed Harry, who had refused to give him more and cursed him for leaving Tangier. Therein, Rutherfield had made a mistake. Cortez wanted more money and intended to get it, by foul means if not by fair. He had fallen at once for the handsome bribe extended by young d'Auvergne.

Then the story about Bill Lindsey being taken in a state of unconsciousness to the home of Mercédès was told to Philippe by Cortez. The Spaniard also admitted that yesterday, on his way from the hospital, he had encountered the Captain, and Lindsey had grabbed hold of him and punched him hard (that was the explanation of the bruise on Miguel's forehead). Bill had 'seen red' and endeavoured to extract a promise from Cortez to own up to the truth. At that moment some friends of Miguel's, half Spanish, half Arab, and entirely criminal, had come to his rescue. They had knocked the Englishman out and taken him to the hovel on the outskirts of the city, which they called 'home'. There, Miguel intended to keep the Captain until he got more money from Mr. Rutherfield, after which he had every intention of leaving Casablanca once and for all and settling in Barcelona. What happened to Lindsey, once he— Cortez—was safely out of the city, he admitted he did not care.

It was after this that he had seen Rutherfield and been denied the money, and later that he had fallen for Philippe's bribe. With the money in his pocket, Cortez took Philippe to the place where Bill was a prisoner. There, Philippe had, for the first time, made the acquaintance of the man whom Fiona loved to such distraction. A bruised, dirty, hungry Bill with his uniform half torn off him and the light of battle still in his very blue eyes, a friendly charming Englishman who had been relieved and astonished when Philippe first introduced himself and then a little embarrassed.

'I feel I've not quite played fair to you, d'Auvergne,' he had said, 'but I must explain—'

'No need for explanation. I understand,' Philippe had interrupted. 'Fiona is free to do as she wishes now. I hold no bitterness against either of you.'

And it was as friends, not as enemies, that

the two men had driven away—first to Philippe's private office, where he had allowed Bill to wash and sent for a clean suit of clothes to replace the damaged uniform, then up here to the Villa des Fleurs.

'It is now in Captain Lindsey's hands to tell the Seamen's Board exactly what has occurred, and to call Cortez and Fiona and any others concerned in his defence,' Philippe told Rutherfield sternly.

Fiona's father crumpled. He hid his face in a shaking hand.

'I'm a ruined man . . . ruined, if all this is allowed to come out,' he mumbled. 'For heaven's sake, Philippe, do something to stop that . . . keep me out of it . . .'

'For Louise's sake,' said Philippe, 'Louise, whom I trust in the near future will be my wife.'

'Louise!' repeated Rutherfield, stupefied.

'Yes, but that can wait. You have only one chance, Mr. Rutherfield, and I give it to you because of Louise and of the reputation of our firm. You will at once communicate with the authorities concerned and clear Captain Lindsey's name. You will tell them that you have proof that he is entirely innocent and you will demand that he be reinstated and given a new command as soon as he is fit and a ship is available. You will also give your immediate consent to Fiona's marriage with him.'

Rutherfield winced.

'Very well,' he said in a low voice. 'It is as you say.'

'You will also resign from our firm,' continued Philippe in his cold, merciless voice; 'it can be done on the grounds that your health is poor and that you wish to leave the Anglia Shipping Line. My father can carry on alone.'

Rutherfield went scarlet.

'Look here . . . that is too much . . .'

'Very well. I telephone M. Voldaire and he orders a public, instead of a private, inquiry into the facts.'

Rutherfield collapsed again. He saw his folly . . . the defeat of his hopes . . . the end to his high ambitions, and he knew, too late, that he had been a fool. For the wrong that he had done his own daughter, he must pay . . . and pay for the rest of his life.

'I will do what you say,' came his hollow voice.

'Good,' said Philippe. 'Then with your permission, sir, I will telephone the Pension Braemar and inform Fiona that Captain Lindsey is safely here and ask her to come at once and receive your guarantee that Captain Lindsey's good name be restored to him.'

Mr. Rutherfield made no answer. White about the gills, wholly dejected, he listened while young d'Auvergne made that telephone call.

Ten minutes later Fiona, flushed, triumphant, unutterably relieved, was back in her old home, and in Bill's arms, held tightly in the circle of his arm. They were alone in the drawing-room where Louise had left them. Bill stroked her bright beautiful head, holding it passionately against his heart.

'My darling . . . my wonderful, adorable darling. I owe this to you . . . entirely to you, was all that he could say. She hugged him to her.

'Bill . . . my dearest . . . are you all right? Did they harm you? Oh, my *darling* . . .'

'I'm none the worse, except for a hunger that is phenomenal and a sore top to my head where those slugs first got me,' he said with a rueful laugh. 'I was just doing nicely with that little Spanish blighter, then his pals came up and got me on the back of my head.'

She shuddered.

'They might have murdered you.'

'But they didn't, dearest. You can't get away with murder easily, even in Casablanca.'

'And to think that Philippe got the truth out of Cortez and faced my father with it.'

'Your father is rather a sick and sorry man at the moment,' said Bill grimly.

'I've no sympathy with him,' said Fiona. 'None.'

'Nor I, darling. But I shall always be grateful to him for being responsible for *you*, all the same.'

'Oh, Bill . . .'

'Oh, Fiona,' he mimicked her gently,

laughed again and sighed as he looked down into her brilliant eyes. 'Do you realise, sweet, that there will be no Board . . . that I am to be totally exonerated and to get command of a new ship as soon as I'm fit again?'

She frowned at him.

'Do you realise, Captain Lindsey, that you are being led to the altar by a designing woman, as soon as the marriage can be arranged?'

'Gosh!' said Bill Lindsey, softly. 'A life sentence, honey.'

She took his hand, her heart brimming over with her new exquisite relief and happiness.

'Let's find Louise and tell her . . .'

But Louise was not to be found, for she was wandering in the garden, hand in hand with Philippe d'Auvergne; a pink-cheeked, starry-eyed Louise, to whom Philippe had said quite a number of things that quickened the beat of her pulses.

'I cannot wait until tonight to tell you that I have discovered a great truth,' he had said, 'which is that I only imagined that I loved Fiona. It is she who must become *ma petite sœur*, after all . . . and it is you, Louise, *ma mignon*, whom I must marry.'

To which her answer had come softly, shyly;

'I have always adored you, Philippe.'

And then somehow she had found herself in his arms and, as so often in her dreams, she lifted her untouched lips for his first kiss of

346

her brother Harry of late. Then she had received a letter from him from Paris which had startled her somewhat. In it he had stated, briefly, that he was ill, had retired from his company and was living for the moment with friends in Versailles. Fiona's engagement to young d'Auvergne, he said, was broken and Philippe had become betrothed to Louise. Fiona, herself, had been married by special licence in Casablanca, the day after he had left, to William Lindsey the ship's captain whom she had originally met in Scotland.

That was all . . . but enough to fling Lady Inverlaw into a state of excitement. After all, Fiona *had* met the young man here, whilst under her charge, and she felt a certain responsibility. She wired to her niece. Fiona wired back: *May we come to you for part of our honeymoon?* To which her ladyship had immediately cabled back: *Delighted.*

So now they were coming. Last night on the telephone Fiona had sounded ecstatically happy . . . bubbling over with it. She had said: 'Casablanca has lost much of its charm for us. We feel we'd like a Christmas in Scotland . . . our first together.'

Upon asking for news of Louise, Fiona had said that Louise was in Paris with Philippe's Aunt Thérèse, buying a trousseau, and was to be married to Philippe in the New Year. Philippe, himself, was now in the French Air Force. They both seemed enchanted with life

passionate love. In her heart she thanked the Madonna for her intercession. Philippe loved her, and all was well, very well, for Louise Rutherfield.

Through the gardens, in enchantment, they walked.

'I am tired of being a civilian and I am going to resign from my father's office and enter the Air Force,' Philippe informed her. 'You will perhaps prefer me, like Fiona's Englishman, in uniform.'

'No . . . I don't mind what you wear . . . and I beg you to take no risks,' was her reply.

'A man must always take risks,' said Philippe. 'In love or in war, *chérie.*'

Miss Macdonald, having first of all found the eldest of the young ladies in Captain Lindsey's arms, then caught sight of the youngest in the embrace of Philippe d'Auvergne, surged in righteous indignation into her employer's study.

'What am I to deduce from all this, Mr. Rutherfield?' she demanded, her face pink. 'Have your daughters lost their senses, or am I not seeing aright?'

Harry Rutherfield, who by this time had consumed three strong whiskies and sodas, growled at the old governess.

'Get out, Mac, and leave me alone. Yes . . . my daughters are crazy . . . and so am I. But I wash my hands of the whole show. They may marry whom they wish. I am packing and leaving Casablanca. There's an evil eye on the place. I shall take the first possible 'plane to Paris.'

'But, Mr. Rutherfield, you told me that this Captain Lindsey is a terrible man and—'

'Get out!' thundered Harry Rutherfield. 'What I said was untrue. I am the terrible man. And I am not wanted in this house or in this country. So I'm leaving it. Now, woman, *get out* . . .'

Miss Macdonald got out. She had already decided that she, too, would leave Casablanca. Something was going on that she knew nothing about, and that was one thing that an honest and straightforward Scottish lady could not stand.

She marched up to her bedroom, and left Harry Rutherfield to pour out his fourth drink and brood over the disastrous consequences of the effort which he had made to ruin an innocent man.

CHAPTER THIRTY-TWO

One month later . . . many long miles across land and water, away from the golden glitter, the blue sea, the shining white minarets and terraces of Casablanca . . . to the chill twilight of a Christmas Eve in Edinburgh.

It was about six weeks after those dramatic

events which had led to the defeat of Harry Rutherfield's plans and the restoration of Captain William Lindsey to favour in the eyes of his superiors.

Jean, Lady Inverlaw, sat alone in the big drawing-room of the house in Moray Place, waiting for her niece, Fiona, to arrive with her husband. They had already reached London the previous night and telephoned to her. They were travelling today from King's Cross and should arrive in time for dinner. But there had been a heavy fall of snow today and the grand old city of Edinburgh lay under a spotless pall. Lady Inverlaw had already warned her staff that the train might be delayed and the visitors were likely to be late.

She was greatly looking forward to the arrival of the newly-wedded pair. So many of the younger generation up here had departed . . . the girls into the Services . . . the young men into regiments drafted to France, or out East. Edinburgh was dull these days except fo the endless routine of W.V.S. work which he ladyship had to do . . . dull, when compare with the pomp and pageantry of pre-war day the Caledonia Balls, all the old social activiti Why, when Fiona and Louise had been he before, only a few months previously, threat of war had hardly reached Edinbu and the young people had still been dan their way along a rosy path of pleasure.

Lady Inverlaw had not heard much

and each other.

'Wonders will never cease,' Jean Inverlaw had exclaimed. 'What on earth got round my brother Harry to make him agree to your marriage with Captain Lindsey?'

For that Fiona had only an evasive answer.

'Oh, he just did, Aunt Jean . . .'

So Lady Inverlaw asked no more.

Dinner had already been dished up and was waiting when at length the front-door bell rang and Thomas opened the door to Captain and Mrs. William Lindsey.

Lady Inverlaw stood in front of a roaring fire to meet the young couple. She held out her hands in welcome.

'You must both be frozen and famished,' she said.

Fiona rushed across to her aunt. Lady Inverlaw saw a vision of health and happiness, Fiona wearing pale rose tweeds, a short mink coat and a tiny mink hat perched on her tawny head.

'We're much too happy to be either frozen or famished!' she said.

Jean Inverlaw embraced the girl, looked into the brilliant eyes and read in them the same ecstasy that had sounded in the gay young voice over the telephone last night. Then she held out a hand to the young officer. Bill, too, looked well, although his left arm was still in a sling. But his brown face was the face of a thoroughly contented man. His blue eyes twinkled at Lady Inverlaw.

'May I . . . Aunt Jean?' he said, and kissed her.

She laughed and patted his back.

'Get away and don't you try breaking my heart, young man,' she said.

Fiona laughed and said:

'Oh, but he will, if you aren't careful, Aunt Jean. He's terrible. I can't leave him alone for a moment but all the attractive girls are trying to get off with my husband.'

'What about me?' protested Bill. 'Look at Fiona . . . do you think I can hope to keep the attractive men away from *her*?'

Lady Inverlaw laughed and shook her head.

'What a pair . . . good gracious . . . go upstairs and get tidy, the two of you, and come down and eat your dinner before it spoils.'

'We're dreadfully happy, Aunt Jean,' whispered Fiona, embracing her aunt again.

'Good for you, my dear. I must say I'm glad it's all come right. You must tell me everything after dinner.'

But Fiona had no intention of telling Aunt Jean 'everything'. Nobody except those intimately concerned in Casablanca, not even Gaston d'Auvergne himself, must know the real reason why Harry Rutherfield had surrendered.

Upstairs in the big bedroom with its decorous twin bedsteads, its mahogany suite and rich old-fashioned curtains, a coal fire was burning . . . a pre-war extravagance to keep out the intense cold of the Scottish winter.

The honeymooners, coming straight from the warmth of French Morocco, appreciated it. They were, despite Fiona's denials, 'frozen and famished', as Lady Inverlaw had put it, after nine hours in the train.

Fiona flung her fur coat and hat on to one of the beds and walked to the dressing-table and began to attend to her face.

'I *must* wash . . .' she began.

But Bill had put down the suitcase he was about to unpack, come up behind her and drawn her into the circle of his arm.

'I haven't kissed you since we left London this morning,' he said. 'I am famished, not for food, but for my wife's perfectly exquisite lips.'

Rose-red, enraptured, she leaned against him. She had been married one week to Bill Lindsey and she was one week more in love with him. Desperately in love.

He said:

'Life is pretty wonderful just now, Fiona, my sweet.'

'So good, I can hardly believe it.'

'Do you remember the last time we were in this house?'

'Yes . . . everything was against us . . . and we found it grey and dreary.'

'And tonight everything is for us, and it's a house of magic. Oh, Fiona . . . *darling* . . .'

She leaned her head against his shoulder

and let one of her slender hands wander over the thick brightness of his hair.

'All that we've been through seems so well worth while.'

'I agree, darling.'

'Tomorrow we'll go into the snow,' she continued dreamily, 'and walk on the crags and look down on Holyrood, which will be like a Christmas card . . . and when we wake we'll hear the bells ringing from St. Giles' and St. Mary's . . . and on Boxing Day we'll go shopping in Princes Street, and I'll buy a postcard to send to dear Miss Ritchie and we'll eat at de Guise's and forget there's a war on, and that eventually you've got to leave me and go back to sea.'

'Darling,' he said, 'when I do, don't be unhappy . . . you will come with me everywhere in spirit. You have been with me, like that, ever since I first loved you.'

'I know, Bill, but I can hardly bear to let you go. It's so good to be your wife . . . to be with you like this now.'

He lifted her left hand and kissed the wedding-ring which so recently he had slipped on to the slim finger.

'It's a glorious Christmas for us both this year, my darling.'

'For Louise and Philippe, too. Dear Philippe, we can never forget what we owe to him.'

'I never will,' said Bill.

Lady Inverlaw's voice floated up to him.

'Come along, you two . . . come along . . .'

'Goodness!' said Fiona, breaking away from her husband. 'We've been wasting our time.'

'If making love to my wife is a waste of time, then time was meant to he wasted,' said Bill stoutly.

'That's a bit complicated, darling.'

'You are so beautiful, Fiona,' he said irrelevantly.

Their hearts beating fast, they smiled into each other's happy eyes.